SEARCH FOR A SHADOW

Further Titles by Grace Thompson

A WELCOME IN THE VALLEY
VALLEY AFFAIRS
THE CHANGING VALLEY

from Severn House

VALLEY IN BLOOM
FAMILY PRIDE
DAISIE'S ARK
SUMMER OF SECRETS

SEARCH FOR A SHADOW

Grace Thompson

writing as

Kay Christopher

This first world edition published in Great Britain 1995 by
SEVERN HOUSE PUBLISHERS LTD of
9–15 High Street, Sutton, Surrey SM1 1DF.
First published in the USA 1995 by
SEVERN HOUSE PUBLISHERS INC of
425 Park Avenue, New York, NY 10022.

Copyright © 1995 by Grace Thompson

All rights reserved.
The moral rights of the author have been asserted.

British Library Cataloguing in Publication Data
Christopher, Kay
  Search for a Shadow
  I. Title
  823.914 [F]

ISBN 0-7278-4736-8

All situations in this publication are fictitious and
any resemblance to living persons is purely coincidental.

Typeset by Hewer Text Composition Services, Edinburgh.
Printed and bound in Great Britain by
Hartnolls Ltd, Bodmin, Cornwall.

Chapter One

The "end of holiday" party at a New York hotel was a success, Rosemary decided, but for her it was an evening she would have preferred to have missed. Party-going was not her favourite pastime and it was only the threat of her travelling companions calling her a party-pooper that made her even try to look as if she were enjoying it. She smiled as a young woman raised a glass, inviting her to accept another drink but shook her head. She glanced at her watch and saw there were still two hours to go before the coach came to take them back to their hotel.

The truth was that once a holiday was near its end she began to look forward to getting back home; the contrasts once enjoyed began to cloy, her new and brief friendships became jaded and tiresome, and as she thought of the green Welsh valley where she had a small, grey stone cottage, it seemed perfection.

Why was it that whatever holiday she chose, she had this wish for it to be ended quite soon after it began? *Hiraeth*, the Welsh called it. Nostalgia, a longing for home.

New York was fun and exciting. She had found the giant buildings almost unreal and she had wondered if they were really empty, only facades, put there simply for the tourists. A visit to the Empire State Building disabused her of that! She knew that when she told her stories back home, and showed the photographs she had taken to her friends, Megan and Sally, she would make it sound as if she had had the most exciting holiday ever. She always did. But after a week, she had begun to tire of it and now she longed for home with an intensity that was an ache.

The girl who had offered her a drink pushed her way through the laughing throng and squeezed into the bench beside her.

"Has this been your first visit to America?" she asked.

"Yes, and I love it, but I won't be sorry to get back home, to recover!" Rosemary smiled.

"And where's home?"

"A tiny village in the middle of Wales, near the town of Aberystwyth."

"Aber – what?"

A young man standing watching the girls from the edge of a group of people near by, moved closer as Rosemary repeated the name and laughingly assisted her companion in the spelling of it. He had noticed Rosemary before but her standoffish body language and her rather formal dress and dowdy colours had given him no encouragement to seek her out and talk to her. Not while there were plenty of livelier girls to spend the time with.

Then she smiled and her face lit up; her remarkable blue eyes brightened the solemn, chiselled face with its surround of harshly cut, straight hair. The angles softened, the "keep off" expression melted away. He watched and listened and began to wait for that smile to come again.

"You haven't enjoyed New York? A week here has been known to change a person's whole attitude to life!" the girl said in disbelief.

"Oh yes! I've loved it! Americans love visitors, don't they?"

"You'd better believe it!"

"No, really, I wouldn't have missed it for anything, but

Search For a Shadow

I'm always glad to go home, even from somewhere as wonderful as America."

"Your home is that special?" the girl asked.

"I doubt you would think so. It's small, and everyone knows everyone else. It's a village and it's—" She frowned as she thought of a way to describe it. "It's delightfully dull. Nothing ever happens there!" Her face lit up with one of her smiles and the man watching her felt the warmth of it.

"It sounds—" The girl hesitated, wondering how to put into polite words what she hoped Rosemary wanted to hear.

"Boring? I suppose it is and that's what I like about it."

"And you're going straight home to wallow in this dullness? Or will you give Europe a chance?"

"I won't be going straight home. In fact, I've booked into an hotel in London for a couple of nights. It's not very grand, by your standards. It's called Grantham's Piece, very small but pleasant."

"Great! You'll see some shows and let your hair down a little before going back to the dull but delightful village?"

"Not really. I want to visit some libraries and museums."

"Fascinating." This time her companion didn't try to hide her dismay. "Tell me, what the hell brought you to visit America? It's so different it must scare the pants off of you!"

"I enjoy talking to people with different life styles, like you. Now, tell me, what do you do?"

"This and that. Temping mostly. Filling in time before I start making a career. I'll do a bit of travelling next year. When I come to London I'll need a reasonably cheap place to stay. What's this Grantham's Piece Hotel like? It has to be near the centre of things."

The man watching was smiling. He ran his fingers through his curly, light brown hair, and glanced at his watch. Excusing himself from his companions he went to find a telephone.

"Hey, I just remembered," the girl said. "My cousin has visited Wales. Come and meet him and – say, that's odd. He was here a minute ago." She shrugged. "There you go, another missed opportunity. He'd have liked talking with you about your quaint little village."

Rosemary glanced around vaguely and sneaked another glance at her watch.

"Say, what d'you say we swop addresses? I'm planning to do Europe next year and you might like to meet up?" As an afterthought she said, "My name is Barbara, what's yours?"

They wrote their details in each other's notebooks and then Barbara drifted back to her friends. Rosemary shrank back in her corner but smiled as she saw Barbara laughing and dancing. It was unlikely that even a dozen visits to New York would turn Rosemary into a social butterfly.

The day following the party was Rosemary's last in New York and she spent it sightseeing with some of the group, committing to memory all the things she had seen and enjoyed. They stopped to shop in Macy's famous store and she bought gifts for her parents and friends. Besides the friends from work, Megan and Sally, she thought of Gethyn Lewis, her next-door neighbour, and his mother, and decided on a tie and a scarf.

It would be good be back with her friends. Three weeks was a long time to be away, although, as she had told Barbara, nothing would have happened. Everything would be just the same as when she had left. That was one of the good things about living where she did. It was safe, secure and unchanging.

A mist hung over the green Welsh hills, giving them an air of grey sadness. The village below was hidden and no sounds rose on the moisture-laden air to reveal its presence.

The old woman staggered a little and stopped as she climbed up the steep path. Catching hold of a tree branch with a hand almost as gnarled as the trunk, she rested to catch her breath. It wasn't the climb making her breathless, but the tears that flowed unchecked down her wrinkled face.

She felt old, much older than she had a few short hours ago. Disappointment and regret had taken their toll as suddenly as a summer storm. She raised her rheumy brown eyes towards the hidden sky, squinting as if to pierce the mist. No brief summer storm this, only a slow, cold realisation that for her, things would never be the same again.

Her life had been one long lie and now she was paying for it. She relieved herself behind a tree where she had rested and walked on, not with any clear intention, but reaching higher and higher into the hills, where once the constant roar of machinery had torn rocks apart but where all was now silent; the quarrying done, men and their machines gone away. Today the silence was absolute, not even a plaintive birdcall broke the stillness.

The air around her breathed a threat, her past sins hovered near; she felt them about to catch up with her. It was useless to try to outrun them now.

Hidden behind the shrouding mist was something she did not want to see. What it was she didn't know but as she moved further and further from home she felt it more strongly. Punishment perhaps for her stupid lies? Or the worse stupidity of confessing them? She was increasingly afraid, but there was an inevitability about the fear and she didn't turn and hurry back down the steep, twisting path but went on, up and up towards the lip of the old quarry.

Anger and regret grew in her. She regretted not retaining the secret she had held for so many years. She had twice been foolish and now everything was ruined. She could not admit to regret for what she had done, only the telling. Breathless from the climb now, the tears ceased. She went up into the thickening cloud that soaked the grasses and made dainty drinking cups of the leaves.

At the edge of the quarry she stopped, her breath harsh and ragged, and looked down into its unseen but imagined depths. A shrunken figure with a long black dress, quite unsuitable for the weather, hanging around her thin frame, clinging wetly to her stick-like legs, making her appear even smaller.

She felt a presence but didn't look round. There was the slight warmth of the hand touching the small of her back and when the push came she knew it was retribution. She fell without haste, down and down, hitting her head, her frail body folding and unfolding, skirts opening like wings, arms raised as if to stave off that final moment. She came to earth with a thud. The final violence. Her body was curled slightly as she lay on the rocky grass as if in sleep. She settled slightly then remained perfectly still.

Gethyn Lewis jumped down from the bus and walked along the hedge-lined country road towards the road bridge. The view of the hills was lost in mist, the houses nearby amorphous: mirages that would vanish on his approach. On the waist-high parapet he stopped and looked down at the stream flowing beneath it. On its banks was a row of terraced cottages. The first one was his home. Number two was empty and he was counting the days before its occupant, Rosemary Roberts, would return from her holiday in New York. He smiled and murmured her name aloud.

Outside number four, old Mrs Priestley was planting some Welsh poppies on the bank close to the high-water mark. Gethyn waved and called a greeting, and the small, neatly aproned figure waved back.

Opposite the furthest cottage was a wooden footbridge that crossed the stream that flowed under the road, and led to the small area where the occupants could park their cars. A lane led up from it to the main road on which Gethyn now stood.

He ran down the steps and walked to where Mrs Priestley was working, her knotted hands muddy as she refused to work in gloves. Her dark eyes were bright with intelligence. Tendrils of grey hair had fallen from the grips, framing her pert face.

"Has Mam been all right? I wasn't too long away was I? Only I did want to see that film. Fell asleep through half of it, mind," he admitted with a smile.

"I haven't seen her for a while, Gethyn," Mrs Priestley replied. "I went in at lunch-time but she didn't want me to stay. I could sense it. Though she didn't actually tell me to go, mind. She seemed upset about something, so I made sure she didn't need anything then came out to see to this bit of gardening."

"Thanks for keeping an eye. Why don't you let me finish the planting for you? It's raw-cold."

Mrs Priestley smiled up at the heavily built, darkly handsome young man. He was neatly dressed, although his clothes were rather old-fashioned and much more formal than most young men of his age wore.

"Gethyn, dear, you're so kind, but you can't look after us all the way you look after your mam! I won't be long and then I'll go in and get myself warm. But thanks for being so caring. Your mam's so lucky to have a son like you."

"If you're sure?"

"Go you, and I'll be five more minutes at the most."

Mrs Priestley planted the last of the yellow poppies and stood up, stiffly, to admire the effect. She was about to gather up her tools and go in, when she heard a roar from number one and saw Gethyn come dashing out, alarm bristling on his face, his dark eyes darting anxiously as he looked all around.

"Where's Mam?" he shouted. "She isn't there and already it's getting dark!"

After looking around the immediate area, through and behind the main street of the village, and along the banks of the river into which the stream flowed, Gethyn went back to the cottage. He searched it desperately again, then went outside to wait for Mrs Priestley and the other helpers to return from their frantic searches.

They moved slowly, the mist aggravating their efforts. Voices seemed closer than they were, cars threatened to touch them when they were in fact yards away. The small band of people who returned all shook their heads sorrowfully.

"It's no use," Gethyn said slowly. "She isn't anywhere I can think of. I've tried all the people she knows in the village and no one has seen her. I'm going to the phone box to call the police."

"Phone from our house," Huw, the tall gangly student from the end house, offered.

Search For a Shadow

Gethyn sat in his living room all night, with the two students, Huw and Richard, for company, jumping up occasionally as he thought of one more place to search. Periodically one of the policemen would return, ask a few questions and leave again.

What was she wearing? Where did she usually go? Could he think of anyone she might have suddenly decided to visit? Did she have a favourite walk? Gethyn explained that she often went up on the hill to gather firewood, even though he had warned her not to.

"Old she is, and not fit to carry heavy baskets. But she wouldn't listen. Ask anyone. Insisted on going up the hill to look for sticks, so independent she was, and always trying to do more than she should."

"Don't talk in the past tense, man," Huw said. "She isn't dead yet."

Gethyn glanced from Huw to the policeman. "I doubt she'd survive a night out in this. No use pretending, best to face facts, don't you think?"

As dawn broke, the new day hardly able to force a glimmer of light through the cloying mist, Gethyn went and stood on the wooden footbridge leading to the car parking area. He looked down into the dark water of the stream, shadowed at that point with overhanging trees and shrubs that grew out of the banks and narrowed the footbridge, forcing those walking over it to bend outwards over the water.

"I'll have to cut these back," he said to Huw, who had followed him. "Rosemary might trip and fall in. I must remember to order her milk. And remind the shop about her morning paper." He seemed to be thinking aloud and Huw stood silent beside him. "And bread!" Gethyn said suddenly. "I must get her some bread!" He turned then and stared at Huw. "It isn't the same without her." Huw wondered if he was referring to the loss of his mother or the absent Rosemary, but he didn't ask, just grunted in reply.

Who was this Rosemary? And why was Gethyn thinking about her milk and bread now, while his mother was missing and probably dead? He thought the man's mind must be wandering, confused by anxiety.

The shawled form of Mrs Priestley came to join them.

"Like a nice cup of tea, Gethyn dear?" she asked gently. "Don't you worry now about your mam. They'll find her. Frozen she'll be and glad of a nice fire. This reminds me of the time my son Leonard went missing," she went on. "He disappeared . . . searched for years I did . . . he has never come back."

"You told me Leonard had gone to Canada!" Gethyn stood up and looked down on the old woman, his dark eyes blazing with indignant disbelief. "Canada you said. I was so hurt when he didn't write to me."

"You weren't very old and we thought it best to pretend."

"You and Mam lied to me?" He ignored the woman's obvious distress and insisted, "You didn't tell me the truth although I loved Leonard like he was my father?"

"We don't know what became of him. He's one of hundreds of people who disappear without trace. How could we tell you that?"

"Better than having me believe he hadn't cared enough to write to me!"

"Don't keep on, Gethyn. The pain is still as fresh to me as if it had happened hours ago, not years. I lost my only son. He vanished, just like your mam's vanished and in all these years I haven't had even the slightest hint that he's alive."

"I'm sorry," he said more calmly, "but that was a shock,

knowing he disappeared and was never seen again. I didn't know. I'm sorry." He turned away from her, the pain of learning he had been lied to showing in the anger glinting in his dark eyes.

"I should have told you the truth but you were so young and it seemed almost certain he was dead. We thought it kinder to keep such a tragedy from you, young boy that you were."

"I thought he didn't care enough to write to me."

"We couldn't tell you. We kept hoping you see."

"Have you given up hope now, that he's alive somewhere?"

"Not completely, how could I? You see—" She hesitated then shrugged as if making up her mind. "Well, I might as well tell you, it'll take your mind of the search for your mam."

"Tell me, please. I can't abide secrets."

"D'you know Megan, Rosemary's friend? They work together in the library. Well, she and my Leonard were – you know – walking out together, and I didn't approve. She was older than him for a start and utterly unsuitable. I've always believed that she was the reason my Leonard left home and found somewhere else to live. I think he might have gone to Canada or Australia, putting as much distance as he could between himself and that Megan. Wicked she was, mind, depriving me of my son."

"Leonard was like a wonderful uncle. Me not having a father, he filled that gap in a thousand ways." He frowned. "And it was Rosemary's friend Megan who made him leave us?"

"I'm sure of it, Gethyn dear. Megan might be a good friend to Rosemary Roberts but she made my son go away from me and I've never heard another word. She deprived me of a son and you of a friend. She ought to be punished!"

They were sitting silently, each wrapped in thoughts of the absent Leonard, when a solemn-faced policeman came into the room.

"I'm very sorry, sir. But I think we have some bad news for you. A body has been found up at the quarry and we believe it to be that of your mother. Can you come with us, please?"

Gethyn stood up, his face pale and drawn, his arms trembling in silent tattoo. "If only Rosemary was here. I'd cope all right if Rosemary was with me," he said softly to Mrs Priestley. "Why did she have to be away at such a time?"

As they walked towards the police car, Mrs Priestley said, "Very fond of Rosemary, aren't you dear? Now don't get too fond, not until you're sure she feels the same way. That only leads to disappointment. Go now and I'll be here when you get back. We'll look after each other now, won't we? Now we've both suffered a terrible loss."

For several days there were visits from the police. Besides questioning Gethyn at great length, they spoke to all the neighbours, but finally they told him that it seemed his mother had either lost her balance or slipped on loose gravel. Or had become confused in the thick mist that distorted the familiar place and walked over the edge.

"Why did I choose that day to go to the cinema?" Gethyn moaned.

"Don't blame yourself. You couldn't have done more for her than you did. Everyone knows what a good son you've been."

"It should never have happened," Gethyn insisted.

*   *   *

Search For a Shadow

The funeral was a quiet affair. Gethyn's mother had once been a well-known figure in the village but in the last few years she had gradually stopped going out. Several of her friends had passed away and fewer and fewer people called to visit her.

The church was not full and the mourners gathered together in the first pews to make the sound of their voices carry the hymns more strongly, and give Gethyn the feeling of being surrounded by friends.

All the time he kept talking about when Rosemary returned. Mrs Priestley wondered what had happened to make him believe that his neighbour was anything more than the friend she had always been. So far as she remembered there had been nothing more. In his grief and loneliness, Gethyn was enlarging that affection and making it into something that was pure invention. Rosemary was not in love with Gethyn and unlikely to be.

"Go into town and get yourself a job, boy," she pleaded one day. "It doesn't matter what you do. You'd be better off with some companionship." She had called to see if he was all right and to offer her assistance in sorting out his mother's things. "Go on the bus tomorrow and see if there's something suitable."

"I've tried, but there doesn't seem to be a place for me. I worked at the offices up at the quarry almost twelve years, straight after leaving school. Knew that job so well I could do it in my sleep. But I don't feel like starting something new."

"Gethyn, you're twenty-seven, not fifty!"

"I'll wait till Rosemary comes home and talk it over with her. She'll understand."

"Rosemary has her own life," Mrs Priestley said quietly.

"Always got time for me, Rosemary has. She and I

are close, always have been. When her gran lived next door she used to come for holidays and we spent every moment together. There's a real bond. No one else would understand how close we are."

The elderly woman stood to leave. She had tried several times to warn him but he refused to listen. Now it was up to Rosemary to explain. She hoped the girl would be kind when she did so.

"I'll give you a hand when you're ready to to clear out your mam's clothes. Not something you should do on your own." She looked at him, but he didn't answer. He was wrapped up once again in thoughts of Rosemary and the homecoming he waited for with a kind of desperation.

Chapter Two

When Rosemary reached the London hotel after her arrival at Heathrow, she felt disorientated and weary. Her rather harshly cut, short brown hair was untidy, her small figure in the crumpled travel clothes displaying less than her usual neatness. She always dressed rather formally, in her favourite colours, the subdued hues of autumn.

She went to the desk and collected her key without looking at anyone in the foyer of the hotel. Head down, her blue eyes staring at the floor, she seemed to want to be invisible. Yet someone was observing her.

At a small table, sipping coffee, a young man followed her progress across the muffling carpet and to the stairs. He was tempted to run and help her with her suitcases but did not. Best, he decided, to wait until the scene he had planned could be acted out. He slowly finished his coffee.

The city of New York had been a contrast so great it might have been on a different planet from the place where she lived. The visit, with its hectic round of sightseeing and museum visits and late night discussions, had been fun, but only for a while. Now she knew she would be content to settle back into the routine of her quiet life and the pleasant job in the library of the Welsh market town.

She threw down her luggage and flopped on the bed. It seemed an effort to undress and bath and she was tempted to simply lie there until sleep claimed her.

The hot, soapy water made her feel marginally better and when she went down to check on the opening times of the libraries and museums she planned to visit on the following day, she realised she was ravenously hungry. She chose a small Greek restaurant; she wished she didn't have to eat alone.

Back in the hotel foyer, she stopped to telephone her friend Megan to tell her she had safely landed.

"I imagined every disaster I'd ever heard of and you were in them all," the softly spoken Welsh voice admitted. "There's glad I am that you're back."

"I'm not back for a few days yet," Rosemary reminded her. "I'm taking the opportunity of doing some research for my next book while I'm here."

"Well, hurry home, girl, we all miss you."

"Has anything exciting happened while I've been away?" Rosemary asked.

"Your neighbour, Mrs Lewis, has died."

"What!" The shock of losing her neighbour, who had taken the place of her grandmother in her affections came like a blow. "But how? It must have been very sudden, she was fine when I left. Oh, I'm sorry to hear that. She was a friend of my grandmother's for years. And poor Gethyn! He'll be lost without his mother. He never was much for making friends, he relied on her for everything."

"Gethyn came into the library a few days ago and asked me when you were due home," Megan went on. "Strange he was, all quiet and lost, and looking as if he hadn't slept for weeks. He seems anxious to talk to you about it."

"I'll see you at the weekend," Rosemary promised. "Tell Gethyn, if you see him, that I'll be back late on Saturday, will you?"

Rosemary left the booth. Standing near her, in the foyer

Search For a Shadow

of the hotel, a young man was struggling to open a map and was spilling some books held precariously under his arm. Instinctively, Rosemary went to help.

"Gee thanks," he smiled. They bent down together to gather the recalcitrant books and rescue the crumpled map. Rosemary saw two brown eyes sparkling with amusement, and tousled brown hair that seemed to have a mind of its own quite as determined as the books.

"American!" she said.

"Well, little lady, how did you guess!" he said in an exaggerated accent.

She joined in his laughter and told him she had just that day returned from New York.

"Like it?" he asked.

"Warm, friendly, exciting, surprising, and utterly different from the quiet place where I live," she replied.

"That sounds like my home town." He smiled.

"You live in New York?" she asked.

"You look as if you can't believe anyone actually lives there! Yes, it's my home. I'm a New Yorker born and bred and I love it, noise, bustle and all." The map was finally folded and he handed it to her and asked, "Can you help me find a place called Covent Garden? I was told to be sure and see it."

Rosemary, attracted by the friendliness of the American and conscious of returning the many kindnesses she had received on her recent stay in his country, said, "If you like, I'll show it to you."

The man held out his hand and said, "Glad to meet you, my name is Larry."

Rosemary took his hand, feeling the warmth of it enveloping her arm and spreading around her body.

"I'm Rosemary," she smiled, wishing she felt less travel-worn, wishing she was as attractive as some of the other women sitting around the foyer. She caught sight of her reflection in a large mirror. Her clothes were out of place here in the capital city. She felt so drab she could vanish into the wall and not be seen. For the first time in her life she was unhappy with herself. She looked well beyond her twenty-five years.

"You live here?" Larry waved his arms to encompass the hotel and she shook her head.

"I live in a small Welsh village. But I'm staying in London for a couple of days before returning home."

"I plan to visit a place called Aberystwyth." He surprised her by his careful pronunciation and she praised him for it.

"My full name is Laurence Madison-Jones and my antecedents are Welsh," he said proudly.

"I am Rosemary Roberts and I'm pleased to hear it!" she replied.

"What do you do, Rose Mary?" Larry asked, as they set out the following morning. He pronounced her name as if it were two separate words and she smiled at the pleasant sound of it.

"I'm a librarian and I write stories for children."

"I'm a historian and I'm here for a few months hoping to learn something about my own family. Perhaps you can help me?"

"If it's Aberystwyth you're heading for, that isn't very far from my home," she told him.

"What a marvellous coincidence! I believe my grandfather was from there." He took out some photographs of his family and included in them was one very old black and white photograph of a baby in a pram, with a woman standing beside it, a smile on her face.

It was taken by a street photographer way back in 1962,

Larry explained. "I'm hoping someone might recognise the woman."

"I recognise the place. It's Aberystwyth," Rosemary said.

"I reckon you're right."

"The woman, she's a relative?" Rosemary asked.

"Kinda related, yeah." Larry was vague, his eyes staring at the photograph.

"That seems very unlikely. That someone would recognise her, I mean."

"Coincidences happen."

"Of course, and I wish you luck," she smiled. He looked at her then, his face relaxing into a smile so warm that she felt as if she were melting. His hand reached out and touched hers.

"Surely you believe in coincidences, Rosemary? Or why are we here together, at this moment? Talking about a small part of the small country of Wales we are both connected with?" He was rewarded with one of her dazzlingly beautiful smiles.

The near kinship seemed to relax the remaining hint of their being strangers in a strange town. Meeting Larry felt like an extension of her holiday and she found the prospect of returning home less and less of a draw.

"I thought London was new to you," she said curiously, surprised that he seemed so at ease with taking shortcuts Rosemary herself was unfamiliar with.

"I studied the street plan before we set out," he admitted, "and luckily, you chose to show me the part I had half remembered."

She was tired but refused to admit it and when Larry suggested they ate she was grateful for the prospect of a rest.

He hailed a taxi and they were driven to a small Italian restaurant not far from Oxford Circus where all the food was home-cooked. The marble floor was bliss to Rosemary's aching feet and Larry teased her by threatening to run off with her shoes. Without the proprietor's seeing, he lifted her feet onto his knee and massaged her feet and ankles in a way that made her forget their tiredness. The movements were sensual but he still had that attractive and irresistible sense of fun in his dark eyes.

"Tell me about your village, Rosemary," Larry asked, when they were enjoying a coffee after their meal.

"Life is quiet and, for someone like you, probably dull. Nothing ever happens. Not even any grafitti or litter to complain of. You can walk for an hour along some of the country lanes and not see a car. Life seems to slip along on a conveyor belt, each day similar to its predecessor."

"But you love it."

"I love it." Her eyes softened as she thought of it, imagining walking along the quiet lanes hand in hand with him.

"You have good neighbours?"

"Oh yes. They're all friends really. It's hard to imagine but there are still doors that are rarely locked, and once you have seen a person twice you can call him a friend. I bought the cottage from my grandmother when I wanted to leave home. I preferred the idea of living in a house I knew rather than renting a flat in the town. The people in the five cottages making up the terrace are long-standing friends, almost part of my family really. Over several generations we've always lived near each other and we are bound up in each other's joys and tragedies.

"When Gran died a year ago, the terrace grieved with us. Yesterday I learned that my neighbour, who had been Gran's closest friend, has died. Gethyn, he's the son, will be devastated. But he won't feel alone. Everyone will support him and share his sadness. Gethyn will be anxious for me to get home; he and I have been friends since childhood and he'll want to talk to me about it."

"Boyfriend, is he, this Gethyn?"

"Oh no. Just a neighbour, part of my extended family, a close friend." Larry's hand tightened its grip. His eyes looked deeply into hers and he asked with a sigh, "There's a boyfriend?"

"No." She smiled and shook her head.

"I'm glad."

On the following day, Rosemary rang Megan to tell her not to expect her until Monday morning.

"I've met this American," she confided, "and I know what everyone says about holiday friendships and I know that's all this is, but I can't resist extending it for another day."

"Gethyn will be disappointed," Megan told her. "So will Sally and I of course, but poor Gethyn is hovering around the library hoping for news of your return. Very impatient, he is."

A moment's guilt was soon washed away as Larry came to join her for their second onslaught on the sights of London.

"Perhaps today," she suggested brightly, ever conscious of her dowdiness, "we might do some shopping?"

Larry's idea of shopping was not hers. She thought of C & A, Marks & Spencers . . . Larry took her to Piccadilly and through Burlington Arcade. They walked to New Bond Street where, under his persuasion, she bought a lemon dress and jacket that cost more than a month's salary and he insisted on buying her shoes and a handbag from Gucci.

"I want you to accept them as a thank you gift for being so generous with your time," he said as she protested. "I know how much you really want to be back in your little grey stone cottage beside the stream."

"No, I've loved seeing London with you," she insisted. The parcels packed in the distinctive Gucci bag hung heavily on her arm like a steadily increasing burden as they walked to their next destination. Somehow, receiving such expensive gifts had spoiled everything.

They had lunch at Fortnum & Mason and tea at Simpson's. Yet, although they talked as freely as before, the gift and the thank you had changed everything. She was nothing more than a kind stranger. She knew that now. His hand no longer searched for hers. After leaving her hand close to his and getting no response, she filled her arms with the parcels to disguise their emptiness.

When they returned to the hotel, Larry carried her parcels in for her from the taxi. At her door she hesitated, inexperience making her unsure of what she should do. Should she invite him inside, or thank him at the door? Then he smiled, his eyes looked into hers as he said, "Open the door, woman! I can't drop all these on the floor, can I?"

"I hadn't realised there were so many."

He put the parcels and bags on her bed and sat in a chair beside it.

"I want to see you wearing the new dress," he said.

"Of course. I'll wear it tomorrow."

"I can't wait that long!" he laughed. "Go on, it won't take a minute to slip it on."

Amused, she went into the bathroom and pulled the dress over her slim figure. There was only a small mirror in the bathroom but even in that she could see that the colour did something for her. The slim, fitted line of the

Search For a Shadow

dress gave her figure a lift, instead of disguising its trimness as skirts and blouses had done. Stepping out into the room, she saw Larry's face show admiration and a blush suffused her face.

"Rose Mary, you're beautiful! Why have you been hiding yourself?" he murmured.

When she removed the dress, Larry's reflection appeared in the bathroom mirror. Immediately panic seized her. Did she want this? How could she accept what was in his eyes? But how could she refuse? He was a stranger and someone she might never see again. But it might be the beginning of something wonderful.

She felt his fingers relieving her of the rest of her clothes, his lips kissing her slowly revealed body. She was losing control and she didn't care. Her own body was responding to his touch in a way that she had never imagined and there was no turning back. This was something she wanted so badly that even if she regretted it for the rest of her life, the here and now demanded she abandoned her fears and give herself completely to this man.

He lifted her and carried her to the bed. His loving was gentle and caring, it seemed as natural as breathing and it transported her to realms of exquisite joy. When she finally slept it was with his arms around her, his breath touching her cheek like a caress.

When she woke the next morning he was lying beside her, his hair tousled, his eyes glowing with rekindled desire. They showered together before going down to breakfast, and then they were driven back to the bed once more. In her eyes, he was her own, her protector; she had given herself to him and now they would never want to part. She marvelled at how quickly it had all happened and knew she was in love.

A stranger until a matter of hours ago, he was already

so important to her happiness that she felt a momentary shiver of apprehension at the thought of him saying goodbye. But he wouldn't. Would he?

Their last day was a dream. Everything was perfect; the weather, the places they visited, the meals they ate and especially the evening, when they once again came back to her room to make love.

"For the first time since I was a child, I'm not longing to finish my journey and get home," she admitted on Sunday evening, the last of their stay.

"You mean you were always as excited at getting home as setting out?" Larry laughed. "Hell, I thought holidays were supposed to be fun! Didn't you enjoy yours?"

"Always! But I still found that going home was something to be relished. There's the post, perhaps something you've been waiting for, or an unexpected letter from a friend. I even found a small Premium Bond win waiting for me once when I'd been away."

"A 'Premium Bond'?" he queried, smiling as she briefly explained. "But this time, it's different?" he probed. She stretched out her hand and he took it in both of his, holding it as if it were something precious.

"This time it's different," she whispered.

His arms reached for her and it was late before they finally slept.

So it was with a feeling of hurt and disbelief that she woke next morning to find herself alone in the bed. She looked around her room and saw in a moment that his clothes, strewn untidily across the floor last night, were gone. She hurriedly dressed and ran along the corridor to his room. The door stood ajar, the room was empty, the maid was

Search For a Shadow

already stripping the bed. It was as if Larry Madison-Jones had never existed.

She walked slowly back to her room and lay on the bed, unable to think. The alarm, set to tell her to rise and go for her train, puttered into life and she stood up and slammed it off, wanting to throw it out of the window, wanting to hit out at something, anything, to vent her anger and humiliation on the world. She prepared to leave, her mind in a daze.

Her brain began to work again as she settled her account and ordered a taxi. She realised that for Larry, she had been just a pleasant way of filling a couple of days. He'd been glad of her company and her ability to guide him around the treasures of London, a mild flirtation and nothing more.

For her, the few days had been magical, an experience she would hold in her heart and around which she would spin daydreams. In time she would forget. She repeated the words, trying to believe them. In time, she would forget the disillusionment and remember only a brief and pleasant interlude that held no special importance.

In the taxi she sat like someone still caught in the muzzy folds of sleep. She didn't look out of the window, she didn't answer when the friendly cab driver offered conversation. She paid him like an automaton and walked to the platform on Euston station, dragging her case behind her.

She followed the signs to her platform and looked about her, eyes dull and with a hurt expression that hadn't left her since she had woken and found herself alone. Footsteps echoing on the hard surface, the morning hollow-sounding in the unbroken day. No curly head or laughing brown eyes hurried towards her.

She was confused, feeling a certain amount of guilt now she was back on home ground in a place where she could never have imagined behaving in such a casual way with a stranger, and with the guilt came bitter regret at the ending of the affair, with embarrassment and hurt. After the train journey, during which she had been lost in her own thoughts, she now wanted to fill the time with talk, and no longer be alone with self-recrimination.

The slow journey through small villages and the richly green fields was balm. The soft Welsh voices were soothing and welcoming. She felt at that moment she would never want to go away again. Sheep wandered the hills like fallen segments of the summer clouds; a heron flew up from a narrow stream and flapped lazily across to the untidy nest it had made in a tree. Above the hillside, a buzzard hovered, smaller birds flying nervously under its shadow. This, Rosemary thought, is all the excitement I need from now on.

As she left the bus and walked down the steps leading from the main road to where the cottages nestled on the edge of the stream, she saw that the door of the first one was open. Gethyn looked up, waved, then ran to meet her. An odd figure, in old-fashioned, ill-fitting clothes and painfully shy, it was good to see him. Tall, powerful and as familiar as breakfast toast, the welcoming smile on his face creased the folds around his dark eyes. He darted glances at her shyly, but with an unmistakable air of excitement at her return. His obvious pleasure almost brought tears to her eyes. His undisguised delight made her distress at Larry's departure fade, become less painful. She was home, among friends, and those who loved her.

"There's empty it's been all these long weeks," Gethyn said, "your house never showing a light. It didn't seem right. Thank goodness you're back safe."

Search For a Shadow

"I've heard about your mother, Gethyn," Rosemary said at once, to save him the distress of telling her. "I'm very sorry."

"I've got milk in for you and a fresh loaf of bread and there's cheese and fruit to see you through till you can go shopping tomorrow," he said. "I put it on the kitchen table."

She was surprised at the way he ignored her words, but knew how difficult he found it to talk about things that really mattered. When she had been home a few days he would want to talk to her, go over the details of his mother's death, she was sure of that.

"Thank you Gethyn, you're so kind. That's just what your mother would have done for me."

He dropped her luggage on the hall floor and with a brief smile which did not include his eyes meeting hers, he went into his house, next door to her own, without another word.

Mrs Priestley from number four arrived with a plateful of cakes before Rosemary had finished unpacking. She held the plate aloft while under her other arm was her old black cat. She announced that she had called to welcome Rosemary home and tell her the news. Rosemary put down the post she had begun to examine and put the kettle on to boil.

"I know you'll be dying to hear what's been happening in the weeks you've been away," she said conspiratorially. "Well now, where do I start? Mr and Mrs Hughes next door at number three are well but they're away at present visiting their youngest in Bala." She followed Rosemary into the kitchen and, still carrying the patient animal, helped Rosemary prepare a tray of tea to go with the cakes. Then, with the cat comfortably sleeping on her lap, she settled in one of the armchairs for a chat.

Resigned to it, knowing from past experience how impossible it was to discourage Mrs Priestley when she was in full flood, Rosemary forgot all thoughts of unpacking and sat opposite her near the empty fireplace.

"The Powells have gone to Canada for a year and the house at the end is let, to students," Mrs Priestley went on. "Very nice they are, mind, not a bit of trouble so far. There's Huw and Richard; he's got a car and I've driven to the shops in style twice already!" she chuckled.

"I feel as if I've been away for months instead of three weeks!" Rosemary said.

"Seen Gethyn next door, have you?" The smile faded and the shrewd hazel eyes looked towards the wall shared with Gethyn's house, she lowered her voice and added, "Gethyn, poor dab, he's devastated."

"He came to help me with my luggage from the bus and he bought some groceries for me just like his mother would," Rosemary told her. "What happened? He didn't seem willing to talk about it."

"One of the shepherds found her. She had been walking home with a basket of logs for her fire. No need for her to do that, mind. Everyone knew Gethyn was always on to her to stop struggling with heavy loads, you know how he fussed over her. But she was stubborn and insisted on going up the hill beyond the church, gathering firewood in that old woven straw basket of hers. Fell into the quarry she did. Found lying there near the decomposing bodies of a couple of sheep." Mrs Priestley shuddered dramatically as she went on.

"Her heart they say it was, we had an inquest and all. She'd had several blows to the head. From the rocks it must have been, although for a while they weren't sure, mind. Going over that steep edge as she did, she was bound to be battered as she fell. Poor Gethyn. Poor dab. What'll be do without her? That's what we're all wondering."

"He's only twenty-seven!" Rosemary defended. "He'll make a new life for himself. Thank goodness he lives in a place like this and not in a town. He won't be alone, he has all of us to comfort him and help him find his feet."

The emptiness of the house hit her when Mrs Priestley had gone. Somehow the journey and the bustle of arriving home, unpacking and sorting through the post, as well as catching up on the local news with Mrs Priestley had deadened the impact of the return. Now, in the silent house, her mind went once more to Larry and his abandonment of her after three days of companionship and two nights of loving. The interlude had blanked off the American holiday so it seemed like something that had happened months before. Her immediate memories were so strong, so filled with mixed emotions that they overrode the two and a half weeks in New York.

She hung up the new yellow dress and stared at it. She had intended to wear it to the library the following morning but now, seeing it without the background of the capital city and the modern hotel room, she decided against it. The idea of changing her image was possible while she was away and with Larry beside her, but now she was home in the grey stone cottage on a low hillside besides a Welsh stream, the idea seemed laughable.

She took from the wardrobe a grey skirt and a pale grey and blue check blouse. The thought of changing had been exciting for a while but it was far easier to stay the way she was.

Gethyn Lewis watched from his front window as Mrs Priestley went into Rosemary's house. He watched as she left an hour later and wondered what they had been discussing. Himself and the death of his mother for sure, he decided. It had been the talk of the neighbourhood since it had happened.

Gethyn wanted to go and talk to Rosemary about it, explain how he felt. She'd understand how it was both a sadness and a relief not to be tied to his elderly mother any more. She had been forty-five when he was born and now, at twenty-seven, he remembered the years of resentment at being known as "The Lad" or "The Lewis Boy". But now she was gone and he could decide who he really was.

He stood up and cleared the remnants of the simple meal he had prepared on the old-fashioned, wooden, scrub-top table. Perhaps he could go in to see Rosemary now? Tomorrow she'd be at work. He pulled a comb through his hair with little effect, and straightened his shirt collar. A glance in the mirror showed him a tidily dressed young man, paler than usual, giving his dark features a rather sickly look. He looked away in doubt.

What if Rosemary didn't feel the same as he did? What if the absence, instead of making her realise how much they meant to each other, had instead had the effect of making her take a wider view and spreading her wings?

At her door he hesitated. Then he lost his nerve. Why would she want to talk to him? She must be tired after her long journey. He couldn't imagine travelling all the way to London, let alone flying across the Atlantic to America. Why had she wanted to go? What was the sense in exploring a place filled with strangers, when everything she needed was here?

He walked past her door up the hill to the woods, then, turning, came down to the church half hidden between the woodland and the hill and stood beside his mother's grave. Tomorrow he would talk to Rosemary. Tomorrow for certain.

Rosemary's return to work was a sham. She forced herself to make an adventure of her weeks in America, exaggerated the laughs she had shared with the people she had met. Made more of the simplest event so that the people she worked with, and the people who called to exchange a book, all enjoyed the telling and believed she had had a marvellous time. In fact, the memories of the visit were already vague, overshadowed by the few days in London with Larry Madison-Jones.

She met her friends, Megan and Sally, and they went out for a meal so they could hear all her news. Sally hadn't been working with them for very long and Rosemary was a little disappointed that Megan had invited her to join them, but she added to the hour, laughing enthusiastically at the humorous stories and listening avidly to the adventure in the London hotel.

Sally was red-haired, loudly spoken and very confident. Rosemary was afraid their personalities would clash but Sally seemed anxious to make a friend of her and went out of her way to please her. She tried to make the leap from new acquaintance to close friend in a matter of hours, to become a confidant without the preliminaries of getting to know each other and that, Rosemary did not like. Sally even suggested they went to Aberystwyth that weekend to do some shopping then go back to Rosemary's cottage for a meal.

"You'll have your photographs by then," she urged. "We'd have a lovely evening looking at them and you telling us all about the occasions. Go on, let's have an après-holiday evening."

Feeling herself pushed into something for which she was not ready, Rosemary refused.

"But I'll bring them into the library for you to see," she promised with a sideways look at Megan. Megan raised an eyebrow as if to say, she'll need watching or she'll take over our lives.

Rosemary got back into the mood of the evening quickly, pushing aside the slight irritation, making them laugh, inventing thrilling stories out of the most ordinary events to give the impression that it had all been such fun, but in fact it was already a part of the distant past. Only Megan, much later when Sally had left them, heard the truth about the few days in London. Older, wiser, she sympathised momentarily then said firmly, "Rosemary, you are a fool. To have an adventure like that with someone as handsome and attractive as this Larry sounds, well, you shouldn't feel sadness, shame, guilt, or any other destructive emotion. You should pack it away in your memories to be enjoyed over and over again. Not treating it as if it were the most terrible disaster!" Rosemary gasped in amazement at her friend.

"I thought you'd be shocked!" She stared at the mouse-like Megan, fifty years old, grey and set in her ways but still with a younger, more modern outlook than her own, it seemed.

"Me, shocked? Jealous more like!"

"But he used me and abandoned me like some tart he'd picked up on the streets!"

"So, you used him! You must have enjoyed it, so why pretend you didn't?"

As she told Megan more and more of what they had done, what they had seen, Rosemary began to see that Megan was right. She had enjoyed it and her only fault was expecting more of the incident than she should.

Search For a Shadow

"Being brought up in a small village and used to the gentle, unworldly ways of the neighbours, imagining that what we see on the television isn't real, has made me unaware that outside the boundaries of this place there's a great big world," she said.

"An exciting one too and there's lucky you are to have touched it for a day or two." Megan chuckled and went on, "I thought I was world class when I won a weekend in Paris! And I came back no different from when I went!"

After work, Rosemary drove home and went into her house. Megan's words had cheered her and put the whole episode into a different mould. She didn't stay in the house long but closed the door and set off again without seeing any of the neighbours. She looked at the row, Gethyn in number one, herself next door. In number three were the absent Hughes's, Muriel and Harry, and Mrs Priestley was at number four. At number five were the students. She must call and see them soon, introduce herself and offer assistance if and when they needed it.

She put on an old anorak and some walking shoes and, taking the flowers she had bought, she walked up over the hill to the churchyard, intending to place one bunch on her grandmother's grave, and the other on the new grave of Gethyn's mother. She didn't lock her door, she rarely did except when she went to work and at night. It didn't occur to her that she should. A key was left with a neighbour in case she locked herself out. It had always been that way, relaxed and easy.

She walked up between the uneven and tilting gravestones in the evening shadows, slowly, lazily, enjoying the soft breeze on her cheeks and the scent of flowers on the air. To her horror, she saw that the new grave had been dug up, earth thrown across the paths and onto the nearby graves. Vases lay smashed, the flowers that had once been arranged in them were torn into shreds and scattered.

Who could have done such a thing? She tidied it as well as she could, planning to buy some new vases the next day. She hoped she could straighten it all out before Gethyn saw the desecration.

Walking back through the village she saw a Citroën car, a red and white "Dolly", and for a moment the driver looked like Larry. She stopped and stared after it, then laughed aloud. She was behaving no better than a lovesick teenager! She reminded herself of Megan's wise words and walked briskly home, admiring the hedgerow flowers and the song of the birds. They were real. Larry no longer was.

The sight of the graves, then imagining seeing Larry, had jangled her nerves. She was unsettled. The result of the holiday and what followed, she decided. A few days home and she would be back to normal. Her normal dowdy self! she thought with a sudden shock.

No, she wouldn't slip back into what she had been before. Larry's admiration was something that had altered her opinion of herself. For a while she had seen herself as an attractive and desirable woman. She mustn't accept that the improvement was temporary. At least then something would have been gained from their affair besides just memories. Tomorrow, she decided, she would make a start by going to a good hairdresser and finding a softer, more feminine style.

Television had little to offer, she was out of touch with all the soaps. She picked up a book and decided to get undressed and bathe luxuriously in some of the expensive bath oils she had bought in Macy's, New York, then go to bed early and read. She'd pour herself a drink – there was some Metaxa left from her Greek holiday. Tonight was a

Search For a Shadow

time to indulge herself. Tomorrow she would begin a new stage of her life. That was something to celebrate.

As she went through the hall she saw a small, white envelope. Curiously she went to pick it up. There was no post this late, unless a letter had been dropped through someone else's door by mistake and pushed in later on. She turned the envelope over. It hadn't come by post, there was no address and no stamp, only her name.

She opened it. Then she gasped with shock. The note was from Larry.

Chapter Three

Rosemary stared at the note in disbelief. Where was he? Why hadn't he knocked? How had he found her address? Questions bowled through her confused brain like straw scattered by a wild wind. Belatedly, she opened the front door and looked out. There was no sign of anyone in the shadowy evening.

Beyond the small front garden with its tangle of marigolds, geraniums, sweet williams and fuchsia, bound together by an unruly marriage of trailing bistort and lobelia, was a footpath. Beyond that, a grassy bank and the small stream flowing calmly down to join the River Dovey. In front and to her right was the wooden footbridge that crossed the stream, half shadowed by trees. To her left the path led to where steps rose to the level of the road which crossed the stream via a stone, parapeted road bridge.

There wasn't a sound. What the locals laughingly called the main road, was rarely full of traffic. This late evening there wasn't a single car to disturb the night. Even the waterfall that came under the road some distance to her left was slow, spilling softly over the worn rocks, rippling to recover then moving quietly on; peaceful and familiar. Rosemary stepped inside and closed the door.

She read the note again more calmly. Larry was in Aberystwyth and wanted to meet her. There was a phone number for her to call, but when she did so,

Search For a Shadow

her fingers trembling with confused excitement, she was told he was not there but would she kindly leave a message. The disembodied voice promised politely to give the message to Mr Madison-Jones the moment he arrived the following day.

"But I thought he was there already?" Rosemary queried.

"Not until tomorrow, Mrs Madison-Jones. He has a room booked for you both for three nights starting Friday," the woman said. "What time shall I tell him to expect you?"

Rosemary stuttered a little, confused and embarrassed by his disregard for the truth.

"I – er – will you ask him to phone? I'd better remind him of the numbers." She added stupidly, "They've changed and he never remembers." She recited the numbers of her home and the library and the woman repeated them and took them down.

"Will there be anything further, Mrs Madison-Jones?"

"Thank you, no." She put down the phone and felt a giggle rising in her throat. This was so ridiculous; more like a farce than real life! The fact that he had booked a double room, naming her as his wife was a shock, but who was to know? The town was far enough away from home for there to be little chance of anyone here finding out, and even if they did she was twenty-five and, since London, no longer a virgin.

But a tiny doubt remained. She would be unhappy if her neighbours thought her anything other than a respectable librarian who wrote children's stories. She smiled at her foolishness. After the mixture of thrill and fear had settled down to happy anticipation, she began to wonder again how the note had arrived at her door.

The obvious explanation was that Larry had asked

someone to post the note through her door, someone who was passing near. Or perhaps he *was* the man she thought she recognised, driving the Citroen Dolly? Of course he wasn't! Why did she look for more mystery than there already was? She went back into the living room and revived the fire. She no longer felt like going to bed. She undressed and sat before the blaze.

She read the note several times but it revealed no more than the first time. Larry was in Aberystwyth and would like to meet her. She had given the woman her library telephone number and wondered if he would in fact ring, or, foolishly, whether the note was some kind of hoax. Why would he let her go without a word then take the trouble to seek her out? A knock at the door startled her and she almost ran to answer it.

"Rosemary," Gethyn said apologetically, "can you spare a moment?"

"Come in, Gethyn, if you'll excuse my appearance."

She saw his colour brighten as he attempted to make a complimentary reply but the words were lost in embarrassment and he lowered his head and said nothing. He was dressed in ill-fitting clothes of a style popular many years before. He had on an over-wide tie, over which he wore a hand-knitted V-necked sweater. On top of that, unbelievable in the warmth of the evening when even the cheerful fire was not really necessary, a tweed jacket. She realised she had never seen him in anything specifically chosen for summer.

"It's about Mam's grave," he said when they were seated near the crackling fire on which fresh logs were beginning to catch.

"What about it?" Rosemary frowned. Surely they hadn't been damaged again?

"Someone has changed the flowers, and the ornament

Search For a Shadow

I bought has been replaced with one smaller and less ornate," he said.

"That was me, Gethyn." Rosemary decided at once that it was best to tell the truth. "I went up there when I came back from holiday and found the flowers broken and scattered and the vases smashed. I tried to replace them so you wouldn't find them and be upset. Sorry, I couldn't find exactly the right ones."

"You did that for me?" Brown eyes stared at her with such admiration that she turned away. This time it was her turn to be embarrassed.

"It was nothing. You'd have done the same for me," she muttered.

"Oh yes, indeed I would, but – Rosemary, thank you."

She stood up, dismissing him, and he stood beside her, tall, strong and suddenly different from the man she had known all her life. She felt his eyes following her as she went to open the door. She saw him out and closed the door against him. What was it about Gethyn that was different?

She felt stirrings of excitement, a heightening of her senses, strongly aware of herself as a woman more than of him being a desirable man. He was attracted to her!

She wondered what had caused the almost imperceptable shift in their relationship and decided that the change was in herself rather than him. It was meeting Larry, loving him, being loved and growing, in a matter of moments, from a quiet, orderly, single girl, to an experienced, more sensual, woman. But was it only herself? Hadn't Gethyn become somehow different too? There was a look about him she hadn't seen before. Perhaps the death of his mother had cut some invisible cord?

How odd, the thought as she doused the fire and set off

up the stairs to her bed. Gethyn, whom she had befriended in her childhood was suddenly an enigma. But not, she reminded herself firmly, not someone who could mean anything. So be careful, Rosemary Roberts, or you'll find yourself in a very awkward situation. Neighbours are sometimes too close for comfort.

Gethyn went back to his lonely house but, like Rosemary the other side of the shared wall, he did not sleep. She was considerate and kind. Imagine going to the trouble of sorting the mess on the grave to save him being upset. Few would do that for him. She must care.

All though the long weeks while she was away he had dreamed of her home-coming, a return to find him waiting, his arms open for her and her suddenly realising how much she needed him. He was her haven and she was beginning to realise it. His mother's death was a tragedy, but it was necessary to clear the way and make room in their lives for each other. It was all meant to be, he thought as he relaxed against his pillow, his hand on the shared wall where he imagined she would be lying; it was all happening for the best.

Beside his bed was a photograph of his mother. The house was full of photographs, in assorted frames, on the walls and on most of the available flat surfaces, some going back to the days when his mother was young. This one was of his mother when she was about forty, before he had been born. He picked it up and stared at it.

She had been, from what he had overheard people say, set in her ways. Because of her age, her attitudes overlapping from a previous generation, his life had been inhibited and filled with older people. She had been more like the grandmothers who had occasionally called at the school to meet their grandchildren and spoil them with forbidden sweets and comics and trips to the park.

He remembered with surprising anger how he had resented being asked if his mother was his gran. He remembered too how Mam had refused to allow him to play with the other children, probably, he thought now, staring at her photograph, because she felt ill-at-ease with the parents. Some of them twenty-five years her junior! "Mamma's boy", they'd called after me, he remembered bitterly.

Perhaps it wasn't too late to change? He sensed rather than knew that Rosemary was not happy about the way he looked. Being out of work meant he didn't have a lot of money for clothes and anyway, Mam had drummed it into him that it was wicked to buy things you didn't really need. The clothes he had were good and with plenty of wear in them. That too, he recognised with a resurgence of anger, was an attitude from a previous generation.

He replaced the photograph on the small bedside table and ran his hand over the shared wall. Behind it Rosemary was sleeping. He wondered if she was dreaming of him.

When Rosemary walked to her car the following morning to go to the library, she heard a voice calling her name.

"Miss Roberts."

She turned to see a tall, slim young man approaching and looked at him curiously. He was fair and his eyes were smiling in friendly greeting. He held out his hand as he reached her and said, "I'm one of the students, living in the Powells' house. Huw Rees, how d'you do, Miss Roberts?" He was looking at her boldly and with obvious interest. She wondered why she was suddenly of interest to the opposite sex when until now, most men had ignored her. Perhaps being half in love with Larry showed on her face and made her more attractive?

"I share number five with a friend, Richard Lloyd, although there's usually several more of us flopped around in sleeping bags. If you ever need anything, just call on us; our skills are varied and we want to be good neighbours." He smiled, released her hand somewhat unwillingly and stood while she walked across the wooden footbridge to where she parked her car.

"Your car?" she asked, pointing to the rather battered Capri. He shook his head.

"That belongs to Richard, it's shanks's pony for me I'm afraid."

As she got into the car she saw the door of number one open and Gethyn came out and waved to her.

"I'll put your milk inside for you, out of the sun," he called. Rosemary chuckled. It seemed Gethyn too was staking his claim to be allowed to help her!

She drove into the town, Gethyn and Huw forgotten, wondering if Larry would phone her. It was Thursday, not much time to arrange to meet if he was in Aberystwyth. Although she had spoken confidently on the telephone when she discussed her arrival, it was bravado; she wouldn't go anywhere unless Larry phoned to confirm.

She decided to use her lunch-hour to go to the shops and buy herself a couple of smart, colourful outfits just in case Larry did get in touch. If it had been some hoax, although she doubted if it could have been, then the new clothes would cheer her anyway and the outlay wouldn't be wasted.

As soon as she mentioned her intention, Sally asked to go with her.

"I love shopping for clothes," she said, "and if Megan

doesn't mind, I can have the same lunch-hour as you and help you choose."

Unable to think of a reason for refusing, Rosemary smiled and agreed.

Sally's comments and enthusiasm did help her to avoid the usual and look at different styles but all the time they were together, the girl seemed to be asking questions. Mostly about the cottage and its neighbours. After a while, Rosemary became intensely engrossed in her examination of the garments on offer and ignored the endless interrogation. She went back to the library having bought nothing.

"Why is she so curious?" she whispered to Megan on her return. "What can interest her about my neighbours, a few people she doesn't know?"

"New to the job and anxious to make new friends, I suppose. Did you get anything nice?"

"No, I saw some lovely things though. But if I bought them it would be a waste of money. It was probably a hoax."

"Why would you think it's a hoax, for heaven's sake?" Megan sounded exasperated.

"Lack of confidence I suppose, not believing that someone like Larry could want to bother with someone like me."

"Have you looked at yourself, lately? Beautiful you are, with eyes like welcoming beacons to any red-blooded male!" Rosemary laughed delightedly and admitted there had been a change in the attitude of a few young men.

"When you next go shopping for clothes, I'm going with you!" Megan said firmly. "And I'll make sure you come back if not broke then badly bent!"

Rosemary laughed.

Larry had walked out of the London hotel intending never

to see Rosemary again. She was confusing him. First he had decided she was ordinary, homely, the kind of dame he wouldn't waste a moment on. Then that smile of hers began to get to him and he had allowed himself to be drawn into an affair he hadn't intended. The fact that she lived in the very area he needed to search was too good to ignore and leaving her like that had blown it.

How could he see her again? Thinking out an excuse for his behaviour wasn't easy. But he was sure enough of his own attraction to hope she would be so glad to hear from him again she wouldn't delve too deeply into his story.

He had bought a car, a small Citroën, and it was easy to slip a note through her door. Finding her home hadn't been so easy, the place was unbelievably dark and it was a miracle he hadn't landed in that brook!

He called the Aberystwyth hotel and was given her message. Just before lunch-time he picked up the phone.

Larry's call came just before Rosemary and Megan were due to leave for their shopping expedition.

"Rose Mary, I was devastated when I got back from my early morning wander around London to find you'd gone! And without leaving your address too. I'd hoped you'd want to see me again." He hoped his fervent voice would make the words more convincing.

"I thought you wouldn't – I mean, I didn't think you – I—" She faltered to a stop and Larry laughed and said, "You thought I was avoiding you on your last morning deliberately? Oh, honey. After we'd had such fun together? And after that wonderful night? I didn't know you were leaving so soon. Honestly. I came back after buying a paper and a few bits and pieces and your room was empty."

She wanted to believe him, oh, how she wanted that,

Search For a Shadow

but she remembered with heart-aching clarity seeing his clothes gone, and seeing the empty room. He had vacated it before she had woken. How could he have been disappointed to find her gone?

"How did you get my address?" she asked.

"I told the receptionist I had a book belonging to you and wanted to return it. She hesitated but in the end she gave me your address. The fact I was coming so near your home was a gift from the gods but I'd have come to find you anyway, you must believe that?"

"I believe that." Rosemary smiled. It was what she wanted, needed, to believe. Perhaps he had taken his luggage down stairs and had gone out, forgetting the time—

"You *are* free for the weekend?" Larry queried.

"The whole of it?"

"You bet the whole if it! I've made reservations at an hotel on the promenade or whatever you call it. Dark grey stone, a forbidding exterior, but warmth, friendliness and comfort inside. Please say you'll come?"

"I'll see you at seven."

"Earlier, please, baby."

"I could drive up straight from the library. I could be there by five-thirty?"

"Great, I'll leave all the sightseeing 'til you arrive. First, we have to climb up Constitution Hill, at the far end of the beach. The locals call it 'Consti' I'm told. Are you game for that?"

"Race you to the top," she laughed. "Loser buys the teas."

The second shopping trip was a whirl of excitement. With Megan's help and Sally's enthusiasm, Rosemary bought dresses for the evening and for the day, summer cottons and silky gowns. Out went the ubiquitous cardigans and sensible shirts, in came smart jackets and colourful tops. Culottes took the place of the comfortable and baggy trousers she wore for walking the hills. She would go prepared for any occasion Larry and Aberystwyth could offer.

Gethyn rarely went into the town. He was uneasy with people and preferred to find what he needed in the small mini-market in the village. Seeing Rosemary set off for work that morning, he decided to go and see her at the library and perhaps, if the situation went well, invite her to go to the shops with him on the following Saturday afternoon. He knew it would be easier for him to ask her by calling in the house next door, but if he were to change his clothes, he must change his attitude as well. Going into the library, her place, strange ground for him, was a challenge he must not avoid. If he were to change then he had to face a new challenge every day. This was an easy one to start with.

He saw her almost at once and knew he could not speak to her. She was laughing with her friends, Megan and the new assistant, Sally, both of whom he disliked. Megan was too possessive with Rosemary and Sally looked too bold to be anything but trouble.

From the shadow of a tall bookcase he watched as she took out a garment and held it against herself for the others to see. It was shaped rather like a pair of dungarees, but in material so flouncy and light and colourful, he couldn't imagine anyone using them to do anything except sit still. She looked stunning, with more colour in her cheeks and excitement shining in her eyes than he'd ever seen. He turned away. It was she who was changing, and much faster than himself!

He felt foolish standing there wanting to talk to her,

Search For a Shadow

now there was nothing to say. Something had happened to her, she was moving far out of his reach.

"Gethyn? We don't see you in here very often." Rosemary, coming up behind him startled him and he stood up and closed the book.

"I was waiting for the bus back and came in for a few minutes. I didn't come in for anything in particular," he added hastily. He left then, feeling angry with himself for not taking the opportunity to ask Rosemary to go shopping with him, but there was plenty of time. Tomorrow would do.

On Friday, he sat in his front room, watching for Rosemary's car to stop at the parking place across the stream. She was late, and he presumed she was still working. Friday was the day they stayed open until eight o'clock. But at ten o'clock she still hadn't arrived and he guessed then that the shopping and the excitement must have meant she was away for the weekend.

But why hadn't she told him? There couldn't be another man, could there? He sat at the window until darkness made it impossible to see even the shadows of the footbridge, then went to bed.

The weather was amazingly good for the weekend in Aberystwyth. As Rosemary parked her car behind the tall hotel, the clouds broke more like morning than evening, and the sun burst out, touching everything with gold as if it were setting the scene for the brief sojourn in the quiet seaside town.

Larry ran out to meet her and his greeting left no doubt that he was pleased to see her again. They chattered as they went up to their room with its wide windows looking out across the sea. They marvelled at the brightness of the sun, the peacefulness of the beach and the promenade.

"It's another world!" Larry said. "It's like walking back into a past where today's troubles aren't even a distant fear."

"Lacks the bustle of New York, doesn't it!"

"It's fantastic! It's a place to come and find yourself," he murmured. Then he kissed her, the excitement of meeting again overcame them and they fell back on the wide and tempting bed.

Larry announced later that he had hired a car, not a large comfortable one as she imagined he would insist on, but the Citroen Dolly, which he described as "no speedster but a lot of fun".

"I thought I saw you driving one through the village, the day you put the note through my door," she told him. But he shook his head.

"I guess there's another handsome fella with the same tastes," he joked. "Just so long as he doesn't want my girl as well!" He smiled at her and added, "I sure am longing to see the village and this cottage of yours. Grey stone and built on the banks of a stream . . . it sounds good to me."

On their first morning, after a leisurely breakfast, Larry drove them up to an area close to Cader Idris mountain.

Thinking about it later, Rosemary realised that by the end of their weekend, although she had chattered about her friends, her neighbours and everything else they saw, Larry gave little away. His conversation was animated and he was obviously enjoying himself, but she knew no more about him than after their first day out in London. He wasn't deliberately evasive, but managed somehow to avoid directly answering a question.

"What do your parents do, Larry?" she asked as they

settled to eat in a small restaurant in the middle of the town.

"Dad's retired, but he keeps himself busy. He does a lot of charity work. The family go to the coast a lot and Dad loves to sail."

The apparently full reply made it difficult to repeat the question without sounding very insistent. The days were too pleasant, his company too satisfying for it to be worth the risk of spoiling it. There would be other days, other opportunities for asking questions. What really mattered was that they were together, here and now.

She realised he was staring at her and brushed her hand through her short hair in slight embarrassment.

"What are you thinking about?"

"Trying to find a single word to describe you, my beautiful chameleon. Yes, that's what you are, I think – yes. Captivating, is the one. You captivated me the first moment I saw you, in the London hotel. You seem to enjoy even the simplest pleasures and you make me feel good." He smiled and took her hand in his. "There, does that answer your question?"

She blushed slightly, remembering that her own thoughts at that moment had been hovering around the fact that he didn't answer her questions!

"I think I would use the word mysterious, for you," she said hesitatingly, half fearing that her words would spoil the day.

"Me? Mysterious? Why, for heaven's sake?"

"I feel I've known you for ever, yet I don't know a thing about you."

"I've been so afraid I'd bore you and drive you away from me."

"Bore me? I want to know everything about you."

"Then you will!" he laughed and began tapping his

fingers as he told her his name, age, address in New York, his occupation – that of a history teacher in a college – and the fact that he was in love with her and wanted to go on seeing her until he was grey-haired and losing all his teeth. Helpless with laughter, they walked arm in arm back along the seashore to their hotel, tired and utterly content.

Yet, as she lay in bed, unable to sleep, going over all they had done that day and all they had said, she still felt a slight unease. Had he pushed that note through her door? If so, why the mystery? There was the car too, it wasn't that common a sight to see a red and white Citroen Dolly in the village. And in London, he had said he was a complete stranger there yet she had the strong conviction on more than one occasion that he knew his way around as well as she did.

She stirred slightly in the bed and his arms tightened around her. His lips touched her cheek and, turning her head a little more, he found her lips. The rest of the night was a celebration of their love. All doubts were swamped and forgotten.

At breakfast on their last morning she was apprehensive, wondering if once more he would disappear from her life and again leave her waiting, hoping for a call or the mysterious arrival of a note.

"I'll call you during the week," he said, as they finished their final coffee. "And if you want to talk to me – please, please baby, *please* want to talk to me – here are the places where you might find me." He handed her a piece of paper on which several telephone numbers were written. "In fact, if you don't have any objection, I might call at your home. Perhaps Wednesday?"

"I'll be there," she smiled. "Come for dinner."

She put the numbers he had given her into her handbag

Search For a Shadow

and felt secure in the knowledge she would be able to ring him at one of them and talk to him should her doubts return to spoil the memories of the weekend.

Driving back and going straight to the library on Tuesday morning gave her an uncomfortable feeling. It was as if she were arriving for work unprepared, casually, and without the responsible feeling she normally wore like a cloak of respectability. I'm neither serious nor respectable any more, she thought with a half smile as she parked her car.

She had arranged to meet Megan and Sally for lunch and they were given a brief and rather dishonest version of her few days in Aberystwyth. But she needed to discuss it, to try and put the exciting events into some calm order, to make herself believe that it was only a casual thing, a wonderful interlude that would pass and leave her with no regrets. She wondered if Megan's wise head would be able to persuade her to believe that was all she should expect.

It was Megan's day off and she had to wait until the evening to talk to her at length and tell her more about the weekend, things she couldn't discuss in front of Sally. She bought a ready-to-eat meal from the supermarket in town and after she had eaten, she settled into her favourite chair and dialled Megan's number.

"It was a wonderful weekend and Aberystwyth was the perfect background for it, so calm and friendly, like—" She sought for the right words.

"Like a full-bosomed, favourite maiden aunt!" Megan finished. "That's how I always think of Aberystwyth."

Although she only gave a description of the places they had seen and the restaurants where they had eaten, Megan sensed there was something else Rosemary wanted to tell her.

"But?" she asked in her forthright way. "There is a 'but', isn't there?"

Rosemary paused before saying, "Megan, did you hear a click then, as if someone had picked up another phone?"

"No, love, I didn't. If it's a crossed line whoever it is will soon put it down again." Megan waited a moment but the sound was not repeated. "There, nothing at all. Now, what was the slightly sour note?"

"Only that, all the time, I was wondering if, at the end of it, Larry would disappear again without telling me where I could contact him, or even if he wanted me to. He seems to be open but he doesn't give anything away. He uses a lot of words to answer a question but they don't amount to much in the way of information. I have to accept that this is only a brief affair, haven't I?"

"But he gave you a number where he can be reached?"

"Yes, but right at the last moment. Megan, I know it sounds silly but I had the feeling he was teasing, playing with me, wanting me to ask him."

"Why didn't you?"

"I don't know. There was something holding me back. He isn't being honest with me. I felt he was undecided about seeing me again. Perhaps I don't come up to his expectations in bed and he couldn't find the words to tell me. Megan! Did you hear that? Someone breathed heavily."

"Nonsense, love. Go on."

"I wondered if – oh, Megan, perhaps he's married. It isn't easy to get him to answer questions, he fills out a reply but without really telling you what you want to know. I would have had to really pester him for answers and, well, I didn't want to spoil the wonderful weekend."

"You think he's married? Is that what's bothering you?

Search For a Shadow

I can understand if that's the case, you don't want to be involved in anything messy."

"Megan, I think someone *is* listening to this conversation."

"Oh, come on, you are getting paranoid. Best you don't see the boy again if he's having this effect on you!"

"There! Did you hear that?" The sound of a stifled cough met her ears, but again, Megan laughed it off.

"Imagining things you are. Overtired I expect. Get to bed now and you'll feel better in the morning.

"See you tomorrow, love," Megan chuckled and she replaced her phone.

Immediately afterward, Rosemary heard the unmistakable sound of another phone being dropped into its cradle.

Chapter Four

On Wednesday Rosemary went to work, having prepared a meal ready to put into the oven, put a bottle of wine to cool and made sure everything in the cottage was as neat as she could make it. At the library she was in a state of excitement, wondering when Larry would arrive. Every time the phone rang she would run to it, so, eventually, no one else even attempted to answer it. When a query forced her to leave the desk, she ran frantically to deal with it to hurry back to the phone and wait again for it to ring.

She allowed herself a long lunch-break with the collusion of Megan and luxuriated in a session at the hairdressers where she had a tint and a fluffy cut that changed her appearance startlingly. She stared at her reflection and marvelled at the change from the sober, rather stiff-faced Rosemary of just a few weeks before, to this modern, and well-presented young woman that stared back at her like an attractive stranger.

At four she left the building and stepped out into a dull, rather chilly afternoon and looked around the town car park with rising disappointment. There was no sign of the Citroen Dolly that Larry had been using the last time they had met.

She reached her car without seeing anyone remotely like Larry and began to drive home. She turned in just

Search For a Shadow

before the road bridge and went slowly down the lane. There was no Citroën to be seen.

Parking on the opposite side of the stream next to the Capri belonging to the student, she looked across, but the house seemed exactly the same as when she had left. There was no one standing at the gate looking out for her. She collected the salad and fruit she had bought at lunch-time and walked across the wooden footbridge and into the house. He wasn't coming.

She opened the door with her key and stepped inside and at once knew someone was there.

"Larry?" she called. There was no reply and she tiptoed along the small hallway and into the living room. He was stretched out on her settee and fast asleep.

She didn't stop to wonder how he had got in. Dropping her shopping onto the carpet, she knelt down and kissed him lightly on his forehead. He stirred slightly and she kissed him again, this time on his lips. His eyes opened and crinkled into the smile hidden from her by their closeness. His arms slid around and held her close against him and she was breathless when he released her.

"Larry? What are you doing here?" she asked, her eyes showing undeniable delight at finding him there.

"You don't mind, do you? Only the queer fellow next door said he had a key."

"The 'queer fellow'? You mean Gethyn?"

"I guess so. Big, dark and kinda bashful?"

"Yes, that's him," she laughed.

"I ran out of gas, would you believe! I walked three miles on empty roads. No vehicle passed me and I didn't see a house. What a wild place this is! Give me New York where you can't blink without missing something! I was almost in the village before I found anyone to help so

I decided to wait here 'til you could come along and rescue me."

As he stood up she saw heavy scratching and a purple bruise on the side of his face.

"What happened to you?" Her voice was light-hearted but she was alarmed by the severity of the bruising.

"I got in the way of someone practising for the shot-put I guess. A rock came through the window of the car while I was stationary. Hey! It's okay! Don't look so worried! Whoever heaved that rock must be feeling pretty sick. It couldn't have been intended. Who around this place knows me well enough to want to crack my head? Come on. It's nothing serious, but it was one hell of a shock at the time. I thought the natives were supposed to be friendly!" He laughed away her concern and insisted it must have been an accident. But privately, he thought differently. What I came to Wales to find out is worrying someone, that's for sure, he thought, as he explained where he had left the Citroën.

After putting the meal into the oven and the salad in the fridge, they set off to rescue the car. The driver's window had been smashed by the rock that had hit Larry's face. Despite further attempts on Rosemary's part to find out what had happened, Larry insisted it was nothing more than an unfortunate mistake.

When they had taken petrol to restart the car and stopped at a garage to fill it up, they returned to the house to find the meal ready. They sat, companionably discussing the irritations of motoring.

It was dark by the time they had finished chatting and Larry yawned and said, "Rosemary my love, it's time I was leaving."

She tried to hide her surprise and disappointment.

Search For a Shadow

Finding him in her home she had presumed he was staying at least for a night or two.

"Where are you staying?" she asked.

"In a town with an unpronounceable name!" he laughed. He showed her on a piece of paper.

"Machynlleth," Rosemary laughingly interpreted for him. It was only later that she realised that once again, he hadn't answered her question.

"I have to go back to London early tomorrow. Can you meet me there, say on Saturday?" he asked.

"Well, I have to work on Saturday morning, but the following Monday is a day off, will that do?"

"Perfect!"

They were standing outside her doorway and he hugged her.

"Where shall we meet?" she asked, touching his injured face gently with curled fingers.

"I'll book a room," he said. "I'll ring you to tell you when and where. Okay?"

Rosemary sighed as she waved him goodbye. She would be spending the next couple of days glued to the telephone once more, waiting for him to tell her the name and the address of the hotel where they were to stay. He was, she decided with a smile, a man who loved childish secrets. And she was a woman in love with a man who loved childish secrets. He was her mystery man, and she knew she should insist on knowing more about him or tell him goodbye, but something about him made her want to trust him, to wait until he was ready to talk. But, she prayed silently, please make it soon. In the front window of number one, Gethyn watched their affectionate leave-taking with a heavy heart. This then was the reason for the change in Rosemary. The words of a song from a recently borrowed library tape, *Aspects of Love*, came into his mind, "Love, love changes everything—" Her love was not for him, but it was going to change things for him, all his soaring hopes were going to fall to the ground with a dull thud.

On a Sunday evening, late in June, when she had succeeded in completing the first draft of a new story, she put aside the freshly typed pages and stretched luxuriously. She had been sitting at her desk for too long. She stepped outside intending to walk along the stream for a while and look at the river, but stopped when she heard a car approaching the parking space on the other side of the footbridge.

It was two weeks since she had been let down over their planned sojourn in London. She had heard nothing from Larry. So it was in disbelief that she covered her eyes against the bright sun and looked across to see his tall figure standing beside the red and white Citroen Dolly.

She forced herself to stand still and allow him to come to her, watching his long-legged stride crossing the wooden bridge. She tried to guess his intentions from the look on his face but failed. He looked just the same as always; warm, friendly, pleased to see her. There was no doubt in his expression that his pleasure and delight at the reunion would be reciprocated.

"Honey, you're beautiful and I've missed you. I'm sorry it took longer than I planned."

"What do you mean?" she asked, stepping back a little from his intended embrace. "What took longer? I have no idea what you're talking about."

"About having to cancel our weekend in London, what else?"

"So far as I remember, you didn't cancel, you just didn't tell me where we were to meet as you'd promised."

Search For a Shadow

"But you had my note?"

Hope flowed through her as she stared into his eyes.

"Note? I received no note, no phone call, nothing. I waited here expecting you to tell me where to meet you and there wasn't even an apology for letting me down."

"I passed through on the way to Heathrow. I had to go back home for a few days on family business. I put it all in the note and promised to ring you when I returned. I came instead. Aren't you pleased to see me?"

"Larry, I had no message of any kind. I thought you'd decided to forget it."

"Are we going inside to talk about this or do you want me to go?"

She led the way in and gestured to the drinks cupboard but he went straight to the kitchen and the percolator.

"Coffee," he said. "I'll have coffee. I've a feeling I'll need all my wits about me if we're to sort this out." He switched on the coffee maker and turned to her. With a hand on each of her shoulders he slowly pulled her closer and kissed her. "Now, my darling Rosemary, tell me what has been happening." Rosemary's resolve began to melt. They soon agreed that the note Larry had placed in her letterbox on Friday had blown away.

She put aside her doubts and, remembering Megan's words, determined to enjoy the moment and not look too far into the future. Larry was good company and they laughed a lot as they shared a meal.

Doubts remained but she cast them aside, convincing herself with ease that it would work out, that Larry wasn't treating her as a casual and convenient pit-stop while he made his enquiries in Wales. She wanted him so much that any niggles of doubt left her as they climbed the narrow stairs to her room, hand in hand, pausing for a kiss on the way.

Kay Christopher

It was strange to have him share her bed. Different from sharing a bed in an hotel where they were anonymous. Here in the house where she had shared a room with her sister, with only the wall between them and their parents, and Gran in the small back room she had been forced to use when the family came.

She felt his presence in the house like a new life beckoning. It was no longer the place where she had spent family holidays, no longer a house in which she had lived alone.

Since she had taken the house for herself, when Gran had moved into a retirement home, she had shared it with no one. Even her parents never stayed when they came on one of their rare visits, but drove to and from home in the same day. She wondered if the neighbours would notice or, if they did, if they would care? Gethyn, Mrs Priestley, the now absent Hughes's and the Powells, had known her since she was born, and would perhaps be surprised. The students were strangers and wouldn't be interested in what she did. Everyone slept with boyfriends these days, didn't they? And even if Gran had been born in a time when behaviour was, at least on the surface, very different, she thought she would understand and not judge her harshly.

Her parents knew he was here; they had spoken to him on the phone and had said nothing to suggest they minded. She wondered if they did or whether, like Megan, they accepted the new morality even if they didn't like it. She knew they would love Larry when they met him. One day she might arrange it, but not yet, it might remind him of how much she accepted him as a part of her life, and run, like Mrs Priestley's Leonard had done!

They went to bed and afterwards they both went into

Search For a Shadow

the small bath. Their laughter filtered through the shared wall to where Gethyn was sitting reading.

Larry watched her with admiration in his eyes and marvelled at the unexpected joy of her. When he had first seen her he wouldn't have given her a moment of his time. It was only the opportunity of knowing someone so close to the area he needed to search that had made him follow her and make her acquaintance. But she had proved herself a beautiful and generous lover and a calm, gentle companion; she hadn't been out of his thoughts for a moment.

He re-dressed but Rosemary put on the silky nightdress she had bought for her London visit. His eyes, watching her as she came down the stairs, showed she had chosen well. The fitting bodice with its generous insets of lace, the scooped neckline that just revealed the swell of her breasts, the slinky, swirling skirt widening out to a four metre hem, all showed her lithesome body to perfection.

"I wonder what the people who know you in the library would make of you if they could see you now!" he whispered. "Sober dresser, formal manners, country-girl habits," he said, with a glitter of amusement in his eyes. Then he went on, exaggerating to tease her, "bookish expression, brogue shoes, dull brown skirts, chilly willie hair cut."

"Larry! I wasn't that bad!"

"Sorry my sweet, adorable chrysalis, for that's what you are, a butterfly that burst out of a 'stay away from me' disguise to dazzle and overwhelm me. But, you're so easy to tease."

She laughed with him, determined to make his stay free of even the slightest difficulty, but she wondered if, behind his banter, there wasn't the hint of truth. Perhaps he saw her still as that brown, quiet, closed-in person she had been when they had met. She was unaware she had sighed, but Larry heard it and was dismayed that his teasing could have upset her.

"I go too far," he said. "I'm sorry. My sister is always telling me I don't know when to stop. It's just that seeing you laugh is such a wonderful sight, such a beautiful sound I want to make it continue and," he ran his fingers through his curly hair, "I go too far. You were never anything other than beautiful to me, although I do think you were a chrysalis waiting for me to come along and persuade you to open out."

"Your sister?" she probed. Perhaps tonight he would begin to talk about himself.

"My sister Rosalie, she's twenty-eight, and the youngest of us."

"How many are you?"

"Four. I have two brothers, older than myself, as well as my sister who is younger. And you?"

"There's only my sister and me." She hesitated, then asked, "What does your father do, Larry?"

"Nothing, he's retired and he plays golf a lot and sails in Florida, where they have a summer place." He had simply repeated what he had told her before. Was it too automatic? Rehearsed?

"Good heavens, he must be comfortably off?"

"Yes, he's comfortable," he conceded. "But I still have to work," he sighed. "Thank heavens for a three month vacation!"

"'He' is comfortable? Don't you mean 'they'?"

"My mother died about five years ago."

"Larry, I'm sorry."

He still hadn't told her what his father's job had been. Perhaps he was unaware of how elusive he was? Or was

Search For a Shadow

she being too inquisitive? Whatever the reason, trying to learn about him was like searching for a shadow in the inky blackness of a moonless night. Trying a different tack she asked, "Have you found out anything about your family's history?"

"Wait there." He went to the Citroën and brought back a file of papers which he began to spread over her table. He began to explain the connections he had so far made and demonstrated how they fitted into his family tree.

"My great-grandfather was a farmer, here in Wales. Why did his name have to be Jones! It's gotta be the most difficult name to research ever known. Still, I've made some progress. From what I can discover, the farmhouse in which he was a tenant was called Ty Coch, red house, right?" She nodded, looking at the details which he had written down and handed to her.

"It's near Aberystwyth," she said, reading the address.

"My parents came here when I was very small," he said softly, "stayed in Aberystwyth, and climbed Consti Hill, just like we did."

"Did they find the Red House?"

"No." He looked tight-lipped and troubled but then relaxed again and said, "Time sort of ran out for them."

"And that's why you came?"

"I promised Mom I'd come back, one day. This year seemed right for me to keep that promise." There was more, she felt it, was convinced of it, but she was equally certain he was not going to tell her.

He stayed two nights and they spent a day in the university library where he concentrated on finding Ty Coch, the Red House. Rosemary worked too, gathering information she needed for a chapter of her book.

"Now you can help me with *my* research," she said when

they were once more out in the air looking down at the magnificent view from the university buildings high on a hill above the town and the sea. "I want to include a walk to Borth in my story, so, tomorrow, get your comfortable shoes on. All right?"

"We'll take a picnic," he said. "I want to do all the things that people living in a wild place like this do, so I can remember when I'm back in my noisy old city."

The reminder that one day soon he would be returning to America was not a cheering one. At least I can make the memories good ones, Rosemary thought, and began to plan what she would cook in preparation for the picnic on the following day.

Before they left in the morning, the post arrived and there was a letter addressed to Larry Madison-Jones. Curiously, Rosemary handed it to him.

"I'm sorry, I should have asked first, but in haste I gave your address to a colleague who has promised to send some material to me. Information on finding great-grandfather's house, I hope." He opened it, read, then shrugged and said, "Nope! No luck. But there are still a few avenues left to explore." He didn't show her the letter but pushed it into his jacket pocket. Something in the way he looked as he read it made her certain that whatever it contained, it was not what he had told her. The letter had made him angry and he had not quite managed to hide it from her.

As they left, Mrs Priestley, nursing her tail-swishing cat, waved them off.

"Mind that ankle, Rosemary," she called. "A sprain can be nasty, mind."

"I will," Rosemary called back, then she turned to Larry. "How could she possibly know I twisted my ankle yesterday? Honestly, her nosiness is unbelievable! How

Search For a Shadow

does she do it? She couldn't have a permanently crossed telephone line, could she? Or perhaps that cat is a walking microphone!"

The walk started off well. They had a ride in the cliff railway to the top of Constitution Hill and set of in the direction of Borth along the cliff-edge pathway. They couldn't walk side by side because of the narrowness of the path, but talked in shouts, pointing out various flowers and birds as they walked.

The day was dull and overcast and the clouds lowered, darkened and threatened a downpour. It began to rain before they were half way and either returning or continuing meant a soaking, so they turned back. It wasn't cold, only uncomfortable so they didn't hurry unduly; heads bent, they walked at a steady pace back to the top of Consti.

In the little cafe there were others who had been caught out by the rain, laughing and shaking the worst of the wet from their coats. One of a group of girls, whom Rosemary guessed to be students, waved and Rosemary looked curiously but did not know her. She turned to see if the girl was waving to someone beyond her but was in time to see Larry smile and wave back.

"A friend?" she asked.

"We met in London," he surprised her by saying. Rosemary began to smile a welcome as the girl stood up and began to walk towards them. Then, to her surprise, the girl walked past them, still smiling, and sat beside someone at the table near the window behind them.

"Oh," Larry chuckled. "I guess I made a mistake!"

"You bet you did," an angry voice growled and a man behind them, previously unnoticed, came up and punched Larry on the mouth.

Chapter Five

Rosemary stared in disbelief as blood spurted from Larry's nose. Then she jerked into action and found a handkerchief for him to hold against his face while the lady behind the counter offered water and tissues to clean him up. Her mind was in turmoil. Larry was a stranger there, how could he have offended someone so drastically that they would punch him viciously and in such a public place?

The man who had hit him so suddenly and without any reason that she could imagine, had disappeared, walking out into the rain and back down the hill to the town. The incident had been so sudden, yet at the same time it had seemed to have occurred in slow motion. The man's arm shooting out like a piston; the expression on Larry's face; the look on the face of his assailant . . . they would stay in her mind for a long time. The man, she would most certainly recognise again.

It was only minutes before the bleeding had eased and Larry managed to talk.

"I don't know," he said in answer to Rosemary's questions. "I don't know the guy and I'm sure he doesn't know me. It's obviously a case of mistaken identity."

"An American," one onlooker whispered, "gangsters, the lot of them!" And Rosemary was relieved to see a cautious smile crease the corners of Larry's eyes.

They went back down the hill in a small procession, as

Search For a Shadow

the people who had been sheltering in the cafe considered Larry their special charge. One old lady tried to cover him with an umbrella, but as she only reached his shoulders he considered himself in more danger from the spikes than from a soaking.

Rosemary was shaking with the shock of it. It seemed so unbelievable that on a summer's day in a small Welsh town someone should suffer such an attack.

"It happens all the time in cities," Larry said, as she once more repeated her disbelief. "You only have to look hard at someone and you get a bottle in the face."

"Told you so," said the little woman who had described Americans as gangsters.

They drove back to the cottage in the Citroën and Rosemary suggested they call a doctor.

"Hell no! I'll be a bit sore for a day or two but that's all. It isn't the first time I've been at the receiving end of a punch," he said ruefully. "I just wasn't expecting this one. Or that rock the other day! Someone around here sure hates my face!" He grinned at her, tried to make light of it.

"Who was it, Larry?" she asked.

"I've no idea, honey. I certainly haven't been flirting with his wife or anything. The guy mistook me for someone else, that's all. Now, let's forget it and think about food. Something I can take through a straw I think!"

The picnic they had planned to eat at Borth, was eaten while sitting on the carpet before the fire. Larry went to bed early and slept through the night, while Rosemary failed to relax for long enough to do more than take occasional dozes. She puzzled over what had happened, wondering if there was more to the attacks on him than he was telling. First that rock thrown at him while he sat in his car, now this unwarranted punch.

Larry returned to London on the following day. His face still showed the results of the blow. He was bruised, his lips were fat and swollen from the cuts he had received from his own teeth, his voice thickened by the damage to his nose. He promised to phone her that evening, and Rosemary was left with a loneliness greater than she expected, but also the fear that there was still a lot about him she did not know. However unlikely and unbelievable, she had the strong conviction that Larry knew the man who had hit him.

Gethyn had given up making regular visits to the employment agency. Since he had left the quarry, where he had worked since leaving school, he had only managed to find two temporary jobs, both in shops and both of which he hated. Uneasy with people, it was soon apparent that customers avoided him, sensing in him the inability to help them. After a short time he was requested to leave.

By spending as little as possible on food, he managed to pay his rent and deal with the few bills that came through his letterbox without too much worry. Entertainment was almost nil. Apart from the television, music and books, he did nothing except sit and daydream about an imaginary, different life which one day he hoped he would live. His mother had left a little money, but that was for when he and Rosemary got together. It wasn't much but it would be a start.

Rosemary was the central figure in his dreams. Although he knew, deep within the core of his imaginings, she would never consider him as anything more than a neighbour, he still grasped at her every word, her every kindness, to perpetuate the dream.

Search For a Shadow

It was all that American's fault, he told himself, unreasonably. If *he* hadn't come on the scene, Rosemary would have come home to him; of that, he was more and more certain. Damn the man with his flattering tongue and pushy ways, forcing himself into Rosemary's life where he had no business to be. He knew he was being unfair and a little childish, but it helped. Having someone to blame for his disappointment eased the pain, just a little.

Larry phoned almost daily now, but did not commit himself to a meeting. From the small front bedroom where she worked, Rosemary saw the postman stepping out of the van with a parcel one morning. He waved at her as he crossed the footbridge and she presumed it was for her. On the rare days Larry did not phone her, he wrote a letter, so a parcel was a possibility, she thought with excitement. She ran down and opened the door but the parcel was for Gethyn.

She was surprised. He never seemed to receive any post apart from official letters. There was no reply when the postman knocked on his door, so she took it, put it on one side and went on with her typing.

When she was eating her lunch, through the shared wall she heard the sound of Gethyn poking his fire and, picking up the parcel, she went around to give it to him.

"Rosemary. Thanks." He seemed a bit flustered and put the parcel into a cupboard without examining it. "Will you come in and have a cup of tea?" he asked. "You're so busy, we never have a chance for a chat."

"Well," she hesitated. There was a chapter to finish if she were to keep to her schedule.

"Please, Rosemary."

"Thanks, I could do with a breather. This chapter isn't going very well."

"You work too hard."

While he made tea Rosemary looked around the room. She hadn't been inside the house for years and was startled at how little it had changed. Nineteen-fifties! she thought to herself as she looked at the faded, heavily patterned wallpaper, faded and in places, torn.

There were photographs everywhere, mostly of people she did not recognise. There were family groups and pictures of children taken on beaches, in gardens and in the room in which she now sat. She smiled as she recognised herself as a child in one or two groups, taken, presumably, on one of her holidays with Gran, who also figured in the gallery of memories. Memories, she mused, belonging to Gethyn's mother. She wondered how long it would take before he took them down. Many were faded and yellow and looked as if they had been there as long as the house!

It was the house of an old woman. She felt a surge of pity for Gethyn, having to cope alone after having his mother to look after everything for so long. He hadn't left home as a teenager like so many people did today, he had stayed to look after her and he was lost because of it. At twenty-seven, he was living like a middle-aged man, in a house that was almost a museum piece.

But how could he not care about the place where he spent so much time? It was a house that was in urgent need of some loving care. How could Gethyn live in such discomfort and with a lack of anything beautiful? Couldn't he see how shabby it all was?

He came out of the kitchen with an enamel tray on which he had set biscuits and tea and one of the cakes regularly supplied by Mrs Priestley.

"The old place could do with a face-lift, couldn't it?" he embarrassed her by saying.

Search For a Shadow

"I suppose I'm lucky, earning enough to keep things nice," she excused, ashamed of her silent critisism of him. "It takes time and money, to do even basic decoration today, and I know it isn't easy for you, not working."

"Time I've plenty of, but not much money."

"Perhaps if you sorted out your mother's things it would give you a bit more room. I'll help if you like," she offered.

"Would you?" His brown eyes glowed as he looked at her. Then he looked swiftly away, down at the dusty carpet. "That would be great. Perhaps later on, when you aren't so busy."

"You tell me when you're ready to do it and I'll find the time, I promise."

He stared at her, she felt his gaze upon her, so piercing she began to feel like a specimen in a jar of formaldehide. Yet, when she looked at him, his eyes darted away from making contact to stare at the walls and the ranks and ranks of photographs. She finished her tea, made her excuses and hurried home. She sighed with relief to be back in her own, clean, orderly house, away from the sadness and emptiness of Gethyn's existence.

The following day, Larry arrived at the library and invited her out for lunch. He looked tired and the bruises on his face were still visible.

"Larry! I never know when you'll appear," she laughed.

"It's a fleeting visit I'm afraid," he said. "But if you're free at the weekend perhaps you'd come to London with me."

"I'd love to, but you look tired, wouldn't you prefer to have a quiet weekend at the cottage?"

"I love it here, you know that, but I think I'd prefer to be somewhere livelier, somewhere where we can find something to do in the evenings. A city is where I feel at home, not a peaceful village, no matter how beautiful. Please, won't you come with me?"

"You've never complained before about the way we spend our evenings," she whispered.

"Wanton woman!" he whispered back.

"I shouldn't, I'll get behind with my work."

From his pocket he took out the folder of Her Majesty's Theatre and from it took out two tickets for *Phantom of the Opera*. "There, will that persuade you if my charms fail?" She hugged him, ignoring the surprised glances from some of the silent browsers.

"I'll ask Megan if she'll take my shift on Monday morning," she said. "Fortunately, I have Saturday free. I'll have to work very hard next week though, I am anxious to finish my story and get it to my agent before the end of August."

"I'll be busy myself next week. I think I'm on the trail of the missing members of my family at last," he said. "I need to go to St Catherine's House for some birth certificates, then I'll be almost there."

"Is the mystery of the Red House solved?" she asked.

"Yes," he groaned. "Goddammit, the whole area's been replaced by a housing estate!"

Larry waited until Rosemary had finished for the day and they went for a cup of coffee before driving home. In a small tea-shop, they were about to sit down when Larry rose suddenly and pulled her out through the door.

"Larry! what is it?" she demanded, a bit ruffled by the peremptory change of plan.

"I didn't think it looked all that hygienic," he said, hurrying her across the road to the cars.

"Nonsense! I've eaten there often and—" She turned to glance back and saw quite clearly, standing in the doorway, the man who had punched him in the face at the top of Constitution Hill in Aberystwyth.

"Come on, Rose Mary, I've a better idea. We'll go home, then try a pub for a meal. Better than tea-cakes," he teased. "What in hell are tea-cakes anyway?"

"Larry, isn't that the man who hit you?" He pretended to look back, then shook his head.

"Nothing like him. The man who hit me was taller, and not so dark."

"But I'm sure—"

"You drive ahead and I'll follow. We'll use my car for the journey to the station on our trip to London. I'm sure looking forward to seeing a city again. All this quiet, it's bad for my nerves!" Joking and chattering as if nothing had happened, he led her to the car, took her key and opened the door for her, then went to his own, parked close by.

When she drove out of the car park, still bemused and startled by the cavalier way he had ushered her out from the tea-shop, she saw the man standing near the entrance, watching them go. She saw him clearly and knew without doubt that she had been right, he was the one who had struck Larry. But why did Larry deny it? He might have been unsure about the man, it all happened with such speed and a blow to the face makes it impossible to remember precisely what happens. But he had been so certain it was *not* the man, surely he would have at least have doubts?

She considered the possibility that he *had* recognised him, and that was the reason he had rushed her out, before the man could hit him again. But why not tell her? And, back to the same question, why would a stranger want to hit him?

She was serious-faced when she got out of her car and crossed the footbridge with Larry beside her.

"Is something wrong? Have I ruined your day by depriving you of a buttered bun?" he joked.

"Larry, it *was* the man who hit you, wasn't it? And you recognised him. That was why we left in such a rush, before he could hit you again? Why?"

She saw the smile fade, his shoulders droop and he admitted quietly, "Yes, it was he. But please, Rosemary, trust me. It's a lot to ask, I know that, but I promise you, one day soon you'll have the full story, but I can't say anything just yet." It was unsatisfactory, but when he pleaded with her, looking into her eyes, love for her showing clearly in their depths, she nodded and promised to wait.

It was easy enough to promise, but not as simple to put aside all her questions. All through the evening, she had to keep forcing her mind back from the many unexplained little quirks, many of them, she was certain, nothing more than simple misunderstandings. But there were problems looming, threatening their relationship, she could see that.

They left early, in the Citroën, and stopped on the way to Aberystwyth railway station in a small village, where Larry spent a while searching through the graveyard, deciphering the names on the almost obliterated stone lettering.

They were both quiet during the train journey after an initial perusal of the London map to plan their days. At Euston they continued their journey on the underground to the same hotel they had stayed at before. They bathed and rested before setting out for the theatre and supper.

Later that night, their love-making was sweet, tender and she knew that whatever problems he had, his love for her was real. No one could pretend to be the way he was with her. Yet the realisation that they were deeply in

Search For a Shadow

love kept her awake for long into the night. How could there be love without trust? How could he love her and not disclose what was worrying him?

The time when he would be leaving was drawing nearer by the minute, although he had not given a date on which he would depart. And the undeclared problems seemed to be coming more and more into their relationship, looming larger and larger and threatening to ruin everything they had. Neither fact could be ignored, not if they were to have any future. She was sure that a future together was what they both wanted. She clung desperately to that thought and slept.

They returned to Wales in a glow of contentment. Rosemary had committed herself to trusting Larry, telling herself that when the time was right he would explain everything and they would be together.

Larry stayed one night then he went off in the Citroën, explaining that he once again had to travel to chase some information. Before he left, he showed her his family tree and she saw recently added information; names, dates and places, and the gaps he was hoping to fill.

While Larry was away, Rosemary and Megan often walked on the hills, sometimes borrowing a friend's dog and spending the day out, eating at a country pub.

Megan greeted her one day by saying, "He didn't stay away from you long this time, did he?"

"What d'you mean?" Rosemary frowned.

"That American of yours. I saw his car parked in Aberdovey, yesterday, and there he was, sitting in a cafe, talking to a man of about fifty; laughing they were as if they were old friends."

"What was he like?" Rosemary asked.

"Big chap he was, fairish hair flopping about like a dish-mop. Know him, do you?"

"Oh, yes," Rosemary said. "I know him. Friendly were they?"

"Yes, for sure! Laughing and slapping each other's back, in the daft way men do."

Rosemary turned and tried to concentrate on her work. Yet another twist to the confusion that surrounded Larry. Not only was he seen in Aberdovey when he had told her he would be in Cardiff, the man he was talking to in such a friendly manner was almost certainly the man who had attacked him in the cafe on top of Constitution Hill.

Chapter Six

There was no sign of Larry during the next few days. Every minute of each hour, Rosemary expected him to appear. Megan was certain it had been Larry whom she had seen, and the car which he said he had hired but which she suspected he in fact owned, was unusual in the area. Then something else occurred to worry her.

She drove home from work one evening, rather late, having taken the shift that finished when the library closed at eight o'clock. She was tired and, seeing the parking space empty, apart from the old Capri owned by Richard Lloyd, with no sign of the Citroën, she dejectedly walked across the footbridge and prepared herself mentally for another lonely evening.

She unlocked the door and for a moment thought he was there, there was that indefinable difference to which she was now attuned; the house felt different, inhabited, yet there was no answer to her call. Something else was different, a smell, there was an unpleasant odour pervading the house; what was it? Her memory reached out to it but failed to name the source, yet it was one she knew.

Putting put down the food she had bought ready for her meal, she flicked on the television. A coldness spilt down her spine: the chair had been moved!

It was always in the same position, the perfect place for

watching the television and for listening to her stereo. She examined the carpet, which confirmed her intuition. The compressed pile showed where it had once stood, the four marks of the legs deep and unmistakable. Someone had been here, sitting in her chair.

There was something else. A book thrown onto the floor, a guide book on New York, bought while she had been holidaying there. The smell was stronger now. She stood up and then saw, on the floor behind the settee, a vase that had fallen. From it spilled flowers, dead flowers. She recognised the vase and the flowers as some she had placed on Gethyn's mother's grave a few days before. They were the reason for the smell, the flowers were dead, their stems slimed with decay and spread on the carpet as if the vase had been placed on the floor and knocked over.

It was Larry! It must have been him. He was perhaps hiding, having parked the car somewhere different to tease her. But although the relief flowed through her momentarily, she knew she was deluding herself. Larry wouldn't frighten her like this. His humour was always gentle, he had never shown any tendency to use malice or cruelty in the name of fun.

She felt a desire to run, her muscles tightened, preparing her for flight. The centre of her back felt vulnerable, exposed, but she forced herself to look further. She thought of Gethyn but she couldn't ask him to come in and search, he'd think her mad, and, if she went from the house, however briefly, whoever it was might get away. For a moment that seemed very desirable, but she knew she would never sleep in the house again if she did not search it now.

Could she be mistaken? Hardly, with the evidence staring her in the face. The flowers had been in the churchyard

Search For a Shadow

and now they were here, in her living room, making it smell like a funeral parlour from some nightmare. She hadn't become oversensitive, there *was* a mystery attaching itself to her; overheard conversations, now someone entering her home and leaving horrible calling cards.

Whatever it was, the problem was hers to deal with. Although she could not imagine how or why, it definitely included Larry. It had begun at the time he had entered her life. For that reason alone she knew she must get to the root of it.

The small front room into which she went first was sparsely furnished and it took only a glance to see it was empty. There was little there that could reveal the interference of an uninvited visitor, but she moved the furniture, examined the carpet just the same, all the time listening for any sound that would reveal the presence of an intruder. Nothing revealed any disturbance.

From the Victorian fireplace she picked up a heavy, brass-headed poker and began to make her way up the carpeted stairs.

She climbed slowly and cautiously, craning her neck to look upwards to the shadowy landing above her. No sound except her own breathing. No shadows moving except her own. The house was silent but not with the quiet of undisturbed tranquility, more, she thought with a shiver, a pause, a holding of breath before something happened.

Her study seemed undisturbed, but there was a sensation of it being inhabited by something other than her desk and her books and papers. She looked at the top sheet. So far as she could remember, it was as she had left it. The final chapter in note-form, was piled to the left of her typewriter. The telephone! Was it a little more to the right? No, she was inventing now.

Her heart beating painfully, filled with the longing to run away and fetch Gethyn, she pushed her feet forward and opened the door of her bedroom. It was empty, but there, on her freshly made up bed, clearly to be seen, was the shape of someone having stretched full length upon it, the man-sized indentation touching her pillow and reaching almost to the foot.

She felt sick and she tore at the bedding, removing everything until the mattress was bare. She threw sheets and pillows down the stairs; it would all have to be destroyed. She couldn't even consider using it again after it had been contaminated by the touch of someone unknown.

Sobs escaping, she struggled to push it all into black rubbish sacks and dragged it outside the door with a shudder of horror. The dead flowers followed, their smell lingering long after they had been placed in the dustbin. She sat down trembling and wondered what to do.

For tonight, at least, she needed to get out of the house. She thought of Gethyn, then Huw. She needed to talk. But it was Larry she needed. After ringing Megan and arranging to spend the night with her, she dialled one of the numbers Larry had given her. She didn't have much hope of reaching him and she almost replaced the receiver before anyone answered.

To her relief, the person at the other end said Larry was there and would she hold on while she fetched him. Within moments she was crying, explaining and allowing him to make decisions. She was only half listening but managed to understand that he would be there the following morning and would change all the locks and add bolts to every door.

"It won't happen again, we'll make very sure of that."

Search For a Shadow

Before packing what she needed and going to stay with Megan, Rosemary knocked at Gethyn's door.

"Have you seen anyone hanging about here?" she asked, trying to hold back her nervous inclination to cry. "Anyone who doesn't belong here?"

"No," he shook his head slowly, trying to think. "Only the American."

"You mean Larry?" She thought again that it might have been him. He could have called, got in and waited a while, then felt a little guilty at going in while she wasn't there and declined to admit it? But no. He would have explained the instant she spoke to him. And what about the dead flowers? No, he wouldn't have frightened her half out of her wits!

"That's right, the American. No one else. Oh, the students were down here doing something but that was yesterday I think, or the day before. Why?"

"Gethyn, I think someone has been in my house."

"Never! I'd have seen for sure if someone had been anywhere near your door. I sit here near the front windows a lot, looking at the birds coming to the stream to drink. I sit reading my magazines and books and can't help looking up when someone passes, although it's rare, as you know. It's so quiet. I'd have been certain to see someone, now wouldn't I? You must have imagined it. You're tired I expect."

Rosemary felt an inclination to smile even though she was still frightened and upset. He sounded like his mother!

"Take it quietly for a few days," he went on, "then you'll forget all about it. Imagination, that's all it is," he soothed.

For a moment, she almost believed him. She nodded. There was no sense in bothering him about it any further, and Larry would change the locks in the morning.

"I'm going to spend the night with Megan. You know, from the library," she explained.

"Oh." For a moment he looked disapproving then he smiled. "More gallivanting!"

She walked across the bridge to the car. Then with a frown on her brow, she went back and asked Gethyn, "When did you see Larry?"

"Earlier today, about midday I think. Why, d'you think he—?"

"Of course not!" She turned on her heels, away from Gethyn and the thought that he might have touched on the truth.

Megan lived in the centre of the small town and in the back bedroom she had a folding bed. It was only two feet across and Rosemary wondered if she would get any sleep at all. The fright she had still had her trembling inside and with a small, hard bed – she hesitated, then a tight ball of defiance built up inside her and she shook her head. She mustn't be driven out of her house. Foul smell and all, she was going back.

"Megan, I know you'll think me foolish but, I won't stay after all."

"I think you should, dear, just for tonight."

"I think someone is trying to frighten me out of the house. Those dead flowers, *ach y fi*! Then there was the time when Mrs Priestley called and asked if I was over my accident, she'd heard I had hurt my ankle falling down the stairs. How did she know? I told no one about that, except you and that was on the phone. I just have the feeling that someone is listening to everything I say, or am I going crazy?"

"Crazy if you ask me, girl! After all, you only have

Search For a Shadow

to ask Mrs Priestley where she heard it from!" Megan replied. "There must be simple explanations for all the small mysteries, and crazy you definitely are if you're thinking of going back to that house at this time of night without even a bed made ready for you to sleep in! Come on, I'll get you a hot drink and you can settle down."

Rosemary shook her head, her lips tightly pressed.

"No. Thank you, Megan, you're very kind, but I'm going back."

"All right," Megan said resignedly, "but I'm coming with you!" She refused to listen to any arguments. She packed the few items she needed for an overnight stay and went with Rosemary to her car.

It was ten o'clock but the day had been a fine one and there was enough light to see their way easily across the bridge and into the silent house. Rosemary went in first and as she reached for the light, a hand came over hers, damp, large and terrifyingly strong. It held her for what seemed a lifetime then released its hold, and she screamed.

Megan was close behind her as a shadow separated itself from the darkness of the corner and launched itself towards them. The shape was large and obviously a man, but it was all a blurr of frenzied movement.

Rosemary was pushed back against the wall swiftly and roughly by a powerful arm. Her head sang with the force of the contact. She pulled herself away from him to stagger against her friend. After a terrifying moment, filled with muffled sounds and sightless struggles, lunging arms and enormous shadows that seemed to grow as they loomed, Rosemary fell to the ground on top of Megan. They fell in a tangled heap and could only watch and scream as the figure disappeared along the path beside the stream.

* * *

Huw Rees was the first to arrive, and he was followed by Mrs Priestley nursing her cat and wearing a blue dressing gown.

"What happened?" Huw asked. "We heard screams." Coming up behind him, dressed in shorts, like himself, was Richard Lloyd. Rosemary was too distraught to give an explanation and it was Megan who told them about their experience.

"Best you call the police," Richard said. "I'll go back and phone, shall I?"

Huw remained with an arm around Rosemary and Megan. He talked soothingly and offered to stay with them all night.

A light came on in the porch of Gethyn's house and the door opened a crack. He looked out, but seeing what appeared to be a crowd, did not venture outside. Rosemary thought she ought to go and explain to him what had happened, but Huw's arms were too comforting.

Megan went to talk to Gethyn and when she had told him briefly what had occurred, she came back and reported to Rosemary that he was "there if she needed him".

"I'd better go and talk to him, ask if he heard or saw anyone," Rosemary said, trying to control the shaking of her limbs. Huw's arms tightened as Mrs Priestley said, "No you don't, my dear. You'll come with me and have a cup of hot, sugared tea and a piece of cake while we wait for the police. Nothing like a bit of carbohydrate for shock." She glanced at Megan, whom she recognised, and pursing her lips in disapproval, added sharply, "Your friend had better stay and wait for the police, hadn't she!"

"No, Megan is just as shocked as me and—" Rosemary stopped. The expression on Mrs Priestley's face showed startling enmity. Not for the first time, she realised, and

Search For a Shadow

recalled that for some mysterious reason neither had explained, Mrs Priestley disliked her friend intensely. She looked from one to the other and decided that in this instance her loyalties were with Megan.

She pulled free of the old lady's arm and returned to stand near her friend.

The police searched the house and when they asked about the unmade bed, Rosemary explained about the previous fear that there had been someone there. After reassuring her that her home was now empty of any unwelcome trespasser, and as secure as they could make it, they left, promising to keep a special eye on the place.

After a brief word with Gethyn, they drove once again to Megan's house, leaving the occupants of the five cottages unable to sleep. Huw and Richard waved them off and from her front window, Mrs Priestley, still nursing her cat, also waved goodbye. Gethyn stood at his door and watched until they were out of sight.

"What I can't understand," Megan said as they drove up onto the main road, "is how anyone can do anything without the rest knowing! Gethyn was in his window watching when we arrived. I saw the curtains twitch."

"No, you must have been mistaken, he told me he had gone to bed early and was woken by our screams," Rosemary said.

"Then what made the curtains twitch?"

"The window was open and there's a bit of a breeze."

"Oh, well, all right then, you're probably right. But," she added, "they're a nosy ol' lot and I bet they'll know soon enough if someone is playing games with you."

The friends drove into work together the following day, and to her relief, Rosemary saw Larry waiting for them.

"I thought I'd get here and do the job as quickly as

possible so you can forget being frightened," he said as he kissed her. "As soon as the stores open, I'll buy what I need and get it fixed. Don't worry. I'll be here to take you two to lunch and by then the house will be as secure as Fort Knox. You have my word."

"I'll have to go shopping for new bedding too," she said.

"I'll help you choose, he said with a grin. "I like the ambience to be right for nights with my special girl."

The morning passed like a flash as Rosemary explained the events of the previous evening to Sally, between attending to her work. Sally was intrigued and wanted to hear every detail.

"Are you sure it wasn't this Larry? He isn't exactly open with you is he? He expects you to take an awful lot on trust. How can you *be* so trusting? I'd have to come right out and demand some answers."

"I don't know," Rosemary said honestly. "I just know he'll explain as soon as he can."

"*Twpsin* you are, falling for a mystery man and too afraid of losing him to protest!" Sally teased. Rosemary didn't reply, Sally was right, the fear of losing him was too great for her to insist on anything. If he was using her for some reason of his own, then she would go along with it until he either told her the truth, or vanished from her life completely.

When Larry came at lunch-time he had news for her.

"It seems you could have been right about someone listening to your conversations," he told her. "The police had a good look around the area and found a box on the telephone pole that shouldn't be there. Someone had tapped the lines of the five cottages."

"The phone lines have been tapped? In our cottages?"

Search For a Shadow

She stared at him in disbelief. In a small voice she asked, "Who?"

"That they don't know. The lines had been disconnected from whatever surveillance position was used and there was no sign of a recorder. Whoever did it has managed to hide his part of the installations, so we'll probably never know. They're interviewing everyone, and that must include you," he said. "But don't worry, I'll be with you and I think they know you aren't likely to be the guilty one."

Megan made her excuses and declined to join them for lunch, and Rosemary sensed in her a slight but growing mistrust for the American. She wondered if it was simply a disappointment that she was less available since Larry had entered her life and taken so much of her time, they had been able to meet less often. But no, she amended, Megan was not the type to be jealous in that way. She wasn't as outspoken as Sally but she wouldn't be afraid to complain if she thought it necessary. Perhaps she thinks in the same way as Gethyn, she sighed. The stranger, the newcomer must be the most likely suspect.

They ate at a pub, Larry cheerful and obviously intent on making her laugh and forget her experience. Afterwards, they searched the stalls of the local market and bought a complete set of bedding for the double bed. Larry insisted on paying for it.

"I must," he said with mock severity. "I should have listened to you when you told me you thought you were being overheard. This is my way of saying sorry."

She was glad he was there when she went into the house that evening. They checked the new keys and Rosemary gave one to Larry. "If someone comes in now, I'll know it was you," she said, "and I won't be afraid again."

"You ought to leave one somewhere," he advised. "There's nothing more annoying that finding yourself locked out of your own home, unless it's being locked out of your car. That happened to me once."

When they were eating a simple breakfast the following morning, Rosemary pointed to the brick shed at the bottom of the garden.

"I've decided to hide the spare key in there like we used to years ago," she told him. "There's a loose brick and no one will think of looking there for it."

Larry examined the place and agreed.

"It seems as safe as it can be, but make sure no one sees you put it there. Until the police find out who was responsible, you mustn't trust anyone, check?"

"Check," she smiled. "D'you think the police will find the man?"

"Surely! In a one horse town like this, with everyone knowing everyone else, it's a certainty. Dammit, I bet the neighbours can hear you changing your mind!" Larry sounded more confident than he felt, but needed to reassure her that the nightmare of knowing someone out there had entered her home and defiled her bed, would eventually be ended. Once the culprit was caught, she would be able to put it out of her mind. She smiled at him, knowing what he was trying to do and grateful for his concern.

A few days later, when Larry had gone and the house had once more settled comfortably around her, the postman knocked. Fear rose again.

"Would you take this in for next door, Rosemary? I can't make Gethyn hear."

"Certainly. He can't be far." She smiled and took the parcel from him.

Search For a Shadow

After an hour, she went outside and knocked on Gethyn's front door. He opened it immediately and smiled as he took the parcel she offered.

"Come in for a moment," he said, stepping back to allow her room to enter the small hallway.

"I don't really have much time—" she hesitated. But then she changed her mind and stepped in saying brightly, "But there's always a few minutes to spare for a chat with a friend, isn't there?" In that moment she had suddenly thought that his refusal to open the door to the postman might have been a ploy to talk to her for a few moments. He was a lonely man, seeing so few people, and it was unkind not to give him a little of her time. He disabused her, saying, "I heard the postman knock but I was in the bath, likely he was too busy to knock a second time. Come in. Excuse the mess."

The room *was* in a mess. The cupboard which had stood against the wall in a corner, had been moved to stand at an awkward angle further along the wall. Piles of magazines and papers were strewn across the old leather couch. He hurriedly gathered them and put them, and the parcel, into the cupboard and pushed the doors closed.

"I've taken your advice, Rosemary, I'm sorting out some of Mam's things. Takes for ever, doesn't it, reading through and wondering what to throw out and what to keep in case it's needed?"

"You've certainly been busy," she laughed. "If you want any help—?"

"No thanks. Best I get on with it myself. Not working, it gives me something to do."

"If you're sure."

"The police haven't found anyone then?" he said as he struggled to clear a place for her to sit. "I didn't expect them to. And there's strange them finding the phone interfered with! In a small place like this you don't expect such carryings on. More like the way Americans behave than people in our village!"

His eyes darted to her face and away again and Rosemary realised it was his way of saying he suspected Larry of being involved. She ignored the remark and instead asked, "Have you found anything interesting?"

"Interesting?" He stared at her with an intensity that slightly unnerved her and she waved deprecatingly at the cupboard.

"You know, papers relating to the family. I think it must be fun, learning facts about yourself and your family that are new to you."

"Nothing like that. Only boring old stuff that should have been thrown out years ago." He seemed unhappy about her remark, and she wondered if it had sounded like snooping. Although they had known each other all their lives, Gethyn was still a very private person, easily embarrassed, even by her.

She stood to leave, rescuing some forms and documents that slid to the floor as she rose, and putting them on top of others on the table. It seemed that the place was filled with paper, everything from complete newspapers to the smallest cuttings and receipts.

"Best I let you get on, Gethyn. I can see you have plenty to keep you busy."

"Come in later on today, when I've got things under control," he said and as he spoke, another pile, this time of yellowed newspapers, slowly collapsed and descended in a slow avalanche, onto the carpet. He shrugged and smiled ruefully. "Better make it tomorrow!"

There was an easing of the secretiveness Larry showed. Now, she always knew where he could be found and

Search For a Shadow

usually, what he was doing. It was searching through the libraries and the archives, where he spent most of his time, although occasionally, when she was not free, he went on sightseeing trips to the mountains and into some of the historical towns of North Wales. They spoke at least once every day and knowing he was within a few hours driving and at the end of the phone helped Rosemary to relax once again. Every weekend he spent with her, only working at his research while she was occupied too.

One Thursday, he asked what she had planned to show him at the weekend.

"I'm in Cardiff now," he told her, "but I'll be finished here soon and for the next week I'll be at Aberystwyth, close enough to come home to you every evening."

She couldn't hide the excitement the words caused and didn't even try.

"Darling, I can't wait. I'll make us a picnic for Saturday," she said. "It's very windy here but so far it's dry. Saturday is my day off and I'd like to show you Aberangell mountain."

"'Aber' means mouth, so it's the mouth of the River Angell, right?" he asked.

"Named for an angel," she explained. "The river was thought to be so beautiful it was named River of Angels. At least, that's what some of the locals believe!"

"And I'll see it with my own angel. Perfect," he breathed.

When she woke the following morning she found two pints of milk had been left for her. She frowned. She always used a pint each day, drinking any that was still left after she had finished breakfast. Only when Larry or someone else stayed did she order extra. Who had forestalled her and placed the order?

"There was a note," the milkman told her later. "Just a block-printed note asking for extra. All right was it? I mean, you did want it?"

"Quite all right, and thank you," Rosemary said.

"Don't look for mysteries where there are none, darling," Larry warned when he telephoned her for an end-of-week chat and was told of the new event. "I expect the previous note was still there and was blown about in this wind. Stranger things have happened."

"But so many things are happening. Can someone still be listening to my conversations?"

"The British Telecom engineers found the box and everything has been dismantled. The police and the engineers will be keeping a look out to make sure it doesn't happen again."

"Of course, but too many coincidences are hard to accept," she said doubtfully.

The wind was strong, and increasing in force, an empty dustbin placed outside number five for the men to empty and which had not been recovered, was sent bowling along the grass near the stream.

Attracted by the noise, Rosemary looked out of her window and laughed to see Huw Rees chasing it and capturing it just before it fell into the fluttering surface of the wind-whipped water. She waved as he looked in her direction, to share the amusement with him.

Larry arrived when the vegetable lasagne she was cooking was sending out tempting aromas. He sniffed appreciatingly as he went straight through to the kitchen to make his habitual cup of coffee. He drank it thirstily then prepared the salad. They ate companionably, sharing news of the hours they had been apart.

Search For a Shadow

She told him about the parcel coming for Gethyn and his inviting her in to see the glorious mess he was in sorting out his mother's papers. He told her of his latest discoveries, including the information that beside being farmers, a branch of his family had once been fishermen.

"Seems I'm not going to discover an exciting link with your Prime Minister or find myself a dukedom!" he joked. He spread out his family tree and proudly pointed out the gaps he had now filled, albeit some in pencil and bearing question marks!

The time she spent with him was both exciting and tranquil, Rosemary decided, as she watched him prepare their after dinner coffee. Tranquil, because she never had to stop and consider what she would say, being able to be completely open with him. Exciting, because the way he looked at her, admiration and love blazoning out of his brown eyes, made her feel like a beautiful woman.

Sensuality was not something she had ever considered, but knowing he loved and admired her gave her an extra perception of her femininity. He had increased her awareness of herself as a woman. Since they had become lovers, there was an added sway to her walk and more provocative nuance in her smile. But for him only. When she was with anyone else, the difference in her would have been hardly detected. Loving was giving, and to Larry she gave unreservedly.

The wind increased in force and howled around the cottage like a crazed thing trying to come in. The trees that grew on the far side of the stream groaned and creaked as the wind pushed the branches against one another in a weird symphony.

"Shall we go to the local pub for a drink?" he suggested. "Those trees sound as if they might fall and I don't think it's wise to travel far, but the pub is only a mile along the main road."

"I agree about the trees, they look precarious, don't they? In fact, it might be an idea to move the cars."

Larry went to the front room and looked out of the window into the stormy evening. Although it was hardly autumn, leaves were gliding down from the trees like giant confetti. Rising and dropping as they were caught and released by the gusts, settling on the banks to roll like hoops or alight on the stream to be hurried along its surface, until finally disappearing under the footbridge. One birch tree was leaning badly, but he decided that if any should fall, none were likely to hit the cars.

The storm continued to increase in severity and as they walked home, they were blown about by the sudden gusts of wind as if some playful giant were taking a deep breath and blowing at them, using them for a game of skittles. As they walked along a dark, narrow section of the road, the creaking and groaning of the trees increased. Something in the wild sounds chilled her and she pulled back, afraid, but without knowing why, an atavistic fear leadening her limbs.

"Come on, Rose Mary, let's get home before one of these trees decides to give up the struggle and – Jesus!"

The rest of his words were drowned by the rushing sound of a tree falling, to rest on the hedges that edged the road. They staggered back in time to avoid the main trunk of the slender ash tree but a snapped branch caught Larry a glancing blow on the shoulder and he fell.

"Larry!" Rosemary screamed. The tree wasn't a large one but it blocked all sight of him from her. She felt under the leaves, frantically calling his name. "Larry? Larry, darling? Are you all right?"

"Shit!" she heard through the wailing of the wind and

Search For a Shadow

the cracking of the settling branches. "Walking on these Goddamned roads is more hairy than jaywalking on Fifth Avenue!"

She smiled. He was clearly unharmed!

A car approached and stopped before hitting the fallen tree and it seemed no time before the police and the fire brigade had arrived and arrangements begun for the removal of the tree.

They hastened home when it was clear Larry was no more than slightly bruised. They laughed and made a joke of their adventure, hand in hand, running and shouting like children; calling up the wind, defying its fury. Larry went straight into the kitchen to make coffee as he always did, and soon after they went to bed.

They relaxed into sleep, with the wind lashing furiously at the house as if seeking entry. Branches were tap-dancing on the roof. Squally showers were beating a tattoo against the window panes. Then, at two o'clock, the wind suddenly rushed through the house. A door banged back against its hinges and the door to the loft fell down against the wall with a deafening bang.

They both sat up in bed and Rosemary clung to Larry.

"What is it? Oh, Larry! Thank goodness you're here."

Larry reached over and switched on the bedside lamp but it didn't work. He climbed out of bed, the sound of the wind filling the room with a ululating drone. He tried the wall switch unsuccessfully, then the landing, the second bedroom and the bathroom. All the lights in the house had failed.

"It must be a power line brought down," he said, feeling for his clothes. "Stay there, I'll just find my pants and go down to see what caused the crash though, there must be a window open."

"I checked them all." Rosemary shivered as she pulled

her dressing gown on. "And what's more, darling, I'm not staying here without you. If you're going anywhere, I'm coming too!"

The banging led them through the house to the kitchen and to their alarm they saw that the back door was open and banging again and again against the wall.

"But, it's impossible," Larry said stupidly. "I made sure the door was locked and everything secure before we went upstairs."

He took her hand and led her to the front door after relocking the back. The door was locked but the bolt was not thrust home.

"I didn't think it was necessary, not with me being here," he said. "But anyway, it's the back door that's been opened and that was locked and bolted, you saw me do it."

"The house sounded angry," Rosemary said quietly as they went back to the living room. "I know it sounds fanciful, Larry, but d'you think the place can have a ghost?"

"Hey, come on!" He held her against him, her body trembling with cold and shock. "No, I do not!"

"But what's happening? I've lived here without incident for years, and now, since—" She tried to remember the date when she first became aware she was being overheard, but Larry misunderstood her hesitation.

"Since I came into your life, is that what you're thinking?"

"Larry, of course not!" She stared at him in consternation. "I was trying to remember the date when I first thought someone was listening! Before the police found the line-tapping equipment. It seems to have gone on for so long. Larry, how could I think it was you!" She hugged him, shivering intensely, cold with the thought that he

Search For a Shadow

believed her capable of suspecting him of causing all the furore. "Not you, darling. Anyone else, but not you."

She left him to make coffee and when she returned, he was sitting on the settee, a solemn expression on his handsome face.

"Darling, it's only your support that's kept me on an even keel during these weeks," she said. She knelt beside him pleading with him to believe her. "I don't believe for one moment that all this is anything to do with you. Believe me, please, Larry. If you abandon me, then I'll never, ever, stay in this house again. Solving mysteries might be satisfying, but for me, all I want is to have you beside me. The puzzle solving I can happily leave to others."

"I'm sorry, Rosemary. I shouldn't upset you more. It's just that I love you and need you so much, I can't bear the thought that you don't feel the same."

"Darling Larry, I do," she whispered as he took her once again into his arms. "Whatever you're involved in, I'm involved too." She was prepared to wait until he was ready to tell her the secret he was keeping from her. She wouldn't ask again.

Dawn came, and the storm died with the darkness. The sky showed sun-edged clouds when Rosemary opened the curtains a little to help her wake. She returned to the settee where Larry's concerned eyes were open and watching her. She knelt beside him and kissed him.

The sun came into the room and shone dazzlingly on something in the room. It puzzled Rosemary in a half-hearted, sleep-dulled way. She looked at the reflected light as her mind uncurled slowly from sleep, wondering what it could be. Daylight strengthened and she recognised the objects with a shout of disbelief.

Kay Christopher

On a chair near the fire where the early sun touched them, were light bulbs. By the size of the pile they made, every single light bulb from the house was there. Someone had come in while they were sleeping and taken each one out of its socket and piled them there to let them know they had been visited.

Chapter Seven

When Larry fully woke to Rosemary's urgent shaking, he stared at the pile of light bulbs, rubbed his eyes and stared again. He examined them, then looked up at the empty socket with wide-eyed alarm. His first thoughts were the same as hers.

"Rose Mary, this means that someone was here during the night while we were asleep!"

He ran to the back door which was closed and bolted, then went into every room, examining every inch of every cupboard, even opening the drawers. He searched the obvious places, the unlikely and the down right impossible, not once, but several times. There was nowhere a person of the most minimal proportions could be hidden. Then he looked up at the trap-door to the loft. He turned to Rosemary who, white-faced and breathless, had followed him around as he searched.

"Could there be someone up there?" she whispered.

"I can't think where else! Dammit, I've even looked up the chimneys," he whispered back. "Where's your torch?"

"Don't Larry! Let's call the police, he's bound to be dangerous if he's cornered!"

"He'll be dangerous, but not half as dangerous as I am!" He took the torch she brought him from her bedroom. There was a chair in the study and he carried it and placed it below the trap-door.

"He's got the advantage," Rosemary pleaded. "You don't stand a chance." She held her breath as he prepared to jump up into the dark space above them. "Anyone there would find it easy to strike at you! You'll have no defence at all!"

Ignoring her, he stood on the chair and raised the flap-door into the attic. His hands on the edge, he hauled himself up and stood in the darkness, shooting beams of light all around him. Slowly, while Rosemary watched with fingers in her mouth to hold back a scream, he disappeared leaving only a flickering light for her to see.

"Darling, are you all right?" she whispered, afraid after only a moment of silence.

"All right so far." She heard him shuffling his feet, stepping over objects, she heard the rustle of paper, held her breath when a box slid across the wooden planking, then cried with relief when his head appeared in the opening, smiling.

"There's no one here, and what's more, there's no way anyone can get from one house to another." He jumped down and she hugged him in relief.

"What I thought might have happened," he went on, "was that in some very old houses, there's no separation between the loft areas. There was one place I heard of where someone could walk the length of the street above the ceilings of unsuspecting neighbours. But," he said firmly to reassure her, "this is not the case here. This partition is the real McCoy, a brick wall that's as solid as you could hope for between you and your neighbours."

"Then how did he get in?"

They went downstairs and Larry put the percolator on for coffee.

"I have more than a suspicion it was me," he admitted. "I think I only locked the front door after we came back from the pub; I didn't push home the bolts."

"Then you think someone already has a spare key?"

"It seems impossible but what other explanation is there? I'm going out to see if the one we hid in the shed is still there. If it isn't I'll have the locks altered again. If it is, I'll bring it in and put it in the Italian vase on the mantle, and there it stays! If you lock yourself out you'll have to call the police to let you in!"

"I'm calling the police now, to tell them about this."

"Perhaps I'm wrong, darling, but I don't think that's a good idea."

"But why not? Someone came in here while we were sleeping!" She shuddered at the thought and repeated, "Came in here, stood in our bedroom, watched us while we slept, then took out all the light bulbs so we'd know he'd been here!"

"He's trying to frighten us."

"He's succeeding!"

"I mean that if he wished to harm us he's had the opportunity. I think he's a trickster, getting his excitement from troubling us. If we ignore the tricks he plays he'll grow tired of them and perhaps think of some other foolish way to entertain himself."

"Or," Rosemary argued, "he might develop his 'entertainment' into something more dangerous for us! If we're the spice in his life, he'll want to increase the dose as the excitement fades, not leave it out altogether!"

"Let's give it another day or two, then, if we still feel the police should be informed, we'll go to them and tell them all that's happened."

Doubtfully, Rosemary agreed.

Neither of them felt like going on the day out they had planned with such excitement.

"But," Larry said when they had discussed it, "we're still

going! Dammit I can't think what else we'd do. Sit here wondering if someone is going to come in and watch us? No, it's creepy and we have to get out. A touch of Welsh mountain air is what we both need."

"How will I face coming back in?" Rosemary shivered and looked about her as if the place was a prison from which she couldn't escape. "If I go out I'll never come back."

"Yes you will, I'll be with you."

"But when you go away tomorrow, I'll be alone and I don't think I could stand it."

"I'm working in Aberystwyth. I promise I'll be back here every evening before you are. You won't be alone in the house, I promise."

"Why didn't you call the police for goodness sake?" Sally demanded, when Rosemary told her friends about the weekend's happenings.

"Yes, love," Megan agreed. "That should have been your first action. How can they help if you don't tell them everything?"

"You're afraid Larry's at the bottom of it all, are you?" Sally demanded. "That's stupid! If you suspect him, how can you allow him to share your home – let alone your bed!"

"He isn't responsible!" Rosemary defended. "Although I think he might unwittingly be the reason for all this."

"Demand an explanation! Talk to the plice, now!" Sally insisted but Rosemary shook her head.

"I wanted to call the police at first," Rosemary told her, "but we decided that someone was tormenting us for peculiar reasons of their own and we should disappoint him by not showing any reaction."

"But someone who could do such things might be dangerous. How can you tell what he'll do next?" Megan asked

Search For a Shadow

anxiously. "He might be unbalanced and he seems to be able to get in and out of your house as easily as walking down the street! Really, Rosemary, you're risking serious trouble by allowing this to continue."

"If I were living there alone I'd have told them, and I doubt if I would ever sleep in the place again," Rosemary admitted, "but Larry is going to stay, at least until he goes back to America, and—"

"When will that be?" Megan asked softly. "Is that something I should, or shouldn't ask?"

"We haven't mentioned it lately," Rosemary admitted. She looked at her friend with some defiance and added, "And I don't care. I'm taking your advice and enjoying it while it lasts!"

"I was talking about a couple of nights in London, love. Not a drawn out affair that could leave you sadder and more lonely than you could ever imagine."

"I still don't regret it."

"I did," Megan admitted, turning her face away from Rosemary's startled expression. "I certainly did."

"You had an affair that went wrong?" Rosemary stared at her friend in surprise. "All this time we've known each other, spent days talking non-stop and I never knew."

"The man concerned lived not far from where you now live, that's why I haven't said 'til now. Long time ago it was. His mother disliked me the moment we met, I was older than him, you see. She had a strong pull on him and, well, he left both me and his mother in the end and went to live abroad somewhere. His mother wouldn't even talk to me and certainly wouldn't tell me where he was."

"But why?"

"We'd spent some time living together and twenty-odd years ago it definitely wasn't the done thing. Especially in a small Welsh village. Put me down as a fallen woman who'd tried to drag her son down with me, or something equally dramatic. What she did was cruel though."

"Why didn't you marry?"

"I wanted to, I begged him to marry me but his mam didn't think we should and he – well, sufficient to say he listened to her."

"Who was it, Megan?"

"Mrs Priestley's son, Leonard."

"So that's why she's always a bit cool with you! I remember hearing something about her son leaving, from Gran. Gethyn thought a lot of him and treated him like a fond uncle. But – I had no idea that you and Leonard – I'm sorry Megan."

"No need, love, it's all a very long time ago."

"And you don't know where he is?" Sally asked.

"He never wrote and so far as I know he never got in touch with *her* either. She blamed me for that too."

"I never knew. She knows you and I are friends but she's never mentioned a word. Megan, you don't think she's at the bottom of what's happening to me, do you? I mean she sees you visiting me and perhaps she has some vague notion of punishing me because I'm your friend? But no. She's a sweet old lady and I can't see her doing anything so terrible."

"Nor can I, not now. Although years ago I thought her capable of anything to keep me from her precious son. She was frighteningly determined and – almost evil in her protection of him against me, the wicked woman."

Mrs Priestley as the mysterious prowler? The incongruity of the scene made Rosemary smile. Mrs P. with her fluffy blue dressing gown and fur-trimmed slippers, cat under her arm, wandering about trying to create mischief? No, it simply wasn't on!

Search For a Shadow

"Stranger things have happened," Sally said, as if reading her thoughts through her smile. "I'd like to meet this Mrs Priestley, Rosemary. Any chance? I hear all this gossip and it's driving me mad not to put faces to the names you and Megan talk about."

"Yes, we'll arrange something – soon." Rosemary was vague but Sally insisted until Megan was finally irritated.

"Leave it, Sally, for heaven's sake leave it! I think Rosemary has enough on her mind without arranging 'get togethers' to satisfy your curiosity, don't you?"

Driving home from work that evening, Rosemary was apprehensive.

She was relieved to see Huw Rees walking ahead of her along the hedge-lined road as she approached the last turning, and she stopped just ahead of him and offered him a lift.

He threw his coat into the back seat and climbed in, smelling a little of the fungus with which he worked, smiling his thanks.

"The holiday work is a bit different from your usual activities, isn't it, Huw?" she said as she moved off. "What are you studying? Not mushroom growing I bet!"

"Electronics is my subject," he laughed, "not much use to me at present!"

He looked at her and guessed something was wrong. Her tenseness was obvious and he asked if everything was all right. Because of the state of her nerves she told him something of the events of the night before the last and before she realised it, found herself pouring out the whole story. The attacks on Larry and the intrusions into her home.

"Is Sally doing some detective work for you?" he surprised her by asking.

"No, why?"

"It's only that I saw her in the village shop and she was asking questions in her forthright way."

"You know her well?"

"Not really, but she always comes to talk to me when I go in the library. Asks a lot of questions, doesn't she and in such a way that it's hard not to answer."

"That's sounds like Sally! No, she isn't investigating on my behalf, but by the sound of it she has questions of her own. I wonder why?" she mused. "No, Larry and I decided not to tell anyone of everything that's happened," she explained, "because we don't know who is responsible. Telling the wrong one might put the man on his guard. Please don't let Larry know I've confided in you."

"I won't tell Larry you told me," he said, "but I'm glad you did. It might be useful to have someone else who understands. If ever you're on your own, or need help of any kind, just call me." As the car pulled up near the footbridge, he added, "Night or day."

There was no Citroën parked nearby and Rosemary's heart began to flutter.

"Huw, can I ask a favour now?" she said in a small voice. "You see, Larry isn't here yet and—"

"And you don't fancy walking into the house alone? Of course I'll go with you. Better still, give me the key and I'll go in first and call you over when I've made sure nothing is wrong."

She watched, feeling a little foolish as the slim, tanned, gangling young man walked over the bridge and approached the house. He opened the door with the key and disappeared inside. Moments later she saw him wave from the front window, then a brief delay before he came out of the door and beckoned her across.

Search For a Shadow

"The place is empty and it all looks normal, if unbelievably tidy!" he reported. "If you like, I'll wait here while you look then you can be certain all is well." He waited at the door until she had satisfied herself everything was as it should be, then she thanked him and he walked along to number five.

Larry arrived within half an hour, very agitated and apologetic.

"Honey-baby, I'm sorry! I looked at the time and realised I'd be late, I tried to phone the library but you'd left." He hugged her, then looked at the meal she was about to place in the grill-pan. "I'm so proud of you! Coming in and carrying on as if the past couple of days hadn't happened."

She smiled and was about to confess to accepting some support from the student Huw Rees, when there was a knock at the door. Larry answered the knock, but she heard Huw ask for her and she went out before Larry could call her.

"Come and see this," Huw urged enthusiastically. "There's an owl in the tree behind Mrs Priestley's house, broad daylight and sitting there as bold as you like!"

"Turn off the grill for me, darling," Rosemary said and followed Huw to where they could see the backs of the cottages.

She felt him push something into her hand, and realised it was a key.

"Sorry, I walked off with it after taking it out of the door," he whispered. "I thought you might not like Larry to know."

Larry joined them and she could only nod to Huw in expression of her thanks, before he asked, "Where is this oddity then? This night bird posing for photographs in the day?" He showed them his camera which he had hurriedly picked up, but Huw admitted sadly that the bird had disappeared.

They went back inside. She picked up the vase where she and Larry now kept it and quickly replaced the key. Larry smiled and came to hug her.

"Brave girl, but not quite as fearless as she pretends," he said, kissing her brow. "She has to rattle the vase now and again to make sure the spare key is still there!"

For the second time she took a breath to tell him about Huw's help but there was a yell and he ran from her to rescue the trout under the grill that he hadn't quite turned off.

"Just a smidgin over-cooked would you say? Oh, what the hell," he said, staring at the burned mess, a boyish grin on his face, "let's eat out!"

A week later, Rosemary's manuscript was ready to send to her agent.

"I have to read it through once more to make sure everything is right," she explained and Larry offered to read it as well.

They sat throughout the evening, reading through, marking any typing errors and remarking occasionally on how she had achieved a particular effect.

"I've never had the benefit of someone else's eye before sending a story off," she smiled as the closed the file on the last pages. "I must admit I enjoyed sharing my thoughts and ideas. You really were a great help, darling, thank you."

"The teacher in me I guess," he said deprecatingly. "It's easier to correct than to create." He stood up as she collected together the pages she needed to alter. "I'll make the coffee, shall I?"

"The last pages can wait 'til tomorrow," Rosemary said lazily, "it's a bit late to start typing. I'll sent it off on Monday."

* * *

Search For a Shadow

"What does he do day after day?" There was doubt in Sally's voice when she began questioning Rosemary about Larry. The blue eyes in the pale face looked quite fierce. "You can't believe he's spending day after day researching his family. Aren't you curious?"

"He's at the library most of the time, and what else would he be doing? You have to remember that he's come on a very expensive trip to do some research into his family's background and he has to make full use of his time."

"Not so expensive," Megan said quietly, "thanks to you he has no hotel accommodation to pay."

"He's appreciative of that and more than pays his way," Rosemary admonished firmly.

"I'm sorry, I know I'm interfering, but there are a lot of coincidences and although I know they happen in life, surprisingly often in fact, it's unbelievable that he's always there when something strange happens, isn't it?"

"Megan's right." Sally spoke more quietly. "His presence could explain everything that's happened. We've discussed it and honestly, Rosemary, you're mad if you can't see it too."

"You don't think he's behind all these frightening happenings, do you? Really, that's crazy! He simply wouldn't do this to me. I know he wouldn't."

"All I'm saying, love," Megan said, "is be careful, and don't believe everything you're told, ask yourself questions and consider each answer with great care."

"I'd know if it were Larry. Whatever you think, I'd *know*."

"All right, consider these for a start." Megan held her fingers wide and touched them as she itemized the coincidences. "You saw him in the Citroën before he or a mysterious someone put that note through your door to tell you he had found you, after walking out on you in

London. Then there was the fiasco of the on/off weekend in London. He said he put yet another note through your door about that, but you never found it. Then there was the letter he didn't show you but which made him angry. It was addressed to him at your address."

"Then what about the cafe on Constitution Hill?" Sally added. "A girl appears to know him then changes her mind. Then he's punched in the face by someone whom he insists was a complete stranger."

"Then there's all these break-ins," Megan continued. "He is seen at the time of some of them, by either Huw or Gethyn, yet insists he was elsewhere. Or," she said emphatically, "he was already there, in the house."

"Invite Megan and me for the evening, we'll persuade him to open up," Sally suggested eagerly.

"No!"

Rosemary didn't wait to hear any more, she looked from one of her tormentors to the other then walked away from them.

When Rosemary walked to the car park at about a quarter past five, Gethyn was standing beside her car, patiently waiting for a lift.

"I'm sorry, Rosemary, but I missed the bus. Stupid of me, I went for a cup of tea and forgot the time."

"Glad I can help." She smiled and opened the door for him to get in.

He chattered easily all the way home and Rosemary was grateful not to have to force herself to make conversation. He spoke mainly about the occupants of the five cottages, explaining about Mrs Priestley taking her new kitten to the vet for injections.

"Lonely she'd be without that animal to look after, going into old age without a soul of her own. Shame she hasn't

Search For a Shadow

a son to look after her, isn't it? Him being driven away from home like that." From the expression on his face she guessed that he strongly supported Mrs Priestley in her blame of Megan, and she hurriedly changed the subject and discussed instead the amusing antics of the young cat. He then went on to tell her that the Hughes's from number three were still visiting their daughter and grandchildren, in Bala. The students he clearly didn't like.

"You can't lump all students together," she laughed when he began to complain about their lack of seriousness. "Huw seems a pleasant young man and I can't complain about their behaviour."

"I've seen Huw standing on the footbridge staring at your house," Gethyn said. "And he can't be looking for that owl. No one else has seen it, I think he invented it for reasons of his own."

Rosemary knew that was true, but she said nothing.

She met Huw again on the way home and he gratefully accepted her offer of a lift, getting in behind Gethyn, who looked decidedly ill-at-ease. When she parked the car beside the Citroën, Gethyn got out, murmured his thanks and hurried across the footbridge and disappeared through his front door.

"Gethyn mentioned the elusive owl," Rosemary said with a frown. "I wonder how he knew?"

"I'm certain I didn't mention it," Huw said, helping her out of the car. "Probably overheard us talking about it. He spends a lot of time in the front of the house, doesn't he, just looking?"

"And that," Rosemary laughed, "is what he says about you!"

Chapter Eight

Sitting alone in Rosemary's living room, Larry began to feel very uneasy. There was no special sound or movement he could explain in words, just a slow realisation that he wasn't alone. The silence around him bore a hint of slow and soft breathing. He knew he was imagining it, yet the fear of it still prickled his scalp. He went into the kitchen and began making coffee. At least out here the sound faded until he convinced himself it had stopped. He flicked on the radio then snapped it off again. If there *was* someone there he needed to know. He daren't risk masking the sound of their movements.

The admission that he really believe he had unknown company made him laugh aloud. He'd been spooked, that was all. Someone was trying to scare the pants off of him and he'd have to stop his imaginings right now or he'd be ready for the funny farm.

As if to prove something to an imaginary companion, he raced up the stairs and threw open every door. Every room was clearly untouched since his previous inspection. He was alone. Any hint that things were otherwise was simply fanciful. He went to the kitchen again and poured out the coffee. Then, he heard a sigh, so soft he thought it was in his own head, then it came again, a plaintive sound, sad and utterly chilling.

Someone driving him away? Warning him he was getting

Search For a Shadow

too close to what he was seeking? Hell, he thought, I will go away, but only up on the hills for an hour to clear my head a little.

After phoning Rosemary to tell her he would be out for a while, he gathered a jacket from the back of a chair and left the house. It was dull, the sky a low grey cover, not a day to enjoy views from high hills. Perhaps he wouldn't go far after all.

As the door closed behind him, the smaller door of the cupboard under the stairs, known locally as the *cwtch dan star*, slowly opened and a figure rose and let itself out of the house; then slipped around the back of the row of cottages and up the hill to the churchyard.

Crossing the footbridge, Larry's shoulders were dampened by the overhanging branches, the leaves already moist with the misty air. He hurried, conscious of the silence broken only by the sound of his sneakers on the wet wooden planks. Following the stream, he walked past where the river and stream joined and strode out purposefully towards the hills.

He tried to pretend, but the feeling of being followed wouldn't leave him. He glanced behind him several times but each time the road was only a wet, empty ribbon. From the fields on either side, sheep watched him pass, their solemn heads turning to follow his progress with idle curiosity. The River Dovey on his right made hardly a sound as it sullenly slid past the banks, held down by the weighty air.

He hadn't really thought where he was going and he began to wish he had stayed put. The eerie feeling in the house hadn't been left behind; it was walking with him.

He touched the fading bruises on his face. It wasn't all

imagination. But how could anyone have guessed why he was here? How could what he was searching for cause such a violent reaction?

He came to a T-junction and he left the road to climb up towards the old quarry. There were still some old buildings there and he was tempted to explore them, more from the need to add some purpose to his walk than from real interest. He would look at them, consider the expedition at an end and go home.

The climb wasn't very steep but the way was difficult because of the small blackthorns and birch trees that were already colonising the abandoned place. The spiky branches tugged at his clothes and the clumps of heather underfoot and the trailing brambles tripped him several times. He realised he was hurrying and he slowed down a little, trying not to listen for sounds coming behind him.

He came out into an open space, where the scars of previous work were still visible, as yet unweathered by lichen and moss and small plants. Then the mist, so unpredictable here in the hills, closed in and he found he could barely see the bottom of the excavations. There was a rustling sound behind him and his heart began to thump fiercely and his body stiffened for action. He hadn't imagined it, someone *had* followed him!

The sound wasn't repeated and he began to relax. It must have been an animal shuffling through the grass, the hills were full of rabbits and the highest layer of the quarry-sides showed evidence of their burrowing. Even a fox might be hunting in daylight, he had seen them several times before, emboldened by the mist and the absence of people.

He remained standing on the lip of the quarry, undecided as to whether to continue or walk back. Then the rustling came again, something – or someone – was pushing through the grass. He tried to look in every direction at once, turning to glance behind him, ignoring how close his feet were to the edge.

A sigh, impatient this time, followed by the rustling of a bush close to him. He heard breathing then, not a sigh but an irritated breathing, with the hint of a growl in its eerie, bodyless sound. He stared into the mist and saw nothing yet the sound seemed to be all around him. Rosemary's thoughts of a ghost invaded his hyped-up brain and he moved suddenly, jerkily. His feet slid on the wet earth and he went over the side with a yell of alarm.

He didn't sail out wide of the sides like the old woman had, but half slid, scrabbling on the edge. He went down half clinging to the side and grasped briefly at a tree growing out of the steep side. The young tree fell with him, but it had slowed his fall enough for him to turn himself and when he fell, he landed on all fours in a shower of gravelly stones, bruised, scratched but relatively unharmed.

He lay for a few moments and listened but there was only the sound of his own breathing. No one was climbing down to follow up the assault, if assault it was. Now, in the silence of the deep quarry, it seemed as unlikely as Rosemary's theory of a ghost.

He moved carefully, trying not to make a sound, still half convinced of the presence of someone else. He walked looking up, his senses ready for flight. Then he tripped over something soft and he stifled a shout of alarm. At his feet was the decomposing body of a sheep. Grimacing his abhorrence he turned away and gave his attention to the almost sheer face of the quarry. He found a place where the jagged edge gave him some chance of climbing up and he began to reach higher and higher.

The air was benign, a bird sang as if to mock his fear. The vicinity of the place from where he fell was silent although he stood and held his breath and listened for almost a minute. He ran down the hill to the further side of the village; panting, wide-eyed, blood-stained and filthy, he burst into the cottage to stand listening for as long as he could hold his breath.

Rosemary came home to find him still filthy, his clothes showing the damage of the afternoon's events. His explanations were garbled. He admitted falling into the quarry but told her he had been watching a small greeny-grey bird and had lost his footing. He made no mention of his belief that someone had followed him up there.

Larry had never discussed the date of his return to America. As the weeks passed and their relationship seemed to flourish and grow stronger, the only insecurity Rosemary suffered was not knowing when it would end. She had moments when she thought it never would end, that their present situation would go on for ever, that Larry would continue searching in the libraries and archives and nothing would change. But there was never a day during which her thoughts did not at least once leap to the reminder that it was temporary, a castle of dreams built on an ethereal pink cloud. One day, perhaps that very day, he would regretfully tell her he was leaving.

She rehearsed a series of imaginary scenarios in which he was broken-hearted and she was brave, or one in which she was on her knees begging him to stay, promising anything just to have him near her. The most common one was that she would arrive home one day, open the door and know with that sixth sense of lovers that he was gone.

There would be a note, affectionate and full of praise for her generosity and signed with kisses, and promises to "keep in touch". But she would know, looking down at the note, the flimsy end to it all, that there would never again be the sight of him welcoming her with his brown eyes full of love and arms held wide to enfold her.

Every day, when she walked across the footbridge and his car was not parked near hers, she would hold her breath, go into the kitchen and look for the note she half expected and dreaded to find. Days and weeks moved them through the warm summer, yet the moment hadn't come.

There were no further events to alarm them and August passed in a haze of sunny days, picnics, days out walking in the green hills and lush valleys. The cooler winds of September began to prepare the countryside for the new season. The scenery was surreptitiously stage-managed; the sharper air, the stronger breezes easing the leaves from the trees.

They seldom talked about the series of bizzarre happenings that had worried them. Whoever had been tormenting them had either given up, or had found someone else as a target for his amusement. But there was one exception. On Sunday afternoon, while Rosemary was editing her script and Larry was cutting the grass behind the house, the spare key, which they had thought to be safely hidden in the vase, was found outside the door by Mrs Priestley, who returned it, saying she thought it was Rosemary's as all the others in the row had keys that were alike.

"I think the locks the rest of us have are the ones put there when the cottages were built," she said, handing the shining key to a startled Rosemary.

"But, where did you find it?" Rosemary asked. Mrs Priestley led her to a slight indentation in the grass verge beyond the footpath, and pointed.

"Down by there and half covered with earth as if it had been there some time and had been trodden down a bit," she explained, in her pleasant lilting voice.

"Thank you for returning it."

"No trouble my dear."

Rosemary held the key and wiped it free of earth with her fingers. Where had it been? And more seriously, how had it been removed from the vase on the mantle? She and Larry discussed it when he came in from cutting the grass on the back lawn. He too picked it up and examined it as if the answer were somehow to be found on its shining surface.

"We'll put it back and stop worrying about it," he said.

He lifted the vase down and unconsciously shook it. It rattled. An anxious examination found their key still inside. Wordlessly they went to the front door and tried the key Mrs Priestley had found. It turned in the lock without any effort. Someone had somehow managed to get a duplicate key.

Coming in the following evening, Larry kissed her and hugged her to him. "I'm sorry I'm late," he said. "I had to go into town." He stopped suddenly as if he were about to say something further but had changed his mind.

"Larry?" she looked at him questioningly. "What is it?" Had the moment she had been dreading arrived at last? Was he trying to tell her he was leaving? He walked away from her to hang his coat in the cupboard under the stairs, avoiding her stare. Obviously there was something on his mind and there was only one thing it could be. He was leaving her.

Now the moment had come she was none of the things she had imagined and rehearsed. Not brave. Not smiling and casual. Not hysterical either; not inclined to drop to her knees and cry and beg him to stay.

"Rosemary, I've booked my flight home. For a week's time."

"Oh, I see. I hope you've finished all you set out to do."

Search For a Shadow

The cold words, sounding like a polite remark to a stranger, startled her, she had no will to say them. They had come out without thought, part of the defensive pride with which she would deal with the pain.

"I'll be back," he said, still not looking at her.

"That will be lovely," she said, again in the cold voice that seemed to belong to someone else. "Now, are you ready to eat? I'd hate this expensive meal to be wasted."

He turned towards her, then made a move as if to pull her into his arms, but the expression on her face, white with shock, stopped him and he gave a half smile, and nervously sat at the table.

The meal had lost its appeal. Rosemary's appetite, heightened by the smell of the cooking, had vanished with his words. The steaks she had bought as a special treat and had grilled just as he liked them, looked too ordinary to warrant the effort of cutting and eating them. The vegetables, so carefully chosen and cooked were left untouched on both their plates.

Glancing across at him as he sat, head down, trying to summon the emthusiasm to eat the food in front of him, she thought he even looked different. The expression on his face was altering him so that already she could feel him slipping away, moving out of her life without leaving a ripple on its surface.

They went for a walk after they had given up the attempt to finish the meal, unable to sit in the silence of their individual grief. Through the village and back along the banks of the river they walked, the darkness a relief, a curtain between them and sheltering them from the rest of the world.

Getting undressed and into bed was as unnerving as if it were the first time. Surprisingly, they made love. The moment they touched each other in the enforced intimacy of the bed, an urge so strong they could neither ignore or even calm it, made their loving as fierce and urgent as lovers separated for a long time. She woke with his arms still tightly around her and saw his eyes were open, watching her, as if he had not slept.

"Rosemary, we must talk, but, I can't find the words to begin."

"Let's pretend it isn't happening, at least for a few more days."

"But it is happening and I need to know how you feel about it."

"Later," she pleaded.

His arms tightened around her and again they lost themselves and their unspoken feelings in deep and satisfying love.

Going to work was hard. She was afraid to leave the cottage, convinced more than ever that when she returned he would be gone. His attempts to say goodbye with any degree of truth, had failed. He would simply walk away from her. Of that she was convinced.

She wanted to talk to Megan but she was holidaying in Italy. Although she was still less happy confiding in the blatantly curious Sally, she knew that given the slightest encouragement she would tell her of Larry's decision.

Sally took one look at her face and guessed something was wrong. Her concern was enough. They went out together to lunch and Rosemary told her Larry was leaving.

"When?"

"His flight is next week, but I expect he will go today," she said quietly, her lips trembling with threat of sobs. "I don't find it easy to cope with after all."

By the time she was on her way home, Rosemary was

almost resigned to walking into an empty house. She met Huw Rees again as he left the mushroom farm and he slid in beside her, saying, "So Larry is going home, then?"

"What?" Rosemary's foot eased off the accelerator and she stopped the car. "How did you know that?" she demanded.

"I think the woman in the shop told me. Said something about not having to buy any more popcorn, which she used to buy especially for him, or something like that. Why are you surprised?"

"He didn't tell *me* until last night!"

"His ticket is booked for a week's time according to Mrs-the-shop. Is that right too?"

"That's right, but how can they have known?"

"Larry calling in for more popcorn?" he suggested, and she sighed with relief.

"Of course. I should have thought of that. He must have gone in to buy something before setting off for the library."

"Why were you so worried? It isn't a secret is it?"

"No, I was being silly. For a moment I thought – I thought someone was listening in to my conversations again."

"The police never found out who it was, did they? Have you any ideas?"

"We did wonder if perhaps someone was hiding in the Hughes's house while they were away, although the police checked and found no evidence of that. Gethyn was convinced it was you," she smiled, "you or Richard."

"The man's an idiot! He probably still thinks exactly as mother told him he must think! He probably believes that all students are agitators for some or every cause! We must spend our time cooking up trouble and irritation for someone!

"I think I'll have a word with Gethyn," he said as he got out of the car. "You never know, he might he persuaded to open his mind to a new thought! Thanks for the lift."

The Citroën was not there, and her heart began to race with apprehension. She said goodbye to Huw, and walked aross the footbridge towards number two. As her hand touched the gate, she heard the sound of the Citroën's engine. It stopped, the door slammed and she heard Larry call her. She waited for him and they went into the cottage together.

He was carrying a brief-case she hadn't seen before. There was an expression in his eyes that looked like excitement and she wondered what he had to tell her. Whatever it was, it could not be as devastating as the announcement of the previous day.

"Don't cook," he said, bending to kiss her. "We're going out. Do you fancy that 'brigands' village' again?" he said, referring to Dinas Mawddwy, where they had been once before. "There's something to celebrate."

She put the shopping away in cupboard and fridge and smiled at him.

"You've made a breakthrough in your research?" she asked. "I'm so glad it's completed before you have to go."

"Not that exactly. Oh, it's no use, I've kept this from you long enough." He opened the brief-case and brought out a file. "It's the manuscript of my novel."

"But – what is it? I don't understand."

"I've been dishonest with you, darling. I *have* been researching my family, but besides that I've been writing a novel based on what I've discovered. Invention mostly of course, but I've had it typed and now, if you will, I want you to glance through it and appraise it. Tell me if you think there's a chance it will be published." He smiled at her, the old, remembered smile of a lover and friend. "Will you read it?"

"I'm so surprised! Why didn't you tell me?"

"Somehow I couldn't. Not until I'd finished it. I was afraid I'd lose the impetus and leave it half done then I'd have been ashamed. So, what do you think? I'm sorry I've been so dishonest, when you've been so wonderful to me."

"I've been a little dishonest too," she told him.

"You? This I don't believe."

"I knew you had to be doing something more than looking up the dates and occupations of your family and I invented all sorts of reasons for your deceit. I even thought that it might be you who was playing all these tricks on me, frightening me by taking out light bulbs while I slept and – Oh, Larry, I'm so glad to know how you spent your time. You can't imagine how relieved I feel."

"I had no idea. Hell, I've been stupid. Of course you'd wonder and of course you'd invent reasons to explain the mystery. But, surely you can't believe I'd frighten you?"

"No, I could never really convince myself of that. Sally suggested it, and although I tried to fit you into the role of mischievous tormentor, somehow I couldn't."

"Thank heavens for that!" He kissed her again, with excitement still present and making the kiss short, casual and unsatisfactory. "And I really am sorry. I should have been honest, I owe you that."

"You owe me nothing," she said. and the words, like the flippant and perfunctory kiss, were a reminder that he was leaving, that soon he would allow his memory of her to drift and fade until she was nothing more than a brief and convenient love affair in a far-off country. Something to tell his friends about, with perhaps a wistful and nostalgic smile.

It was late before they went out. They sat on the settee

and discussed his book. Rosemary was animated by the unexpected shared interest; Larry gaining the confidence to talk about it now his secret was out. She didn't read it, but listened while he explained the story he had woven around what he had discovered about his family.

"Let me look at it, Larry, please," she asked, pretending to pull the papers from him. But he shook his head.

"I'm overly sensitive I guess but, will you look at it when I'm not with you?"

"All right," she smiled.

"Come on woman, I'm starved. You go to the car, I'll just ring and book us a table. Meet you at the road bridge, check?"

"Check."

All through the meal, they talked about the book.

"We should have brought it with us," she said when a question came up that they couldn't fully resolve.

"Safer to leave it at home," he said. "I'd hate to lose it now."

"You have a copy!" she said in alarm.

"I've sent it to Dad, back home," he told her.

The mention of his home was a reminder of his imminent departure and she felt the joy of the evening sliding from her like a loose, ill-fitting cloak. They drove home and went inside with Larry, as always, going first to make coffee. Rosemary went upstairs and looked in her study hoping to have sneaky look at the manuscript. Then she gave a scream that sent Larry racing up the stairs two at a time. He groaned when he saw what had upset her. His manuscript was torn into thousands of pieces and spread all over the carpet.

It was hopeless to even try and put together the pieces. Whoever had destroyed it had done an excellent job. Larry ran his fingers through the fragments, then resignedly began to gather them and put them into a plastic bag for the refuse collection.

"Why would someone do this?" he asked as they picked up the final pieces.

"How, is more my worry. You have a copy, thank heavens, but how did it happen? Haven't you realised? Someone has been able to get in again!"

"This place is definitely creepy. It's like a huge radio transmitter that broadcasts all that happens here." Rosemary remembered then the conversation with Huw.

"Did you go to the shop this morning?" she asked.

"No," he said after a pause. "No, not this morning. I'd promised to go and see the typist early, to go through the book with her, make sure she hadn't left in any errors. Why?"

"Huw knows that you are leaving next week. He was told by someone in the shop, this morning." Larry stared at her, then as she began to say, "Someone is listening," he cut off the words before they could be said, by a sudden and rather fierce kiss.

From his pocket he took a notebook. On the first page he wrote:

"I agree, darling, but we'll say nothing. I'm going to catch this bastard, right?"

"I'm frightened," Rosemary wrote in reply. "What else could he have overheard?"

"Only that I love you and I haven't tried to keep that a secret," was the written reply.

Then the notes became more and more silly as they each

tried to take the other's mind off the sensation of being overheard by a stranger. Loving messages and silly messages, then, after a moment when they sat silently, arms around each other, Rosemary forgot the need for silence and said, "Does the typist still have your handwritten copy?"

"It's in my brief-case in the closet—"

The thought that it, too, could have been damaged made them both get up and hurry to the under-stairs cupboard where they kept the coats.

As they opened the door a strong smell of fresh paint hit them and they looked at the brief-case. Someone had poured paint over the neatly written pages. The copy was ruined.

They rang for the police and two constables arrived within a very short time. They asked questions about all the neighbours and one of them left them to go and interview each of the cottages.

"Next door, number three is still empty," the constable reported. "Next door the other side, at number one, the man has seen nothing that can help. God-'elp, there's a mess he's in poor dab. Says he's sorting out after losing his mam. Pity for him. He needs some help, but insists he'll manage on his own."

"I've offered to help him," Rosemary said, with a return of guilt over her neglect of him, "but I think he's happier just taking his time and getting things done the way he wants them done."

When the two policemen eventually left, carrying the ruined brief-case and manuscript, they offered the advice: "You should change the locks again."

"Is there a possibility we're being overheard?" Larry asked and the policeman shook his head doubtfully.

"Number three's empty, and number one," – he checked on his notebook – "Gethyn Lewis, has no telephone. Besides, the telephone engineers have checked regularly and there's been no further sign of anyone tampering with the lines." He pocketed his notebook again and added comfortingly, "Go to your beds and rest easy, just make sure everything is locked and bolted. Then tomorrow, change the locks. We'll look in again and of course, let you know if we have anything to report." Did he stare extra steadily at Rosemary, when he said that, or did she imagine it?

They felt reassured and when they were alone again, they forgot their fear that they were being overheard and spoke normally.

"I'm going out early in the morning," Larry told her. "Very early, before six. I want to make a phone call to my father and ask him to let me know the minute he receives the manuscript. I want him to make a copy of it."

"Why early?" Rosemary asked. "And why not from here?"

"I – I want to catch Dad at home and the best time will be early morning our time and late at night theirs."

Rosemary felt that he was, if not lying, then evading telling her the full reason, but the hour was late and the evening had been so confused and alarming that she was too tired to wrestle with another problem.

"Come to bed," she said.

Larry rose before the alarm went off and he turned off the switch and hurriedly dressed in a tracksuit and a dark sweater. On his feet he wore his sneakers, silent and suitable for running if necessary. Rosemary slept on, and he touched her cheek briefly with his lips before going down the dark stairs. He did not use any lights, knowing the house well enough to make coffee and find a cookie without any noise.

Getting out of the house without a sound was more difficult and he pulled faces in the dark as he eased the bolts on the back door and went out into the chill pre-dawn. He closed the door after him, turning the key in the lock and pocketing the key.

He didn't make for the car, but crossed the back garden and went to the door of number three, the house owned by the Hughes's, and reputedly empty. Opening a window was simple, a long thin blade moved the round catch with ease and he climbed over the sill and stepped down inside the living room.

He risked an occasional flick of the torch and made his way through the silent room and into the hallway. The rooms seemed empty of any other presence, but he had to make sure.

Passing the bathroom, he moved cautiously along the landing towards the front room. The atmosphere in the house was musty and distinctively eerie, it had been empty for weeks and the air was stale. He imagined the dust rising as he walked on the neglected carpets, and hoped he wouldn't ruin his meticulous caution with a sneeze.

He began to gain a little night sight after turning off the torch he carried, standing on the landing in the darkness and listening for any sound. Once he was certain there was no one else there, he would begin to search, but for what, he wasn't really clear. He began to move again, cautiously, taking small steps and all the time listening for a giveaway sound to suggest he wasn't alone. As he passed the bathroom door, a sudden intake of breath alerted him but not in time. Hands grabbed him and pulled him down. Strong hands, covering his mouth so he couldn't shout out.

He struggled, but the man had been well prepared and

Search For a Shadow

soon Larry was on the floor, his face pressed into the dusty carpet, with his assailant sitting on his back. His arms were held tightly and he was unable to move.

"Now, Mister Larry Madison-Jones," said Huw, his accent unmistakable. "Why don't you tell me what you're looking for?"

"Huw? You sonofabitch! What in hell's this for? I'm doing the same as you, you damned fool, trying to find out who's upsetting Rosemary."

Huw released him and he stood, breathing fast in his anger, waiting for Huw to speak.

"I came in here after the police had gone," Huw said. "Rosemary is convinced someone is listening to her and I believe her."

"You thought this house, being empty, was a likely place for someone to hide? I had the same idea."

"Have you found anything?"

"Hardly! I was jumped on before I'd started to search!"

"We'd better search together, although I doubt you'll find anything. I've looked everywhere. There's no sign of any electronic equipment."

"Hell, I didn't even know what I was looking for! I just hoped to come upon something suspicious."

"Something the police missed."

"I suppose it does sound kinda crazy, but I must do something. Rosemary's being scared half out of her wits here and I have to go back home soon. I can't leave her in this situation."

"What are you going to do?"

"Talk to my father for a start, tell him I'll be delayed for a while. I'm going into town, calling on Rosemary's friend, Sally, to ask if I can telephone America from her place. A damned cheek I know, but, in case we're right about being overheard, I don't want to use Rosemary's phone."

"Come on, you can use ours." Huw switched on his torch and after a less than thorough look in all the rooms, they went out, closing the window as well as they could.

They walked across the backs of the houses to the end one and there, Larry spoke to his father. Unashamedly, Huw listened to the conversation. It was something about a parcel which Larry had posted home. The final remark was, "Dad, I won't be coming next week after all. It's going to take longer than I expected." Larry thanked Huw and gave him money to cover the cost of the call, then prepared to leave.

"I still want to talk to Sally," he said. "Rosemary has other friends but since Megan's gone away, it's Sally she confides in. If I go now I'll be able to see her without Rosemary being any the wiser. I want to ask her to make sure that if I'm delayed or have to go away overnight, that Rosemary isn't left alone in the house." Huw watched him go and he was frowning.

"But," he muttered to himself, "she's alone now, isn't she?" He went out to stand in the shadows of the trees, prepared to watch number two until dawn broke and lights began to show in the five cottages.

A few hours later, Larry left by the front door and walked across to his car. He got in and started the engine. As he released the hand-brake the car slid forward and he pushed down hard on the foot-brake. He stamped on it urgently, his eyes wide with shock, but it had no effect. The car continued to slide forwards. He pulled up the hand-brake, but it had the unnerving result of turning the car to one side. With slow inevitability, the little Citroën went, almost apologetically, tail-first into the stream.

Chapter Nine

Rosemary heard the sound, hardly a crash, more an extended squeal, a groaning and a shuddering. She looked out of the front window and although the darkness prevented a clear view, she gradually made out the incongruous picture of Larry's car, sitting up begging like a dog asking for a biscuit, in the flowing water of the stream. She stood transfixed for a moment then she opened the door and ran down to see if Larry was inside it.

She had woken to find him missing and guessed he had gone to make the phone call he had mentioned.

Larry was trying to force open the car door, which was blocked by a small shrub growing out of rocks on the bank of the stream. There was blood on his face but it seemed, by his furious actions, that he was relatively unharmed.

Huw appeared and ran up behind her. He waded through the water to pull at the shrub and ease open the door. Larry fell out, skidded on the sloping bank, teetered on the edge of the stream but was held by Huw before he could slip into the water.

"Shit!" Larry said loudly and with feeling.

"Send for an ambulance, please," Rosemary shouted as Richard, Gethyn, then Mrs Priestley came out to see what had occurred.

"No, it's all right, I'm not hurt, only angry," Larry

assured them. He took a handkerchief offered by Mrs Priestley to stem the flow of blood coming from his nose and walked to Rosemary and hugged her.

"I'm all right," he reassured her. "I hit my face on the steering wheel and my nose is bleeding, but that's all."

"I suppose it's useless asking if anyone saw someone snooping around my car?" he asked. He and Rosemary watched as one by one the others looked at each other and shook their heads.

"I'm only guessing," Larry said angrily, "but someone has almost certainly tampered with the brakes."

"Why would they?" Huw asked. "It would only have meant a soaking at worst. You were bound to find out as soon as you released the hand-brake. There's no way you'd have driven into a dangerous situation."

"I don't know Goddammit! I only know someone has been messing with my car and I'm going to find out who!" He stormed off with an arm still around Rosemary, and when Gethyn asked if he should go for the police, he didn't even turn around. "No, what's the point?" he growled.

"Larry, we must," Rosemary urged.

"Leave it, Rosemary, I want to think," he said.

"Let me bathe your face. Then you can sit quietly and think all you like," she said, "I've some thinking to do too."

She was surprised to find bruises on his chin and under the left side of his jaw.

"You must have been thrown around a bit more than you realised, darling," she said as she washed away the blood. "You look as if you've been in a fight!"

"I have, sort of," he said.

"A fight?" she said, startled into harsher movements

that made him groan. "Who with? What happened out there?"

"I slid down the bank in the car, that's all. I hit my face on the wheel," he repeated.

"But this bruise under your chin. How could that have happened like you said?"

"Like I said, a fight – to stop the car from rolling. Me nil the car one I think, don't you?"

"Definitely round one to the car," she agreed.

He offered no further explanation and Rosemary presumed that was what he had meant when he referred to a fight. He was very shaken and very angry and she didn't want to press him further.

"What d'you think of Huw?" Rosemary asked when she had finished her ministrations.

"He always seems pleasant and polite, why?" he asked cautiously.

"I asked at the shop and no one there can be sure who told him you were leaving. In fact, they thought the information had come from Huw himself."

"He couldn't be behind any of this. It has to be someone who comes in, how else could they have gotten that key from the vase? Huw has never been inside the place. That has to let him out."

"I didn't tell you, but Huw had the key in his possession, but only for about an hour. I know it's unlikely he could have one cut in that time, but – oh, I don't know. All this is beyond me."

"What d'you mean, he had possession of the key? When was this?"

"Remember the day he said he'd seen an owl? It was the day after the light bulb incident and you were late. I was afraid to come in alone and I gave him the key so he could come in and look around first. He just forgot to hand the key back when he'd taken it from the lock. He made up the story about the owl so he could return it without you knowing."

"Why without me knowing? Rosemary, you have to tell me everything if we're to crack this."

"I'd been careless and he was saving me a little embarrassment, that's all. And in the short time he had it, he couldn't have got a spare made, could he?"

"He could if he has access to a workshop." He looked thoughtful, a frown darkening his face.

"I'd better get to work," she said putting away the first-aid box, "although I don't really feel like leaving you like this." She looked at him, lying back against the settee, eyes closed again, his face battered and swollen. "What will you do, stay here?"

"First I have to arrange to get the car pulled out of the water," he said.

"And the door-locks, will you see to them?"

Suddenly he sat up, gestured to her to be quiet, and began to talk about unimportant things while he rapidly wrote a message to her on his note-pad.

"I'll take it easy I guess," he said. "My nose feels like a split water-melon. My head is one fat, excruciating ache. I'll have a lazy day. The locks can wait, can't they darling? I'll be here all day, no one will try to get in. I'll get around to dealing with them, in a day or so, but there's no hurry."

As he talked, he wrote:

"Don't say anything important. If you're right about being overheard, we don't want to give anything away. We'll talk in the car."

Fear returning after a brief respite of forgetfulness, she

Search For a Shadow

nodded, her blue eyes showing her trepidation, the half smile for him, demonstrating her bravery.

"Phone the garage now. I'll wait to hear what they advise then I'll have to rush," she said, as casually as she was able. "Do you need anything from town?"

"No honey, I just want some rest."

"That you shall have. I won't phone you 'til this afternoon." She kissed him goodbye and he walked with her to the door.

A shout of alarm startled her and for a moment she didn't know whether to run, or throw herself to the ground. She turned, half crouched and saw Larry running towards her.

"Keep away from the car! God help me, how could I be such a damned fool!" His voice so loud, so urgent, plus the look on his damaged face that made him look wild and dangerous, frightened her so much she hardly heard the words. Only when he went to her car, gestured furiously for her to stand back and demanded the keys, did she realise what had frightened him. Her car, parked next to where his had stood, could have been tampered with too.

He took the keys from her trembling hand and opened the door. He looked inside and then sat in the driving seat. He experimentally pushed the brakes, eased the hand-brake and touched them again.

"The brakes are all right, I think," he said. "I'll just take her around the village before you drive off."

With a fearful premonition of disaster, Rosemary watched as he drove her car up to the main road and towards the village. She saw the top of it above the parapet of the bridge where the road crossed over the stream, then listened as the engine faded in the distance. She sobbed with relief when she saw him returning.

He cut off the engine and as he stepped out, he nodded his satisfaction.

"Larry, if you'd had any doubts, you shouldn't have done that!"

"I don't think this man wants either of us dead. I just think he wants me out of the way," he said with an attempt at a smile, which, on his distorted features, was more of a grimace.

Rosemary drove to work and at Larry's insistence, left the car at her garage to be thoroughly checked. It was late when she reached the library and had never felt less like starting work. She was so weary that every bone and muscle in her body ached. She wished Megan were still there, she missed her wisdom and the fun she was able to make out of the ordinary events of their lives.

There were two visitors to the library that day who stopped to talk to her. One was Huw and the other was Gethyn.

Gethyn waited until she was free and asked if "the American" was all right.

"I saw him getting out of the car after it had slid down the bank and he looked badly shaken. Something he did to the car earlier, was it?" he asked. "Best we leave cars to mechanics I believe, don't you? Every man to his own trade."

"What d'you mean, Gethyn?" Rosemary asked. "Larry wasn't 'doing anything' to the car, only attempting to drive it. The brakes were faulty."

"Oh, I must have been mistaken, only, I couldn't sleep and I saw him, or I thought it was him, like, walking across the bridge and doing something to the car. Long before it was properly light, so I suppose I was mistaken. Some

Search For a Shadow

ol' tramp looking for somewhere for a kip perhaps. Yes, it must have been a tramp."

"Yes," she said vaguely, her mind closed against the possibility that it was Larry he had seen. It was impossible. He wouldn't have deliberately made himself crash. Unless, she thought traitorously, unless he wanted to hide those bruises he refused to explain.

She stamped Gethyn's books, one on the history of some Welsh gardens, and two spy stories.

"Like to read about gardens, do you, Gethyn? Not much room in ours for anything very grand, is there?"

"No," he agreed. "But it's nice to imagine. I think I'd be content not working if I had a garden to enjoy."

"I'm leaving at four if you want a lift home," she offered.

Huw came in to order some books for his new term's work. He asked if Larry had recovered and offered to help with the car if needed.

"He's spoken to the garage. Hopefully it will be back on dry land when we get home tonight. Want a lift?" she offered again. "Gethyn might be coming but there's room for one more." She filled in the forms for the books he wanted and stamped the ones he had chosen. "I'll be leaving at four," she told him and he thanked her and tucked his books under his arm. He stood at the counter and she knew there was something else he wanted to say. She smiled up at him and waited expectantly. What he did say was a shock.

"Tell him to go, Rosemary." His voice was low but the words pierced her brain like a scream.

"Larry?"

"Of course Larry! Ever since he came things have happened that we can't explain. He must be at the root of it, there's no other way to look at it."

"Huw, don't be ridiculous! I *know* him, you don't!"
"Tell him to go, please, before anything else happens."
"I don't believe I'm hearing this!"
"Nothing untoward happened before he came. Tell him to go. Things are becoming more and more frightening. I fear for you." He leaned closer, his eyes showing an expression that was more than friendship. Softer voiced, he added, "I'd hate anything to happen to you, Rosemary. You're far too beautiful to suffer even the slightest fright. Let me look after you, tell Larry he must leave."

She was tempted to shout so everyone in the quiet room could hear her, but she controlled her anger and spat back,

"That is what whoever is behind this *wants* me to do, get rid of him! But I'm stubborn enough to want to know *why*!"

"I beg you to think about it. You have plenty of friends who care about you, we'll do everything we can to look after you, but while Larry is there in your house, we can't protect you. Don't trust him, tell him to go, at least temporarily, until we get to the bottom of all this."

"Thank you for your advice, Huw." Her mouth was a tight line, her voice sounded almost prim. "Now, if you'll excuse me, I have to work."

"Of course. See you at four then."

The two men arrived at ten minutes to four. She saw them standing side by side and remarked at the difference in them. Huw, tall, lean and confident, in slashed, shabby jeans and sweater, was looking around him observing all that went on, smiling easily when she caught his eye, amused when someone complained or dropped a book.

Search For a Shadow

Gethyn stood ill-at-ease, head bent, afraid of meeting anyone's gaze but hers. He always looked as if he were apologising for being alive, she thought with compassion. He was wearing a good quality but old-fashioned navy suit, tie and blue shirt. His shoes were the type her grandfather had worn for best; lace-ups with a shining toecap. He looked like a film actor stepped straight out of a 'fifties magazine. Yet there was a warmth and a gentleness about him that she found appealing. Confidence in himself was all he needed. Huw was still the recipient of her anger, his accusations of Larry still simmering.

A third person came to talk to her that afternoon and made an offer for the house. What was said made her withdraw into herself to think about the implications and even the lively and determined Sally couldn't persuade her to discuss it.

The three of them walked together to the garage close by and collected the car. She explained the reason for it being there and said, "Gethyn thought he saw someone skulking around Larry's car early this morning, didn't you Gethyn?" Gethyn only nodded. "Larry and I decided it was probably only a poor tramp looking for somewhere out of the cold wind."

"You should tell that to the police," Huw insisted. "They need every clue we can give them."

"We didn't report it," Rosemary said. "It's rented and covered for accidents. He'll tell them his foot slipped or something I expect."

"Rented?" Huw queried. "What makes you think that? He bought it when he first came here."

"Oh, yes, I get confused," Rosemary smiled, but the smile was tight. It was as she had suspected, and another unnecessary lie.

The Citroën was back in its parking place and Larry

was standing in the doorway of the cottage to welcome her.

"Sorry about punching him, Rosemary," Huw said as they drew near enough to see the bruises now in glorious technicolour on the side of Larry's face. "I didn't know it was him. I just jumped on a shadowy figure."

"When was this?" she demanded.

"This morning, in the Hughes's place. Apparently we both had the same thought and went to search in case someone was hiding there and stage-managing all this." He stopped and turned her to face him. "You didn't know! Why didn't he tell you? How did he explain the marks of a fight?"

"He didn't want to worry me any more than he had to, I suppose," she said, but her eyes were wary as she went to accept Larry's affectionate greeting.

"I've decided to sell this house," Rosemary announced to a surprised Larry after they had eaten their meal.

"You what? But I thought you loved the place?"

"I do, at least, I did. I don't feel safe here any more and after you leave, well, can you see me sleeping here? Can you see me even walking through that door without the fear that something unpleasant, terrifying or downright dangerous might happen? Unless we find out who and what is behind it all, then I'm selling."

Larry switched off the radio that had been blaring music out to drown their conversation. Forgetting about their fear of being overheard, he said, "I phoned my parents this morning. I told them I wouldn't be coming home as planned. I've made a decision too. I won't go home until this is all settled. That is," he added, "if you don't object to my staying."

She smiled, kissed him lightly and said, "Of course I

don't object. It's such a relief that I won't have to stay here alone."

"Then don't do anything about selling up, not just yet. Okay?"

"The offer I had recently seems so opportune, I think I'm going to accept."

She wondered what Larry's private thoughts were. Why should he care whether or not she sold the house? She could live in the town, nearer to her friends and with less inconvenience. Living in a small village with few amenities was attractive, but town had its advantages too, the main one being that she would never feel alone.

Larry had delayed his departure but he was still going to leave her and there had not been even the suggestion they kept in touch. He would leave and there would be an end to it. She glanced at him; lean, athletic, boyishly handsome in a way that would probably remain until middle age, and so deeply ingrained in her everyday living she did not know how she would cope without him. Moving house would give her mind something to wrestle with, a reason to go on.

"You said you've had an offer for the house?" he said. "How did that come about?"

"Someone who used to live in the village and who now lives in Birmingham called to see me and asked if I knew of a house for sale in the village. They want it as a holiday cottage." Rosemary spoke normally, the decision making her forget momentarily the suspicion they were being overheard.

"Tell me about the offer," Larry asked. "Is it genuine?"

"I think so, they're offering a sum which the local estate agents believe to be fair, even generous."

"And you'll take it?"

"I haven't finally decided, it was rather a surprise, although I confess I had considered moving away from here. I think the house is, what do you Americans call it, 'pixilated'? And it's telling me to go."

"Nonsense, my gullible one. Houses don't get pixilated, and I don't believe in ghosts. Or in houses having spirits. No way."

"Neither do I, at least, I didn't. Yet there is something like a ghostly presence in the house, isn't there?"

"Removing light bulbs and loosening the cables on my car you mean," he teased. "Some ghost that would be! A real tourist attraction!"

"Whatever price the customers are offering, double it!" he went on, laughing loudly. "Insist that the ghost comes as an extra with the drapes and covers!"

"All right," she said, sharing his laugh. "I'm being stupid, but there is something, if not a ghost then someone. That's even more frightening, isn't it? Larry, I've known this house all my life. I came here for wonderful holidays as a child and continued to do so until I bought the place when Gran went into a rest home. All the shadows and memories should be my own, shared with my family and without a moment of sadness or even dismay. I've never been anything but happy here."

"Then stay."

"I don't think I can. Not any more."

They sat listening to music for a while, then Larry made them some coffee. As they were sitting enjoying a record of Michael Jackson, there was a series of bangs next door and then a longer drawn out crash. It sounded as if furniture had fallen or was being banged about. They ran outside and knocked on Gethyn's door. Rosemary knelt and tried to peer through the letter box.

Search For a Shadow

"Gethyn? Are you all right?" she called.

"I guess we'll have to break in if the poor guy doesn't answer," Larry said. "He must have fallen."

They listened anxiously and heard more bangs and what sounded like things falling, some were dull like wood, others metallic, as if saucepans were rolling on the stone kitchen floor. Going next door to investigate, they found Gethyn bending over a cupboard, its glass smashed in, the wood cracked, but when they offered to help, Gethyn refused. Resigned to his stubbornness, they returned to their own home.

The next day she didn't have to go into work, and she sat with Larry lazily listening to some tapes. The smell of a wood-fire invaded the house and she stood up and looked out of the back window where dark smoke swirled in an uneasy wind.

"Gethyn has a bonfire," she reported. "Perhaps he'll burn the rubbish I've collected as well." She went out through the back door and saw to her amazement that the fire was enormous. "Larry," she called, "come and look at this. Gethyn is burning some of his furniture."

Through brief gaps in the thick smoke they saw that there was a large cupboard feeding the hungry red heart of the fire. The doors of the cupboard had been smashed in, the panels split in a row of jagged teeth through which flames were licking like a dozen tongues.

"Jesus H! What is he burning?" Larry gasped. "It looks as if he has half the house in that pile."

"It must be the cupboard he damaged last night."

"Damn right it is and several others besides. Is he destroying the whole house?"

They watched for a while, seeing Gethyn appearing and fading from view as the curtain of smoke filled the air then moved aside. He didn't look their way and they didn't speak to him.

The fears of being overheard had faded. Several days had passed without anything unusual happening. Larry's father had reported the safe arrival of the manuscript which had been photocopied. Larry spent the days while Rosemary was at work tidying the small garden, or walking in the colourful autumn countryside, taking endless photographs, which, he told her, he would use to give slide evenings when he got home.

Gethyn called one day when Larry was out and asked if there had been another parcel for him. She assured him there had not and offered him a cup of coffee. She decided it was a good opportunity to tell him that she was considering selling the house.

"Someone has made an offer," she explained. "A letter came from the local estate agents, confirming the offer previously made. It seems heaven sent when so many things are going wrong."

"Nothing's been right for you since the American came, has it?" he sympathised.

"It can hardly be his fault," she laughed.

"We'll have to see if it stops when he goes back to America," he said softly.

"That's nonsense, Gethyn! What would he gain by frightening me? He's a friend."

"Yes, well. So you're thinking of selling. Only thinking of it? You'll wait to see if things settle down after he's gone, won't you?" he said.

"I don't know. I can't see myself being content here ever again. These people want to come before Christmas, so I have to make up my mind soon."

"So long as they aren't planning to use it as a holiday cottage."

"I think they are."

"Rosemary, you can't sell and ruin the place for the rest of us!"

"Hardly ruin it, don't be melodramatic, Gethyn," she scolded quietly.

"But it *would* ruin it! How would we be if the Hughes's decide to stay in Bala near their daughter? And the Powells decide not to come back? If they sell, our little row would be half empty, I'd be stuck without a neighbour for most of the year and especially during the dark months of winter! There'd be no sound of friendly voices, just a cold, empty house next door."

Rosemary didn't answer. She had heard all these arguments before but had never heard it with actual people that she knew being represented.

"I hadn't thought of it like that," she admitted. "Perhaps I'll reconsider. Not the idea of selling, but perhaps I'll wait until a buyer from the village can be found." She looked at Gethyn, unusually talkative and earnest.

"Fancy prices for holiday homes will put it out of reach of the locals, as well you know. What if the Powells decide to stay in Australia? What then? What if they too sold to an absentee landlord. The place would be like one of those 'ghost towns' we see in American films. The students are only in number five for another year. Nothing to stop the Powells from selling then, is there?"

"All right, Gethyn, I take your point," she sighed, not bothering to tell him she had already thought of all this.

"You'll wait 'til the American goes back then?"

"I'll wait for a while," she promised.

One evening, when Rosemary came home from work,

Larry told her the water pressure had been reduced temporarily.

"I think someone must have turned off the water to do some repair and when they turned it on again didn't turn it high enough."

"Oh dear, someone with a problem." She smiled. "I expect Mrs Priestley will be down soon to tell us who it was and all about it."

There was one stop-cock for three houses and another for two.

"It was probably Gethyn," Larry said. "He's on the same supply as us, unless someone didn't know and shut it off by mistake. Either way, I turned the thing up a little and it's now fine."

They didn't think any more about it and went to bed early.

Rosemary woke to the sound of dripping water. At first she thought it was the clock ticking, it was so regular.

Without disturbing Larry she slipped out of bed and went to investigate. He had probably left the tap running. She put on the landing light and as if it were a tap, the sound of dripping which seemed to come from every direction once she had left the bedroom, became a roaring, gushing torrent. Every tap in the house was pouring water!

She looked down in utter disbelief at the carpet at her feet which was soaking wet. Turning her head she saw that water had filled the wash-basin and flowed over onto the floor. The dripping sound was the cascade flowing down the stairs.

"Larry!"

He was awake in a moment and, standing beside her, he stared wildly about him.

Search For a Shadow

"Shut off all the taps if you can!" he shouted. "I'll go downstairs and see what's happened."

Rosemary ran into the bathroom, turned off the taps and pulled in vain at the plugs that were tightly in place in both the bath and the wash-basin. They were so tight she thought they must have been glued there. The water covered her feet but she was so stunned she couldn't feel the chill of it.

She ran down the stairs and went to the kitchen. Water had flooded from the running tap and was over the carpet in a silvery film. The plug there was fixed and as unmovable as the others.

The water reached the front door and was soon seeping underneath and out in a gentle stream, making its way to join the larger stream in front of the house.

Chapter Ten

While Larry hurriedly threw on a few clothes and ran up to turn off the water at the stop-cock, Rosemary knocked on Gethyn's door and he came dressed in night-clothes and an anorak, to help. He was shocked by the sight that met his eyes and said so. He glared at Larry, making it clear Rosemary knew whom *he* suspected of causing the disastrous flood. But he worked alongside them, needing only a few words of explanation before he set to and helped them drag out what they could, in the hope of saving at least some of the furnishings.

She was so distraught she was unaware of how incongruous she looked in lacy-necked nightdress, pink dressing gown and wellington boots, but she couldn't bear to stop and dress more suitably. The priority seemed to be to save her home. "Who would do this to me?" she kept asking, but neither Larry nor Gethyn offered any answer.

They carried out the largest furniture which seemed hardly touched by the water, and then tore the carpet from its pins and pulled that out and placed it as straight as they could on the grass outside. It was difficult, the water gave it extra weight and made it very heavy. In tears, Rosemary said, "It's all hopeless! We're just adding the mess of mud to the problems of water! There'll be nothing worth having. It's all ruined."

Search For a Shadow

"You'll see, we'll save most of it," Larry promised. "A couple of weeks and you won't see a sign of tonight's disaster."

Gethyn took a brush and was standing at the back door brushing the last of the water out when the police arrived. He had worked hard and his breath was uneven with the exertion of it.

"About time you sorted all this, isn't it?" he said to the constable.

"We're mighty glad to see you," Larry said, "but, who sent for you?"

"Mrs – er—" The constable looked at his notebook and when he said the name, Larry said it with him.

"Mrs Priestley!"

"Yes sir, seems she was woken by voices and looked out of her bedroom window to see you vacating the house. Moonlight flits being no longer fashionable, she thought there was a fire, then decided that it was water that was the trouble."

The night had all but gone before they had decided there was nothing more to be done. They were all filthy, dishevelled and weary and when Larry suggested they abandoned the rest until the morning, there was no arguments. Dawn was not yet breaking but the subtle change in the darkness heralded its approach. The eerie half-dark showed the devastation more clearly.

The immediate landscape, usually smooth grass and a few flower beds, was filled with unrecognisable shapes and shadows. The grass was distorted by a covering of pale carpet, the piled up chairs and small tables. Rosemary stared for so long they almost became commonplace, an extention to the house, a new room, an excepted oddity at the end of a peculiar night. But the rest; ornaments, a television, a box of records, cushions and a hurriedly stacked pile of books looked bizarre.

Her first thought, when they stopped to rest, was to arrange for the council refuse collectors to come and take it all. She remembered the despoiling of her bed and shivered. Someone was driving her out. But who? And why?

While Larry and Gethyn went inside and made coffee, she sat on the front doorstep and mentally listed her friends. She had known them all for years. There was no one who could do this to her. No one.

No one, a voice inside her warned, except Larry. He had told so many lies, how could she be sure of him?

He came out then and sat beside her after handing her a cup of steaming hot coffee. Behind them stood Gethyn.

"It's livable," Larry said, hugging her. "The damage is slight although it looked such a mess. The bare floors make it look as if it's been abandoned, but the floors will soon dry and we'll be able to get new carpets down in a matter of days."

"I don't think I want to," she said dully. "I don't want to go inside ever again."

"Don't say that, Rosemary," Gethyn said. "It's your home, you belong there, it will be all right soon."

She wondered vaguely if he meant the water damage or the whole mysterious run of disasters and frights. She sighed. How could he understand how she felt about the place now?

"I'm not staying here tonight," she said, still in the low, subdued voice. "I'll stay with Sally."

"No, darling," Larry pleaded. "I'm with Gethyn on this. Don't let whoever it is drive you out. The rooms are liveable and I'll get the furniture back inside before you come home this evening."

Search For a Shadow

She shook her head.

"I think I'll accept the offer and sell it as soon as possible."

"No, you won't get your price," Gethyn said quickly. "Best you forget selling for a while, until the damage is made good."

"That's sound advice," Larry looked at Gethyn in surprise.

"I don't want you to sell," Gethyn went on, turning his shoulder to exclude Larry, "and you ought to get inside before you catch cold!" He handed the coffee cup to Larry, took off his anorak and put it around her, then went back to his own house without another word.

"That guy is strange, isn't he?" Larry whispered. "He seems to be unable to support a conversation most of the time, except when it concerns you. In fact, that's the most I've ever heard him utter."

"He's a good friend," Rosemary said, snuggling Gethyn's coat around her, unconsciously appreciating the recently vacated warmth. "I have such good friends. Yet," she added sorrowfully, "one of them must be doing this to me."

"Come on, baby, Gethyn is right, you're freezing sitting here in just your night clothes."

She looked down at herself as if only just realising how unsuitably dressed she was.

"If I can force myself to go back inside, I'll shower and get ready for work," she said.

"Before five o'clock in the morning?" he laughed. Talking cheerfully in an effort to rouse her from her depression, he guided her back inside.

"It even smells different," she said with a sob. "It isn't my home any more."

"It will be, I promise." He led her upstairs and ran the

151

bath. The room smelled of dampness and disturbed dust. He leaned over and chose some scented bath foam and poured a liberal amount into the running water. The glued plug had been cut away but he held the water with a coin wrapped in a cloth. When he helped her to remove her clothes he was startled at how cold she was.

"Honey, you're like ice."

"That's just how I feel," she said. "Frozen so I won't feel anything, ever again."

She lay in the warm water and he sat on the edge of the bath and talked to her, not about what had happened, not about anything in particular, he just talked.

He described his home in New York.

"A large apartment on a busy, noisy street. A kitchen you'd love, and rooms that are large enough to lose this place completely. Constant noise, the city buzzing all around, life racing past at hundreds of miles an hour for twenty-four hours of every day.

"You'd hate it after this place. The greenness of Wales is what you'd miss most I guess."

She seemed not to be listening to him but the words were going into her brain like hammer blows. He was telling her gently, but quite clearly, that there was no place for her in his life. His future lay in the American city where he was happiest, and hers was here, in the quiet green hills of Wales. She began to shiver. She wished they had never met.

"Out you come," he said, seeing her shiver and presuming it was because of a chilliness. He helped her out and lovingly dried her. She went to gather some fresh clothes but he led her away. "You, my sweet, are going back to bed."

She didn't protest. He pulled back the covers and she slid into the harshness of the cold sheets. He undressed and got in beside her. His warmth was wrapped around her and she felt the thawing of her depressed spirits. He lay, just holding her and talking soothingly to her, until she slept.

The alarm woke them at seven-thirty.

"I can't face any more of this," she whispered.

"You don't have to, it's over. I feel sure that whoever has been doing this won't bother us any more. The police will be watching carefully now and this morning I'm changing the locks, again. Dammit," he said angrily, "I should have done it ages ago."

"But we bolt the doors. How could a key have helped?" She was wide awake now and thinking over what had occurred.

"I forgot," he admitted. "I forgot to throw the bolt on the front door. I don't know how, it's become such a routine, but I did."

"It's as if someone is following our every move, even knowing when we forget to bolt the doors! It's no use, I can't stay here any longer. I'll ask Sally if we can stay there. I'm sure she won't mind."

"She won't have *me* there!" he said with a crooked grin. "I'm not one of her favourite people. Suspects me of terrible deeds, does Sally."

"Of course she will. It won't be very comfortable, but we can manage for a few days, until we've decided what to do."

Larry was correct in his assumption that Sally wouldn't make him welcome.

"You can stay with me for as long as you want, Rosemary, you know that," she said. But her eyes slid away as she added, "But as for Larry, well, I don't think I've the room and—"

"And you think he's at the back of all this, don't you?" Rosemary accused her quietly.

"Well, it does coincide with his coming here, doesn't it? Everything was all right until he came. I admit I can't think why, unless it's something to do with the family he's supposed to be looking for."

"How can his family roots have anything to do with me?"

"Perhaps they lived in your house and he wants to buy it back?"

"That's nonsense."

"I know it's nonsense. I'm thinking aloud and trying to invent a story to fit at least some of the facts. You must admit it has to be something very unusual to explain it all?"

"Very unusual," she agreed.

"Could someone be in love with you and Larry is driving them away by all this?"

"How would that fit into a story?"

"I don't know. If he can get you away from there, away from whoever he's jealous of—"

"Larry and I don't have a future together, so that theory's out. While I was bathing early this morning he was talking about his home. He spelled out the differences so I'd understand clearly that I would never fit in there. He also made it clear that Wales with its green hills and blacker than black nights was not something he could ever become used to. No, either way you can count Larry out."

"Then who?"

"I can't believe the trouble comes from one of the neighbours. There are the students, strangers until recently, with no known connection with me or any of the others that we know of. There's Mrs Priestley, three is empty, then there's Gethyn and me. Who amongst that lot can

Search For a Shadow

you see as a villain?" As Sally shook her red head she added, "No, neither can I!"

"I suppose Huw Rees or Richard Lloyd might be involved in some way; Richard is very quiet and seems distant from the rest. But I'd still like to know what Larry is really doing here! Oh, Rosemary, why won't you listen to what I'm saying?"

"He's been looking for his family and writing a novel. At least that is explained."

"Is it? Did you *see* the novel?"

"Yes I did!"

"Apart from the pieces spread over the floor, did you *see* it?"

"Well, no, but—"

"Puzzling, isn't it? At least admit it's puzzling."

Rosemary drove home that evening with an increased feeling of dread.

Larry wasn't there, the Citroën was not parked in its usual place and at once the fear of walking into the damaged house hit her anew. She stopped the car and stared across the stream at the row of five cottages. All silent, no sign of anyone there, yet she had the fanciful notion that all the windows were shielding someone, that pairs of eyes were staring across at her and their expression was malign, and threatening, warning her to stay away.

She stepped out of the car and walked across the footbridge. As she approached the houses, she heard a door open and looked up expecting to see Larry. His car was somewhere else; he hadn't allowed her to walk back into the house alone. She smiled and began to hasten her steps, but it was Gethyn who came to meet her.

"Rosemary, I have to talk to you."

She didn't want to talk to him, she wanted to go inside

and see if there was a message from Larry. Had he left her? She glanced expectantly across the stream to his parking place as she followed Gethyn to number one.

The inside of his house was a mess. A cupboard that had once stood against a corner wall was standing awkwardly, further into the room against the shared wall. It was held closed with a tie of string. In front of it was an armchair on which were piles and piles of magazines.

"Sorry about the mess, but I had to see you. I've just had this letter." His eyes darted away from hers as he handed it to her. It was an official note, and she at once recognised the name of the senders. It was the firm from whom her grandmother had bought the cottage.

She opened it and read with dismay that Gethyn had been asked to vacate his tenancy in two months' time. The reason given was that the tenancy had been in the name of his mother and, having no instructions or even a request to transfer the tenancy, they had no alternative but to ask him to leave, he having no legal entitlement to remain.

"I'll go with you to a solicitor tomorrow," she said after reading it through twice. "But, Gethyn, I think they're correct. You have no right to continue to live here, but why didn't your mother ask for the transfer?"

"She did mention it but she wasn't ill, not so you'd say really ill, only a bit of heart trouble. We thought there was plenty of time."

"We all think that time is infinite and things will remain the same. But nothing does. Everything comes to an end and for you, your mother's life ended too soon."

He wailed then, an almost childish wail of pain and fear, and she stepped closer and put an arm around his shoulders. His head bent and they stood there for some time, she the comforter and he the comforted. Then a subtle change came over him and he stood tall and looked down at her, his face calm and his eyes unwavering.

"I'll help you to sort out what's happening to you first. Only then will I worry about this," he said. "I've been neglectful of you, leaving you alone thinking that with the American there it's none of my business, but you *are* my business, Rosemary, and you always will be. My problem is small compared with yours. Let me be your strength, Rosemary, lean on me, I'll support you."

She leaned on him literally and they stood together as strength seeped into her, realising as if for the first time that in spite of his shyness, Gethyn was strong, or would be for her.

A shadow filled the doorway and Larry entered, saying, "Can I come in or is this a private party?"

"Larry!" Rosemary was startled out of a dream in which none of the happenings of the past weeks had really happened, she and Gethyn were standing together and she had been telling him about the strange dreams from which she had woken. But seeing Larry, she knew where her heart lay, and once again, she had encouraged Gethyn in a cruel way by staying within his arms as if she belonged there.

"Gethyn has just heard he'll have to leave this house," she said, her voice fast as she extricated herself from Gethyn's embrace. "The rental was his mother's and it wasn't altered to make it his."

"Gethyn, I'm real sorry. Is it difficult to rent around here?"

"Impossible." Rosemary had recovered from the foolish aberration and stood now beside Larry. "When a place becomes empty it's usually sold, I'm afraid."

"Then you must speak to the landlord and persuade him to change his mind," Larry said cheerfully. "Difficult but not impossible. Mind you, I suggest you tidy up a bit before he comes to see if you're taking care of his property. Jesus, this place looks worse than next door, and we've had a flood!"

They left Gethyn, still staring at the letter, and wondering how to deal with it, and went into number two. Larry had been inside and opened all the doors to allow the slight breeze that smelled slightly of the sea to waft in and take away the damp and musty smell of the carpet-less house.

"Did you ring the insurance people?" he asked.

"Yes and they're sending a form for me to fill in," she said. She stood at the door, unwilling to enter. It smelled different, looked different and she couldn't accept that it was her home.

"It's no use, I can't walk in. It isn't mine any more."

"All right, stay there and look at the brook and I'll get the fire started." He disappeared, whistling cheerfully, coming out a few moments later with a cup of coffee and a chair. He grinned at her and she smiled and sat down, wrapping the blanket he had also brought, around her knees. He disappeared again and then brought out a sandwich and a chocolate biscuit. "Picnic time," he announced and went back inside still whistling cheerfully.

Larry made everything into such fun. Even a tragedy like the ruination of her home was an excuse for humour. What was funny about sitting outside her door with a chair and a cup of coffee, was difficult to explain, but the way he did it made it impossible to remain sad. His light-hearted approach to everything gladdened her.

Inside, the sticks were snapping and cracking as flames took hold and soon she saw the redness on the logs that was the forerunner to flames. He turned and saw her and smiled, pushing the fair hair out of his eyes and leaving a black mark on his face so he looked like a pirate with an eye-patch.

"Good girl," he said and winked before returning to building up the fire.

"Wash your face," she said, winking back.

The floors didn't look quite so strange by the time they had spent the rest of the evening there, familiarity gradually bringing acceptance. But the stairs sounded odd, creaky and hollow, as they walked up them to bed. She deliberately did not ask him if he had bolted the doors and he didn't mention it either.

Before they slept, they talked not about the water of the night before, but about Gethyn and the problem of his accommodation.

"What will the poor guy do?" Larry asked. "I can't comment, I don't know the situation here. If the landlord is giving him the runaround, can't he buy the place and make himself secure?"

"I've no idea how much money his mother left, but I doubt it was enough to buy a house."

"You know him well enough, ask him. If he could buy it, then he might be able to make a bit of cash for himself by letting a room or two to students, like Huw and Richard. They'd know someone reasonable to recommend."

"I'll ask, if I can word it so it doesn't look as if I'm being nosy," she said. "But if he can't buy it, what then? I think he'll curl up and retreat from life altogether if he had to live in one small bed-sitter, and anyway there's no one around here who rents rooms so far as I know."

"Ask Mrs-the-shop," he suggested. "Or Mrs Priestley. I guess she'll know what's available!"

"I'll make enquiries at the Citizen's Advice Bureau tomorrow."

"I thought that *was* Mrs Priestley!"

*   *   *

The night passed peacefully and although she did not expect to, Rosemary slept for most of it. Larry planned to go into Aberystwyth but promised to be home in time to have the fire burning and a meal cooking as it was a night on which she had to work late.

"Then," she told him, "I have two days off."

"Make it three and let's go to London," he suggested.

He took her to an exclusive hotel which advertised itself as "The Best Kept Secret In London". The Montcalm was an impeccably cared for house in a beautiful Georgian crescent only a few minutes' walk from Marble Arch.

Their twin-bedded room was spacious and attractively decorated. In soft shades of green and cream it was light and airy and everything spoke of a disregard for expense in the search for perfection. Nothing had been spared that might improve their comfort. The food, they learnt at dinner that evening, was a dream.

Twice, during their brief holiday he left her. Once he said he had to visit St. Catherine's House for another item of information for his family tree, and again on the way home. They had left the train at Aberystwyth and he asked her to wait while he used the telephone. He didn't explain his absence and she preferred not to ask, but when he returned from the phone his smile was wide and impossible for him to hide.

When they returned to the cottage, everything looked ordinary from the outside. The ruined carpet was still draped disconsolately over the grass, and the few spoilt items were cluttered together in a corner near the front door, ashamed of their appearance. When she opened the door Rosemary noticed a completely different smell from the one she had prepared herself to cope with. There was not the smell of dankness, of an abandoned house, only woodsmoke and the unmistakable odour of new carpets.

Sitting in the armchairs beside the blazing fire were Sally, Gethyn, Huw and Richard, and Mrs Priestley. A new carpet had been fitted and a white fluffy rug replaced the old one in front of the fire. A tray had been set with glasses and on the polished table, were plates of cakes and biscuits.

"Welcome back to your home," they chorused.

"But how did you arrange all this?" she gasped. "Oh, thank you, all of you!" She hugged them in turn, then squealed with joy as a familiar voice said, "Me too? Don't I get a hug then?"

"Megan, you're home at last! Thank goodness!" Rosemary felt tears of relief spilling as she greeted her friend. Seeing her made the surprise welcome just perfect. "Oh, Megan, there's so much to tell you."

"I'm sure, love, but not now. I've heard most of it from Huw anyway. And today is a celebration of everything getting back to normal, so no gloom, eh?"

"No gloom," Rosemary promised. "Oh what a relief to have you back home!"

"*duw* girl, anyone would think I'd been away for months, and you with so many friends you couldn't have even missed me!"

Gethyn watched them as they came in, seeing the joy on Rosemary's face and believing that he was at least partly the cause of it. She had kissed them all to show her appreciation, but her kiss for him had been different.

The new carpet had been Larry's idea and he had given Huw a key and asked him to open the door for the fitters.

Then Mrs Priestley had heard about the surprise and had suggested to Gethyn that they added to it by giving a small welcoming tea-party. Larry had been in full agreement and he arranged to telephone when they reached Aberystwyth so everything could be in readiness for their arrival.

In the first moment of surprise, Rosemary had the unkind thought that Sally had achieved her aim. She'd got her feet over the threshold and was sitting here in her living room, talking to her neighbours. And from what she could see, she and old Mrs Priestley were already firm friends. They sat close together obviously exchanging information about each other and Rosemary guessed that it would be Mrs Priestley who did the most talking. Sally would sop up, like a sponge, all she needed to know.

Then the moment had passed, Megan had appeared in the kitchen doorway and the slight misgivings were forgotten. The relief of having Megan back filled her with a glow.

Gethyn stood back from the rest, glad of the need to replenish plates and tea cups. Larry, of course, had gone straight to the kitchen to make coffee. He hadn't developed a liking for tea. Well, let him. It was one more small reminder that he didn't fit, that he was the interloper here.

He offered a plate of sandwiches to Richard but pulled up in surprise, it wasn't Richard, but Larry. He hadn't realised before how alike they were. Larry took a sandwich and looked coolly at him. Gethyn lowered his gaze, his intention of making Larry feel the interloper wasn't working. Larry was making him feel like the hired hand!

But soon he would leave them to return to his own place and then, when all the mischief had stopped, Rosemary would return too – to him, Gethyn, where she truly belonged.

Search For a Shadow

Rosemary came and took the plate from him and insisted he sat near the fire near the others.

"Come and tell me how you and Huw arranged all this without me knowing," she said. She took his hand and smiled at him and he knew that whatever love she felt for the American, theirs was less fraught and more comfortable and would outlive the interloper's brief sojourn in their midst.

Chapter Eleven

A day later, Larry told Rosemary he had made plans to return home. Her face paled visibly. "For a week or ten days only," he added quickly. "I have a few things I must settle if I am to return and stay a while longer with you."

Larry's luggage was light. Many of his clothes he left hanging in the wardrobe. This fact alone gave Rosemary a slender hope of seeing him again. That, and his words of love at their parting.

To her surprise and delight, there was a letter when she reached work a few days later. It was an air-mail envelope and even seeing, after a cursory glance, that the writing was not Larry's, didn't make her doubt it was from him. But she was disappointed. It was from someone she had met at a party near the end of her visit to New York. The girl, Barbara, whom she only vaguely remembered, explained that she would be coming to England soon and would like them to meet. The reason the letter had gone to the library was that she had lost her address, remembering only the town, and knew that the library where she worked would find her. The final paragraph startled her so that Sally, who was hovering curiously nearby, asked her if it was bad news.

"In a way it is," Rosemary said, white-faced. "She asks if I kept in touch with Larry Madison, who was

Search For a Shadow

so smitten with me and had asked so many questions about me."

She ran to find Megan, handed the letter to her, then stared at her friend, confused by the revelation and trying to fit it in with Larry's appearance in her life.

"He was at that party! I wasn't a stranger when we met in London! Apparently he asked lots of questions about me, pretended to be 'smitten', then," she gave an involuntary shiver, "then he followed me, all the way to London."

"Don't be an idiot!" Sally scorned, peering over Megan's shoulder to read the note. "You aren't that devastatingly gorgeous! She was mistaken, wasn't she, Megan? She must have been. He couldn't have got a ticket on a plane and arrived at the same hotel so quickly as all that. She must have muddled him with – She must have—" She shrugged. Rosemary didn't believe her attempted explanations and neither did she!

"So, the falling books and the disobedient map, it was all arranged so he could meet me? But why?"

"I don't know, love." It was Megan's turn to shrug. "And now he's gone again and you'll have to wait for him to come back before you can ask him!"

"He'll phone, won't he? You can ask him then," Sally suggested.

"He said he will, but d'you know, I've been so trusting. I don't even have his home address. Larry Madison-Jones of New York! That's hardly likely to find him, is it?"

She found a letter waiting for her when she reached home and this time it *was* from Larry. In it he explained that he had met Barbara and had heard about her letter.

"I couldn't explain this on the phone, darling," she read. "But I confess I did cheat a little. I saw you at that party and when I heard where you lived I couldn't believe the coincidence. If I'd told you I had family in the area in which you lived would you have believed me? It would have seemed like the most obvious 'come on' of the age! I genuinely had a flight booked for London, and all I did was change it for the day before you were due home, and book myself in at the hotel you conveniently told Barbara you'd be staying in. If you knew how long I sat in that damned foyer watching for you to appear!"

The letter went on about how wonderful it had been to find how much he adored her and how guilty he felt at deceiving her in the way he had. But the original thought, the chance of having a base among the local people in the area, who might then be more willing to assist him, had been simply too good to pass up. To find in her the wonderful friend and partner in love was a touch of heavenly magic.

He ended by telling her that there was still something else he hadn't told her and he hoped once that was out of the way, there would be nothing between them except open friendship and love.

The letter did not comfort her very much. All he was saying was that he had deceived her to enable him to get a place to stay, in the area where he hoped to discover his family's history. To get to know the local people and persuade them to talk was the whole reason for him being there.

She had been dull, unattractive, boring and ordinary and he had pretended an interest simply to use her. The love and friendship at the end was like a slap in the face, unexpectedly hurtful. Love and friendship were part of the same thing and a loving relationship between friends was perfection, but the way he had written it was not like that. It was the friendship that he seemed to emphasise, not the love. He loved his dog, whom he referred to as "the mutt", and she felt that his love for her was no greater than that.

A few days later, having a free day, Megan, Sally and Rosemary went into Aberystwyth to do some shopping. The sea was dark, reflecting the low, grey clouds above and they shivered as they left the car and walked to the bottom of Constitution Hill.

"Are you sure you want to walk up there today?" Rosemary asked.

"Haven't done it for years. I can't resist it."

There were still flowers showing colour as they began the climb. Red and white valerian, scabious and a few late thrift. Dandelions startlingly cheerful among the mounds of bramble bushes, where opportunist children fed on the luscious berries.

They had to bend forward to avoid the worst gusts of wind as they were in danger of being spun off their feet, but they reached the top without mishap and sat looking down over the town. As they watched, the first few rainspots fell. The rain increased to a heavy downpour and they scuttled for shelter.

They waited a while, sheltering against the walls of the cafe, then decided to run for the car.

"Soaked we are and there's no sense in standing here. We might as well get wet running for shelter," Sally shouted, above the drumming and shushing of the heavy rain.

They hurried down the steep path, laughing at their stupidity at climbing "Consti" when rain was so obviously imminent. Then, as they reached the beach again, the rain ceased as suddenly as it had begun. Around them everything shone as water flowed across the paved surfaces and rushed down the drains until it was gone, apart from a few drops lingering like bright jewels on the edges of leaves and grasses.

They could have been the only people in the world as they walked to the car. There were no people in sight and not even any traffic. Even the ubiquitous seagulls had disappeared, and no birds sang. Everyone and everything had hidden away from the rain-storm and was waiting, to be certain if was finished, before venturing out again.

It was a scene renewed, The silent, parked cars were gleaming and the steps of the hotels were washed clear of the dust and sand that had covered them. Everything was still, even the one yellow shirt that still hung out of the students' accommodation window was wet, bedraggled and lifeless, sticking to the wall like spilt paint.

A car started up from a row parked near theirs and Rosemary's heart gave a leap as she recognised the sound of the engine. A Citroën drove past them, the rain-smeared windows giving only partial view of the driver.

"Rosemary!" Sally gasped. "That was Larry!"

"I thought so too," Megan said more quietly. She repeated the licence number and Rosemary nodded. She had seen him too.

"He must know we saw him. Why didn't he stop and explain?" She stared after the car and then shook her head firmly, pretence aiding her disappointment and dismay. "No, it couldn't have been Larry. He must have lent his car to someone. No, the more I think about it, the more certain I am. It wasn't him. Not tall enough. Darker. Thicker set. No, definitely not Larry. What a shock though, wasn't it?" Gabbling to convince herself, she ignored the doubt that made Sally's forehead furrow

Search For a Shadow

like a newly ploughed field and brought sad understanding to Megan's kindly face.

Gethyn was standing outside the door when she returned home later that afternoon. She was wet and uncomfortable after being soaked and then wandering around the shops getting partially dry and she needed to go straight in and run a bath. She hurried towards him, hoping to give the impression she had no time to talk.

"The American's back then," he startled her by saying.

"Oh, I – er—"

"Saw him on the main road not an hour ago," Gethyn said. "Didn't stop, mind, just drove through the village and on towards Machynlleth."

"Yes, I've just met him in Aber," she lied. "Gethyn, I have to go, I'm soaked and I need to change."

"I thought you'd have had enough water without walking about in the rain."

She looked at him, wondering if it was an attempt to joke about the disaster of the flood, or whether he was serious. His face creased into a smile and she shared it and said, "Some people never learn, do they, Gethyn? We walked up Consti and got drenched."

She added a few details and made light of the small adventure and hoped he wouldn't mention again about Larry being home. What could she say? Wasn't she expected to know what his plans were? He lived with her for heaven's sake! How foolish he was making her feel, coming back home and she not knowing!

She threw down her shopping and went straight upstairs to run a bath. After she had soaked in the warm, scented water for a while she relaxed. It seemed she had two choices. She could either tell him to go away and never come back; that way she would be free of his mysteries forever. But she would be saying goodbye to the one man she could imagine spending the rest of her life with. Or she could tell him she loved him deeply and wanted to share whatever it was he was involved in.

Either way she was taking the risk of losing him, but the second alternative was the one with at least a chance of working things out and staying together. Even knowing he had lied to her didn't change the fact that she wanted that more than she'd wanted anything in her whole life.

Chapter Twelve

Rosemary was uneasy as she doused the fire and went up to bed. The house seemed once more unfriendly, threatening.

Sleep wouldn't come for a long time. She read for a while, closed her eyes then, after a few minutes of lying there listening for the slightest sound, she took up her book again.

The sound, when it came was so faint she thought, after the initial grip of panic, that she had imagined it. She didn't move, she knew that if she opened her eyes the room would be quiet, empty, the glow from the lamp showing that all was well. But she couldn't open them. Her heart was racing, she imagined that the bedclothes were moving in its frantic rhythm. Then she felt something alight on the bed. She sat up and screamed.

Whatever it had been was gone. A dream, she kept telling herself. It was a bad dream. Then the window curtain, that hung to floor length, moved as if someone were shaking it. She picked up the clock, a miserably small weapon but better than nothing at all, and slowly stepped out of bed.

She took a deep breath as she lifted the curtain aside and held her arm holding the clock high above her, ready to strike.

Out walked Mrs Priestley's cat.

She sobbed, a mixture of crying and relieved laughter. The cat looked alarmed, its eyes black as it too showed its fear. Talking soothingly, suppressing the fear-filled laughter that threatened to overwhelm her, she picked it up and went downstairs.

Putting a coat over her nightdress she unbolted and unlocked the front door. Outside, the moon was giving some light and she saw a figure bending down, calling softly.

"Mrs Priestley," Rosemary whispered. "If you're looking for your cat, then she's here. And a fine fright she gave me!" Mrs Priestley seemed not to hear her and Rosemary stepped out and walked to where Mrs Priestley crouched with one hand outstretched to entice her cat to come to her.

Rosemary followed the woman on, across the footbridge to the other side of the stream. She didn't put the cat down but instead followed her neighbour, after her fright, wanting, needing, to talk to another human being.

She ran soundlessly over the damp grass on her slippered feet and called again when she reached the bridge. She didn't want to give Mrs Priestley a fright too.

"My dear!" Mrs Priestley said, reaching for the cat. "Where did you find her? Queenie! You naughty, naughty girl. Hiding from me like that!"

Leaning on the handrail of the bridge, Rosemary explained what had happened.

"She must have come in just before I went to bed. I remember putting some rubbish in the dustbin last thing. It must have been then," Rosemary explained.

"And I've been searching for her for ages! Naughty girl," Mrs Priestley scolded the purring cat. "Come on, it's a bit late for your supper but I suppose you still want it."

Search For a Shadow

Saying their goodnights, the two women separated, Mrs Priestley, still scolding Queenie, walked to number four and Rosemary, hurrying, conscious of the chill night air, into number two.

She was smiling as she rebolted the door and went back up stairs. She was shivering so much her teeth were chattering uncontrollably. Having been standing outside in only a thin nightdress and a coat thrown casually over her shoulders, she decided that a shower might be a good idea, to warm her, if she weren't to lie sleepless for hours.

The shower, hot and fast, revived her and she walked, naked, into her bedroom and found a fresh nightdress. She thought she would need to read for a while after the fright of finding her "intruder", but her eyes grew heavy and she soon slept.

A shrouded figure moved slowly up the stairs and stood looking at the sleeping girl. Barely visible, just a deeper shadow in the doorway of the room, it didn't move for several minutes then melted away, leaving only a slight smell of perspiration that was soon dissipated and which didn't touch the nostrils of the sleeper.

Rosemary slept on in the silent room.

When she next glanced at the clock, now returned to its place on the bedside table, she saw that it was three o'clock. She wondered what had woken her. Then she became aware of music. Music? At three in the morning? She got out of bed and looked out of the window. Surely there wasn't anyone out there with a radio on at such an unearthly hour?

The night was still, a rime of ice showed sparkling on the window sill. No moving shadow disturbed the silent scene before her. The music had stopped. It must have been someone walking past carrying a radio, she decided.

As she slipped back into the welcoming warmth of the bed, she heard it again. Louder now and quite definitely near. As she listened with bated breath she realised that, even allowing for her fanciful mood, the sound must be here, in the house.

It was Ravel's *Bolero*, a favourite of hers. Then her flesh began to creep as if thousands of insects were crawling over her, as she became aware of an added sound. Someone was accompanying the melody by whistling.

A smell teased her senses. The smell of cooking. She reached for the clock again, stared briefly and disbelievingly at its face, then hurriedly pulled on her slippers and a dressing gown; the need for clothing as important as a weapon. The vulnerability of being scantily clad making the precious moments spent adding clothes an unconscious essential.

As she opened the bedroom door the sound increased. There was no doubt now. It was definitely coming from downstairs. The sound of Ravel's *Bolero* soared up to meet her. The whistling had stopped.

Her legs felt like wood as she forced them to move down the stairs; one hand gripping the banister like a lifeline, the other holding the small clock. A draught shook her nightdress as if someone had just opened a door or a window. She stayed perfectly still, afraid to move, yet more afraid not to. Her back felt chill. What if someone had been hiding upstairs and was watching her from behind? Slowly, looking both ways in turn, she moved down the stairs.

She reached the small hallway and looked at the front door. It was unbolted. She knew with utmost certainty that she had been careful to rebolt it after after returning the cat to Mrs Priestley. Since then, someone had been inside.

Search For a Shadow

While she had stood talking to Mrs Priestley, within yards of her house, someone had entered. He had been in the house while she had showered, and walked around naked. He had watched her as she slept. She felt sick and waves of faintness threatened to overwhelm her.

Her face was stiff with fear as she moved on. The living rooms were empty of any presence but her own. The newspaper she had read was still on the armchair. She went cautiously into the kitchen. There, unbelievably, a kettle was just coming to the boil. She sobbed and looked all around her but there was no one there. She stared at the kettle like someone in a dream. Perhaps she was dreaming? Just then a sharp snap behind her made her scream. She covered her head with her arms, but the sound wasn't repeated. Turning, expecting something to be about to descend on her head, she saw that the toaster had just delivered two perfectly browned rounds of bread.

She ran to the front door and threw the bolt across. The music was reaching its manic crescendo, filling the house with its intense, swaying rhythm. She pushed a chair so her back was to the wall, and sat. Too terrified for sleep, too terrified to do anything except sit there and wait for the night to pass. At six o'clock she rang Megan.

Her explanations were too hysterical for Megan to understand at first, but as Rosemary calmed down, and she understood what had happened, she said, "Why didn't you call the police?"

"They didn't believe me last time. They think I'm a hysterical woman who makes up stories to draw attention to herself."

"That's nonsense, love, and you know it," Megan

argued briskly. "Who would think that of someone like you?"

"Whoever is *doing* this must look normal! Not the type to play such terrible tricks! Someone, sometime, will say, 'Who'd have believed it of him!' Won't they?"

"I'll be with you in half an hour."

"Thank you. I don't think I can face leaving this chair unless you come."

To Rosemary's surprise, she felt hungry. She was afraid to touch the toaster. Her imagination gave it a mind of its own. She couldn't eat a slice of bread that had been near it. Nor, she decided with a shiver, could she touch the loaf of bread that her visitor had left on the bread-board after he had cut the two slices for the toaster. Nor the kettle that had joined in the weird, middle-of-the-night ghost's picnic!

She boiled some milk in a saucepan and made a milky coffee, and while it cooled she ate two apples, biting into them with uncharactistic greed. Then she sat and waited for Megan.

Only ten minutes had passed since she had telephoned so she was surprised, then frightened, when she heard someone at the door. It wasn't Megan. The caller was too furtive.

She heard a key being inserted. Definitely not Megan. It must be the midnight prowler! The man, who ever he was, was trying to come back in!

Instinctively she hid. First flat against the wall then foolishly behind the door. Then, as she calmed from the immediate panic, she knew he could not possibly see inside, the heavy curtains were tightly drawn, and with the bolt once more firmly in place, couldn't open the door. She ran to the back door to make sure that was bolted although she had looked at least three times since she had come downstairs.

Search For a Shadow

Fingers tapped the window and she covered her mouth to hold back a scream, then she sobbed with relief as Larry's voice called, "Rose Mary? Honey, it's me. Are you awake?"

She was crying with relief as she pulled back the bolt and opened the door to him. She threw herself at him and sobbed uncontrollably so he had to carry her back inside.

"Bolt the door," were the first words she uttered that made any sense. Not letting go of her, he did so, and then he guided her back to sit beside the dead ashes of last night's fire.

He didn't ask any questions, but talked soothingly to her, holding her tight and kissing her face and her hair, telling her he loved her and wouldn't leave her alone again.

The roar of an engine broke the silence of the early morning, the M.G. sports car slowing and coming to rest on the opposite side of the footbridge. There were footsteps then a knock at the door and Rosemary tensed, then remembered and said, "That will be Megan."

Gradually Rosemary told them the whole of the night's bizzarre events. Larry and Megan examined the toaster, the record player and the kettle and announced that so far as they could tell, there was no electronic skills used. They had simply been turned on before the intruder had left. What Rosemary had told them seemed to have been the truth.

They tried all the combinations of people to work out who was responsible.

"Huw Rees could be helped by Mrs Priestley," Larry suggested. "She could easily be involved. What looks more innocent if she had been seen, than calling the cat in?

She could have used the cat to distract you for Huw or Richard to come in and do these things to frighten you. Or, Gethyn, he could have been watching and simply taken advantage of a situation that offered itself. He's always at that front window."

"Or you, Larry?" Megan looked at him quizzically. "What about you?"

"Hell, why would I want to frighten Rosemary? Besides, I've just come from the airport. I landed at Heathrow some time after nine o'clock then I caught a train to Aberystwyth where I picked up my car."

"We saw you in Aberystwyth when you were supposed to be in New York. Gethyn has seen you driving through the village." Megan was quietly insistent, her voice strong and firm. She was staring at Larry, willing him to tell them the truth.

"You're mistaken," he said. "I didn't leave New York until yesterday." He ran his fingers through his hair in that familiar gesture and looked at Rosemary. "Surely you don't believe that I'd—? Hell, there's more than one Citroën in the country for heaven's sake!"

"You were driving it," Rosemary's voice was almost a whisper.

"Rosemary, it wasn't me! You've gotta believe it!" Both women looked at him, Megan, tight-lipped and defiant and Rosemary almost pleading, wanting to believe him but they said nothing further.

"I'm making coffee, anyone want one?" he asked and went into the kitchen.

Rosemary was tired and her head ached intolerably.

"I think I'd like to sleep, as long as you stay here," she said. Both Larry and Megan nodded agreement and she went upstairs and slept the moment she rested her head on the pillow.

Search For a Shadow

Downstairs Megan looked at Larry and waited.

"What are we going to do about all this?" Larry said.

"You could tell the truth for a start!"

"I swear to you this wasn't my doing."

"Come off it. The moment you appeared things began to happen. You didn't come from the airport tonight, did you?"

"You gotta believe me, I'm not responsible for what happened here tonight. I arrived just before you did and that's the truth."

"Really!" she said sarcastically.

"Really!" he insisted. He stood up and walked away from her, anger in his expression, to check on Rosemary.

"Why didn't you call me?" Gethyn asked a few days later when Rosemary met him on her way back from the village shop. "Mrs Priestley told me what had happened when she brought me some cakes. I don't mind being woken at night, not if you need me, Rosemary."

"I was afraid to go outside," she explained, not liking to tell him that it hadn't occurred to her to seek help from any of the neighbours. That Megan, so far from the scene, was the only one from whom she felt she could ask help.

Huw Rees was friendly and charming but an unknown quantity, and his friend Richard Lloyd had made no effort to be either friendly or charming! Mrs Priestley, with her wandering cat, was a possible suspect, although in her calmer moments Rosemary thought the idea was ridiculous. And Gethyn, although he would have been supportive and kind, would only use the opportunity to reinforce his dislike and suspicion of Larry.

"Come in and tell me all about it," Gethyn invited. He went to his house and held the door open for her, hoping she'd be unable to refuse. She showed him her shopping.

"I have to get in and start cooking," she said. "Larry will be back from town in less than an hour."

"Then wait for him here. You don't want to go in on your own, I'm sure."

"Don't, Gethyn."

"Don't do what?" he asked.

"Don't unnerve me any more than I am already." He was at once apologetic.

"I'm sorry. That was insensitive and stupid of me."

"No, *I'm* sorry, I shouldn't have said that."

"I'll come in with you, you can check all is well, then I'll come away and leave you to get on cooking for the American." He closed his door and followed her to her own.

"His name is Larry," she said wearily. "Why do you call him the 'American'?"

"Don't like him, that's why," he admitted with a slow, unrepentant smile.

He followed her into the kitchen and he made them instant coffee to drink while she went on with her preparation for the meal. She explained what had happened on the night that Larry had returned and he listened attentively, staring at the kettle and the toaster intently, as if they could show him something the others had missed.

"You told him we'd seen him when he says he was in New York?" he asked.

"He *was* in New York, Gethyn. We were mistaken, there are other Citroen Dollies, as he pointed out, and the driver simply looked like him. We only had a moving view of the driver in an enclosed space, and a brief one. And we expected it to be him when we saw what we believed was his car. No, Larry was not the driver. He was in New York." She avoided mentioning the licence plate number.

* * *

Search For a Shadow

Megan was alarmed by the most recent of the happenings in Rosemary's house and was afraid for her. She wondered whom she could tell. Breaking her promise not to discuss it was not difficult. She was well aware of the danger Rosemary might face when the person concerned changed his tactics from mischief to deliberate harm. What was a promise compared to that?

She decided on Huw Rees. He seemed an intelligent young man and was obviously attracted to Rosemary. If only Larry weren't there, she thought he might be more than a friend and neighbour. He would surely help her, if only to show Larry up as the trickster; because Megan was more and more convinced it was he. There were too many coincidences and although she knew they happened, it was hard to swallow so many within so small an area and in such a brief time.

When she knew Rosemary was safely at work, she arranged to meet Huw and discuss the recent events. To her surprise, Richard was with him. She frowned as she went to the table in the seaside cafe in Aberystwyth where they had arranged to meet.

"Sorry, Megan, but I've told Richard everything you told me. He has something to add that you'll find interesting," he explained, as he held out a chair for her to join them.

Richard, who rarely spoke, said in his deep, attractive Welsh voice, "This man Larry, he's obsessed with finding some relative or other and I think it's sending him round the bend."

"Tell him about your father," Huw coaxed.

"He approached my father and tried to tell him that I was a stolen child, not his son but Larry's long-lost brother, would you believe!"

"You do resemble him a little," Megan said, "fair hair

and dark brown eyes and you're about the same height and build, but surely that wasn't enough to make him think you and he were related?"

"The man's cracked. My father recommends we warn Rosemary to stay well away from him. We don't know what turn his obsession will take, do we?"

"Larry doesn't seem the obsessional type, but then, Rosemary and I were saying only a few days ago that when this man is found, people will almost certainly say, 'Who would have thought it of someone like him?'" She looked from one to the other and asked, "What can we do? If we try to tell Rosemary we think Larry is dangerous, she won't believe us. She'll probably stop telling me everything that happens and that would put her in greater danger. No, I think it's best that I concentrate on remaining her friend and confidant. If she doesn't have me to talk to she'll really be on her own – and in greater danger!"

"Not on her own," the quiet Richard said slowly. "That's the touble, she's with Larry. He shares her home, her food – and her bed." Megan thought the remark upset Huw. He lowered his head as if unable to face that fact.

The following weekend Rosemary had to check the proofs of her new book and on the Thursday evening while they were preparing for bed, she suggested that Larry should go off and explore some more of the Welsh hills.

"I'll be working all day throughout Saturday and Sunday," she said. "It will be so boring for you. I'll ask Megan or Sally to come and sleep here if it makes you any happier, but I'll really be all right. Once the doors are locked and bolted for the night, I won't open them for anyone. Not for Mrs Priestley's cat, not even for you," she joked.

Search For a Shadow

"I particularly want to see something of Snowdonia while I'm here," he said, and Rosemary felt the coldness of their imminent parting at his words, "While I'm here." She could pretend all she liked but the day when he would leave her was only a few weeks away at most. "But," he was saying, "I was hoping to see it with you."

"Next weekend I could go with you. But not this one."

"I don't want to go without you, but if you think I'll interfere with your concentration . . ." He kissed her as he spoke and smiled deep into her eyes. "As you spoil mine." He kissed her again and said dreamily, "What was I saying—?"

"You were saying that you'd leave me to get on with my work. And incidentally," she said, sitting on the bed, "what about your own story? Have you submitted it to a publisher?"

He shook his head.

"It seems to have been lost in the post."

"Darling! Why didn't you say? Have you any notes? Anything at all to help you to rewrite it?"

"Not even the will to try again. It's taken the heart out of me having it ruined like that. Dammit, who's doing all this to me?"

Rosemary turned away from him and pretended to rearrange the pillows. Her heart was sad. She knew that was untrue. His lies were getting weaker. He had already told her it had been safely received by his father.

The weekend passed uneventfully. As Megan pleaded a previous arrangement, it was Sally who came on Friday evening at six and stayed with her. Rosemary was relieved to discover that the sometimes overbearing girl didn't interfere with her intention to work on her book. On Saturday morning she was at work and on Sunday she stayed in bed late, spent a little while talking to Mrs Priestley of whom she seemed to have become rather fond, then went for a walk before coming back to cook lunch for the two of them. The work Rosemary had to do was completed and packed ready for posting by four o'clock and they sat then and talked and waited for Larry to return.

Sally didn't discuss Larry at all, nor did she even hint at her firm belief that Larry must be doing the things that had frightened Rosemary. She knew of the conversation Megan had had with Huw and Richard but it remained a secret from Rosemary and her strengthening fears were unuttered. She hoped that if she could somehow stay another night, she might pick up something from Larry's conversation or his behaviour that would help her prove that he was involved. To this end, she suggested inviting Huw and Richard in for a drink.

"I don't know," Rosemary said doubtfully. "Larry will be back by seven."

"He isn't antisocial, is he? I'm sure he wouldn't mind you having a few friends in. Ask Mrs Priestley and Gethyn as well, shall we? I'm sure Larry can't object to a little light social chatter?"

To everyone's surprise the gathering was a great success. So few people and everyone different, yet the thing gelled and the house was soon buzzing with conversation and laughter. Huw had gone to buy drinks, and Mrs Priestley had thought to bring some extra glasses. In a hasty search of the store-cupboard, Sally had found the makings of a savoury rice salad and some tins of meat. A green salad filled a large bowl and with the addition of crisps and biscuits, the table looked festive. By eight o'clock the room was warm, and Rosemary had no fears about opening the front door and leaving it open.

Search For a Shadow

Rosemary was pleased to see that there was no lull when Larry arrived. He sat on the end of the settee and chatted to Mrs Priestley as if they were all old friends.

"I hear you've been walking in Snowdonia," Huw called across. "Bet you didn't walk to the top?"

"I sure as hell did," Larry replied.

Larry left Mrs Priestley and her cat and went to sit between Huw and Richard. The three heads close together were companionable, and it was only when Richard raised his head to laugh, that Rosemary realised how similar Richard and Larry were.

"I saw you in town yesterday," Huw called to Gethyn, who was helping Rosemary and Sally pass food between their guests. "Who were the fireworks for? Not planning on having a little party on your own, are you?"

Gethyn looked slightly uneasy. The words weren't unkind, but there was, in the suggestion that a man of his age could enjoy fireworks on his own, a hint that Gethyn was perhaps a little odd.

"I was hoping you'd all contribute and have a bonfire party," Gethyn said quietly. "I had in mind something to cheer Rosemary and – well, now you know, I suppose there isn't any point. I was planning it as a surprise for her."

The teasing with the slight edge had been turned neatly round, Rosemary thought.

"Gethyn! What a lovely idea! Let's still do it, shall we?"

They didn't hear anyone knocking on the open door. A man walked in and apologetically asked if he could speak to his son.

"Dad," Richard said rising at once to go and greet him. "Come in and meet the neighbours." Rosemary stared in shock. The man was the one who had hit Larry at the cafe on Constitution Hill.

"Sorry to barge in," the man said. "My name's Peter, by the way. I have to see Richard, briefly. There's a part he wants for that car of his and I need to know exactly which part he needs."

He was offered a drink. Then he caught sight of Larry and his face changed.

"I see the madman is still with you," he said. "As I've already told your friend, Megan, it's time you told him to go, young lady."

Chapter Thirteen

There was a silence as if Peter's words had been a small explosion and the aftermath had people stunned.

"Dad," Richard said. He took his father's arm and led him outside, still carrying the drink he had been given. To those left in the breathless silence, there came the murmur of voices, occasionally raised so they could hear words, like, 'Obsessed'. 'Crazy'. 'Dangerous'. Larry stood staring at the open door, his face a mask of shock.

"Why should he talk like that?" he asked finally. "The guy came up and punched me on the face one day. That's right, isn't it, baby? And he calls *me* crazy?" He put an arm around Rosemary's shoulders and forced her to smile. "It seems he resents my looking a bit like Richard, though I'm better looking of course! Now how d'you deal with a queer fellow like that?"

Rosemary touched his shoulder and smiled at him to take the angry look from his face. Mrs Priestley stood up as if to go and Larry stopped her.

"Don't leave, Mrs Priestley, there's plenty of food left and we can go for more drink if it's running low." He filled her glass and then began to talk about his experiences over the weekend. "This is some country," he said. "There's a different scene around every corner."

"I'm sorry about that," Richard said, appearing in the doorway.

"No matter." Larry, playing the gregarious and friendly host, pushed a foaming glass into Richard's hand and waved a hand at the food. "Come on, people! Let's eat and drink and be merry."

"For tomorrow we – cry?" misquoted Mrs Priestley.

"Hell, who cares about tomorrow!"

"Have you made any progress with your house-hunting?" Richard asked Gethyn later in the evening.

"Yes and no," Gethyn replied. "Yes, I've made progress, but no, I haven't yet found anywhere. The trouble is, I want to stay here."

"It doesn't hurt anyone to have a shake up now and again," Huw interrupted. "It can be worrying to have to make a move, but sometimes it works out for the best. You can be in one place too long."

"Not in my case," Gethyn said, then he lowered his voice and added, "I want to be here to keep an eye on Rosemary. We're all enjoying Larry's company, but I for one don't forget for a moment all that's been happening to her since he arrived."

"I'm uneasy too," Huw whispered back, "but what can we do? She loves the man, and there's nothing we can say that will persuade her to doubt him, or encourage her even to check on all he's said."

"Don't let my father's reaction make *you* overreact, mind," Richard warned. "I think they had a misunderstanding, that's all."

"But he could be right," Gethyn said. "Someone is tormenting Rosemary and, who else could it be?"

"You look serious, all of you!" Rosemary called, and Larry looked at the three solemn men and echoed her words.

"We're afraid the booze will run out," Huw said, the

Search For a Shadow

solemn look not leaving his face.

"Come with me and we'll buy some more," Larry said at once. He patted his pocket to check that his wallet was there and they went out together.

It was midnight before the party finally broke up and Mrs Priestley had to be escorted into her house by Rosemary and Sally. They saw her in and made sure she was all right before leaving her sitting in front of her cold grate, insisting that she was, "As warm as toast and twice as tasty!"

"You wouldn't like us to see you upstairs?" Sally asked.

"No, thank you! I'm not drunk you know, only very excited and happy. We'll be all right, won't we, Queenie? But thanks my dears, you're both very kind to me."

Reluctantly, they went out, reminding her to lock and bolt her door.

"We'll wait 'til we hear it done," Sally shouted as they pulled the door to. "Bless her, she needs looking after, doesn't she, Rosemary?" she added in a whisper and Rosemary smiled agreement, curious at the friendship between the lively girl and the elderly woman. The bolt was thrown and they went back to number two as Richard and Huw were leaving.

Gethyn and Larry were in the kitchen, filling black plastic rubbish-bags with the empy cans and wrappings, and Sally knew that there was no way she would be expected to leave before morning.

"It'll be all right if I stay another night, won't it?" she said.

"Sally, need you ask!"

"Only one stipulation," Larry said. "Don't call us before eleven!"

"What a hope," Rosemary laughed. "Some of us have to work you know!"

Gethyn looked at Rosemary and frowned. He was imagining her sleeping beside Larry, and didn't like it one bit. He left the remainder of the clearing up and went home, forcing a smile and a thank you to his hostess but managing not to say even goodnight to Larry.

The impromptu party-givers settled to sleep, Larry and Rosemary in the double bed. Sally on the put-u-up in Rosemary's study. Sally stared at the ceiling and wondered if her suspicion that Larry was playing some dangerous game were true, and if so, what his reason could be. She touched her fingers and counted, noting every incident in which he could have been involved, trying to see some pattern to explain what had happened. At three o'clock, she turned over and slept, none the wiser.

Together in the double bed upstairs, Larry and Rosemary whispered softly to each other.

"Miss me, honey?" he asked.

"Of course I did. I was jealous too. Jealous of you meeting new people and seeing new things without me." She cuddled closer to him.

"Next weekend I'm free," she coaxed. "Where shall we go?"

"Walking around these hills, eating at one of your pubs, that'll suit me."

"No, I think we should see the Gower. We'll stay with Mam and Dad, if you don't object?"

"Meet the parents? Gee honey, that'll be great." He looked suitably alarmed. "The Gower you say, that's in the south, isn't it?"

"I love Gower in the winter, when the scenery is widened by the lack of leaves. Everything looks different, there's more of everything. Different season, different view."

"In the city it's better, every *day* is different," he said, teasing her and expecting to provoke an angry response, but her even breathing told him she was asleep. He kissed her lightly and settled to sleep himself.

Sally and Rosemary got up early to prepare themselves for work.

At eleven o'clock Larry rang.

"Honey, there's been a phone call from your mother. They're coming here on Sunday. Is that all right? I said it probably was, but that I'd ring if you still preferred to go there."

"That's fine." Rosemary was pleased that her parents were visiting. "Try and persuade them to come on Saturday and stay over," she suggested.

"I'll do that – even if it does mean I'll have to be a 'good boy' for a night or two! Love you darling." He squeaked a kiss and rang off.

They were watching for the arrival of her parents' car on Saturday morning when another car turned down the narrow path and stopped on the parking place. There was only room for three cars and Rosemary began to cross over the footbridge to ask the strangers to park elsewhere, when she recognised the vehicle. It belonged to the Hughes's in number three. They had returned, at last, from their visit to their daughter in Bala.

"Rosemary, how are you, my lovely girl?" The rich, deep voice of Henry Hughes boomed across to where she stood waiting to welcome them. He bent from his six feet two and helped his wife out from the passenger seat. Muriel Hughes was plump and always laughing. She laughed now as she waved across at Rosemary and shouted, excitedly.

"Darlin', it's great to be back, we've missed you. I'll

be in now in a minute to hear all the gossip. Got time, have you? *Duw*, there's cramped it is in that car. I feel like a concertina that hasn't been used for years!" She laughed loudly and happily, full of excitement at being home again.

"I'll help with the luggage, shall I?"

"Here, let me do that, you and the lady can get on with the talking," Larry called, having seen and heard the reunion.

He came to where Rosemary stood watching as Henry Hughes began dragging bags out of the back of the car, talking non-stop as he did so. Muriel stared at him admiringly and asked, "Hello, Larry, love! Seems you've got plenty to tell me, young Rosemary."

Rosemary offered her hand to Larry and they walked to the car smiling.

"You know each other? But how?"

"Larry came and saw us at our daughter's place, didn't you Larry? Wanted to know all about the people in the village for a project he's working on. How's it going? Nearly finished it I expect." She laughed as she hugged him and then looked at Rosemary. "Are you two? You know." She winked. "Well," she demanded, as neither answered her. "Come on, you can tell your Auntie Moo!"

"Yes, Muriel," Larry replied, hugging Rosemary, "we are – you know—" And he winked back.

"Well-well! Fancy that! You've grown up a bit while we've been away, girl," was Henry's comment.

Rosemary took one of the smaller bags and went with Muriel to her house. As they opened the door, Muriel gasped.

"There's stuffy it is. I'll have to live with the doors and windows open for a bit to get the staleness blown out. Lucky I'm good and fat, or it'll blow me out as well!"

Search For a Shadow

Laughing she led the way in and opened the windows. "Damn me, one of them wasn't locked! Don't tell my Harry, he'll only blame me and make a fuss."

"You should have left a key, someone would have opened the windows now and then to freshen it before you came back," Rosemary said.

"Not if what we've heard about the goings on at your place are even half true!" Muriel said. "Come on, love, there's milk and biscuits in this bag, put the kettle on and tell me what's been going on."

It seemed impossible to refuse and as Muriel kicked off her high-heeled shoes and loosened a button on her skirt, Rosemary attended to the kettle and began to relate some of what had happened.

She told the story as if it were a humorous one, making more of the funny side of things and playing down the fear and panic she had experienced.

"I'm so glad Larry was there most of the time," she said finally. "I'd have felt very alone, with only Gethyn on one side and your empty house on the other."

"And Gethyn's mam," Muriel said with a loud laugh. "Not that she'd be much good, poor dab, being over seventy, but at least it's another woman."

"You – you haven't heard?" Rosemary said quietly. "Mrs Lewis. She's dead."

"What? What happened for goodness sake? She was all right when we left."

"Fell, up on the mountain somewhere. Gethyn doesn't find it easy to talk about it yet, and I haven't got the full story myself."

"Fell, you say?"

"Apparently no one found her until she had been there long enough to get severely chilled. Poor love. She was Gran's friend and I miss her. It was like having a link with

Gran, being able to talk to Mrs Lewis. I was in America when she died. I couldn't even go to the funeral."

"Where was Gethyn?"

"What d'you mean? He was at home as always."

"When she fell, where was Gethyn?"

"Gone into town, I think," Rosemary said, trying to remember what she had been told. "It was early the next morning before they found her and it was too late to save her." She frowned at the jolly-faced woman who was staring into space. "Muriel, why did you ask where was Gethyn? Where did you expect him to be?"

"Oh, I'm being melodramatic, darling, you know me. But just before we went to Bala, they had a terrible row. Her and Gethyn. He wasn't speaking to her, she told me that. I wondered if an argument could have got out of hand."

"You think Gethyn could have hurt her? Never!" Rosemary said emphatically.

"No-no. Not hurt her, heavens above, no. Just didn't bother to look for her, mad with her and letting her see he was upset."

"He waited on her hand and foot. He's such a gentle, kindly man."

"Yes, but this quarrel, she wouldn't tell me what it was about, but she was very distressed that day. Said she'd 'lost him', she felt sure he wouldn't ever talk to her again."

"I wonder what happened? Poor Gethyn, how awful to lose someone just after a bad quarrel without having the chance to put things right."

"She put on him, mind. Perhaps she went a bit too far, elderly people can, you know."

"Perhaps he'll be able to talk about it soon, it's nearly five months now. Time to have faced all the grief, the horrors and self-recriminations."

Search For a Shadow

"What about this Larry of yours then?" Muriel asked with a sparkle in her dark brown eyes. She had the kind of cheerful and mischievous face that made a smile irresistible and Rosemary forgot the sadness of Gethyn's bereavement and responded to the inquisitive wink that accompanied the question.

"We met in London when I came back from America. It was an amazing coincidence really," Rosemary told her. "He wanted to find out all he could about his family roots and I came from here, the very area where they had once lived."

"It was a ploy, really," Larry said, as he came in with the luggage behind the large figure of Henry. "I'd never heard of the place but Rosemary's legs are the sort to make you really confused when it comes to geography!"

"Larry!" Rosemary laughed.

As they were drinking their second cup of tea, Gethyn came to tell them that Rosemary's parents had arrived and were knocking at the door for admittance, and complaining that their key wouldn't fit.

"Gethyn, love," Muriel said, getting up to hug him. "There's sorry I am about your mam. You must come up later and tell me all about it. Why didn't you write to tell us? We'd have wanted to come to the funeral and pay our respects. Been neighbours for years we had."

"It wasn't easy to think straight for a while. It was sudden, and completely unprepared for," Gethyn said. "Quick for her and that's the thing to remember. The doctor said it was sudden."

"I thought – didn't you say that if she'd been found earlier—" Rosemary began.

"Went out like a light. Worst for me it was, not finding her for those hours, but no, it wouldn't have helped her."

"So you not finding her for a while didn't really matter?"

Rosemary asked.

"No, she died quickly."

"Thank goodness for that. It would have been worse for you if you hadn't done all you could, you being such a good son." Muriel patted his arm affectionately, but in her intelligent brown eyes were questions waiting to be asked.

Rosemary felt an undercurrent of dread. For some reason she couldn't fathom, Muriel wasn't easy about Mrs Lewis's death. It had been an accident. She had walked up on the mountain and fallen, there was no more to it than that. Surely the strange disasters and accidents connected with her house hadn't begun earlier, and in Gethyn's house?

She hurriedly offered to help Muriel if she were needed, and ran to where her parents stood leaning against the door in mock despair.

"Rosemary, thank goodness," her father said. "Our key no longer fits and we were beginning to think we'd be sleeping on the banks of the stream!"

"Muriel and Henry are back," Rosemary explained.

Larry was still helping the Hughes's to empty the car, which seemed to contain enough clothes for a dozen people for a year, but he ran across, hugged and kissed her mother and shook hands with her father in his friendly yet polite way.

When he had finished trekking backwards and forwards from the car, her parents went to greet the Hughes's and she and Larry were alone. At once she told him of Muriel's comments about a quarrel between Gethyn and his mother.

"They never quarrelled," she told him. "Not in all the years I've known them. Gethyn looked after her every moment of the day. He couldn't have done more."

Search For a Shadow

"Perhaps Muriel was right, she overdid the dependency. It happens, the worm turns and bingo, she gets a slap."

"Gethyn was never treated like a worm," she protested. "Neither did Mrs Lewis take advantage. Gethyn offered to do things, I don't think I ever heard her ask for anything. He knew what she wanted and arranged it without waiting for her to ask. To me he seemed a highly sensitive son who hated his mother to feel she was in any way a nuisance. He forestalled her need to ask. She would never have been a whingeing, whining sort.

"Besides, she wasn't an invalid, far from it. She went to the shops, did a bit of weeding and even went for walks occasionally, up on the mountain, like she did on the day she died. Usually she had Muriel for company." She smiled. "Muriel is so overweight that she was breathless long before Mrs Lewis!"

"It must be odd having a mother almost as old as the grandparents of his friends," Larry insisted. "I bet that rankled, at least when he was younger."

"I've never seen a sign of it," she said emphatically.

She began to prepare the meal for her parents and themselves when suddenly she threw up her hands in despair, scattering flour over the stone floor. She had never told her parents all that had happened in the house, determined not to worry them unduly. Now, she had forgotten to warn Muriel not to discuss it. They would most certainly have been told everything that Muriel had gleaned, and if her past record was a guide, that would be plenty.

"What is it, love?" Larry asked.

"Mam and Dad, they'll be told all that's happened here. I forgot to warn Muriel."

"Too late to worry now. Besides, I guess it's time they were put in the picture."

"I guess you're right."

After they had eaten, squashed together in the small kitchen, Larry told them he had a few surprises. From his travel bag he produced gifts for them all. A sweater for Rosemary's father and a scarf for her mother, both bought from Macy's, the famous New York store. To Rosemary he gave a watch. In platinum, it was small and delicately crafted and she gasped at the sight of it.

"Larry, it's lovely. I – oh, thank you!" She hugged him and her parents looked politely away as they kissed. She slipped it on her wrist. She sparkled like a small child at Christmas, they told her.

Rosemary was particularly thrilled with the presents as it proved that both she and Gethyn had been mistaken; Larry *had* been in America when he said he was, and not driving around the country in his Citroën. They must have simply misread the licence plate number.

For that alone the gift was special. She took it off as she went to her lonely bed, thinking about Larry on the sofa downstairs and trying not to allow her thoughts to drift too far into the future. He loved her, she was certain of that and for the moment it was enough. If he went back to his family, then it wasn't necessarily the end, she told herself. The world was small and shrinking all the time. She stared at the watch on the bedside table beside her until she slept.

The next day was chilly but the early mist was already clearing and giving them the prospect of a pleasant day.

They drove to Aberangell in Mr Roberts' spacious Rover and walked up between the tall conifers until a valley opened out before them in the silent world where cars were neither seen nor heard, where the soft murmurings of a stream seemed deafeningly loud and the birds seemed to be subdued and in awe of the wide sky and the miles of rolling hills around them.

Holding Larry's hand, Rosemary proudly showed him her favourite places. They stood and looked down at the blue pool and the waterfall, and teased Larry when he jokingly called it a rival to the Niagara Falls. They laughed stupidly as they watched children in the distance, playing roly-poly down a steep hill, almost wishing they could join in the fun. They watched as rabbits browsed, unafraid, in the soft green grass, marvelled at the narrow, green lane through Aberangell that had once been the main street.

They ate in their favourite pub in Dinas Mawthwy. Everything was exciting and fun; Rosemary couldn't ever remember being so happy.

It was late in the evening before Rosemary's parents left. As she walked with them to their car, she could see that her mother wanted to say something. She hoped it was not disapproval of Larry. She had not kept it a secret that she and Larry lived together.

"Thanks, love," her father said as he put the bag into the boot of the car. "I'm tired out mind, but very content. You and Larry have given us a day that's as good as a week's holiday."

"We've enjoyed it too, Dad," she smiled as she kissed him. Then she looked at her mother and asked, "You too, Mam? Did you enjoy it?"

"Very much, love. Thank you. Both of you."

"But—?" Rosemary asked. "There is a 'but', isn't there? I can always tell."

"But I'm worried about Gethyn."

Rosemary was so surprised, she laughed.

"I know he's a grown man," her mother defended, "but

his mother's death was a terrible shock. He'd been so wrapped up in looking after her he's a bit lost now she's gone, and so suddenly too. Keep and eye on him will you, love? Don't give up on the old friendships to make room for the new, you need them all. It seems that he quarrelled with her on the very day she died. That must make it terribly upsetting."

"I'll make more of an effort," she promised. "I've been too wrapped up in my own life lately to remember how he must feel."

"Devastated he was, by his mother's sudden death."

"He's very fond of you, Rosemary," her father added as he fired the car into life. "Very fond, and that means you can help him more than most."

"I'll give him more time, I promise," she said, hugging them and closing the car doors.

Behind them Mrs Priestley, and Muriel and Henry, stood at their doors waving goodbye. The students were busy working on Huw's car, and they too called a farewell. At his window, they saw Gethyn watching. He had called earlier to say his goodbyes and would not come out with the others.

"It's such a friendly place, everyone knowing the rest and watching over each other," Rosemary's mother smiled as she turned to wave yet again.

"Lucky you are to live in a place like this," her father agreed. Rosemary wondered what they would say when she told them she had decided to sell. Once Larry had gone, she wouldn't stay. The people who had approached her asking for a first chance to buy were still interested and she would give them the go-ahead the moment Larry said goodbye.

Larry stood beside her and waved until Mr and Mrs Roberts were out of sight.

Search For a Shadow

"I suppose I'm the reason you've neglected Gethyn," he said, putting an arm around them as they walked back to the cottage. "If that is the case, well, I'm not sorry. I can't have you consoling bereaved young men, not when he's under the impression you're his property."

"He doesn't think that," she laughed. "But we've been friends and constant companions from childhood."

"Until now, darling," he said, kissing her cheek. "Until now."

"Jealous?" she asked.

"You betyer sweet life I am! Gethyn might be a queer fellow but he's quite handsome in his quiet way, and about the right age, and what's worse, he lives right next door to my girl!"

On Monday morning, Rosemary dressed for work and went to pick up the new watch from the bedside table where she had put it the previous evening. Then she changed her mind. Perhaps, for a while she would treat it like something too exclusive for daily use. She would save it for evenings and special occasions. It was special, much more than a watch. It was proof that he hadn't lied about being in New York.

Larry was there when she returned from work and she sensed he was upset about something. She didn't ask, always preferring to leave it for him to decide when to open up and discuss what was on his mind. But he said nothing, and she was in such a state of euphoria after the wonderful weekend and the gifts Larry had brought for them, that she was almost unaware of his rather subdued mood.

They were going to eat out that evening, their first alone since Larry had returned, and as she dressed in a newly bought suit in Larry's favourite yellow, she reached for the watch. It wasn't there.

"Larry?" she called. "Have you seen my watch? I left it here, on the table beside the bed."

"I wondered when you'd miss it," he said softly. "Here it is." He held out his hand and on it was the watch, or what was left of it. It was completely ruined.

"But—" She looked stupidly at the table as if expecting it to materialise, whole and perfect. "Larry, I left it on the bedside table. How could it have been broken? Where did you find it? I don't understand. If it's a joke then it isn't funny," she sobbed. She picked up the distorted bracelet and then the shattered watch. The glass was smashed, and the hands torn out of shape. "What happened? Please, tell me," she said as the vision of the broken face shimmered and disappeared behind her tears.

"On the road where you carelessly dropped it," he said. "Rolled on by several tractors by the look of it. Rosemary, how could you be so casual with such an expensive and beautiful thing?"

She began to argue, to tell him she hadn't been careless, that it had been safely left in its box beside her bed, but as the words came out of her mouth they seemed to disperse in the chilly atmosphere as if she hadn't spoken.

"What else have you done and then pretended it was done by some mysterious intruder?"

The look in his eyes made her blood turn to ice. There was no sign of the love that had been there the last time she had looked into their brown depths. She was looking at a stranger. Emanating from him was unutterable anger. It was as if he had no words left to describe how he felt, but the expression told it all. She felt a shudder of dismay run through her body and knew that whatever she said, Larry would not believe her. Larry thought she was the trickster, playing the tricks on herself.

Chapter Fourteen

Rosemary sat in her chair as a wall of unresolved anger grew around her. Larry went for a walk and he didn't invite her to go with him. The meal they had planned was forgotten. She hadn't moved when he returned and announced formally that he was going to bed. She didn't move while he showered and undressed and stomped into the bedroom. She heard the sound of the light being switched off and the isolation that had been growing all evening closed around her, an aura of despair.

The silence of the house was complete, isolating her from everyone and everything as the last sounds from the bedroom above ceased.

The tapping began without her being aware of it for some time. The sound was so soft that it seemed no more than a part of the night. Then it grew louder. But for a while she was nothing more than mildly, sleepily curious.

She gradually realised it was two different sounds. Some taps were soft and slightly echoing, others harder; it was as if something was being knocked against two different surfaces. There was no distinct rhythm but somehow she sensed rather than understood, that there was a phrase being repeated. Her sleepy, half-conscious state prevented her thinking about where it came from for a few moments, then she felt the blood drain from her face as she realised that someone was knocking and it was in the house.

She stared around her, wondering where it was coming from, then at the clock, as if the hour of the night could somehow offer an explanation. She went to the door to run upstairs for Larry but stopped. What would she see if she dared to open the door?

But that was ridiculous. To run for help, with Larry here in the house? Besides, she daren't leave the house. Although the threat was within the walls, there was a spurious security in being inside. Who knows what might await her out in the darkness? What if someone wanted her to leave the house? Was waiting outside for her to run out? The tapping continued.

She went once more to the door leading to the hallway and stairs but again she stopped. There was no way she could open the door. Outside might be frightening, but whatever it was that was haunting her was here within the house, locked and bolted in with her. And it might be standing on the other side of the door.

Wild thoughts filled her mind. The ghost, or whatever it was, wanted her, no one else. It was trying to tell her something, her alone. It had waited until she was by herself and now it was trying to communicate. Could it be Mrs Lewis who had died so tragically up on the mountain? Could her spirit be unable to rest?

The pattern of knocking was becoming so clear that she found herself silently following and anticipating the taps. Nervously she side-stepped to the settee and picked up a pen. She wrote down the soft sounds with a cross and the harsher sounds with a circle. The tapping was indeed repeated; she recognised as she saw that she had copied a pattern of sounds for the third time.

She stared uncomprehendingly at the lines of crosses and circles she had written, then took a deep rasping breath.

Search For a Shadow

Above her a door opened. Someone was coming down the stairs.

As the door opened, she pressed herself against the wall. The tapping had ceased.

"Larry!" She didn't wait to see who it was, telling herself it was him and no apparition, no ghost of Mrs Lewis.

"Rosemary," his tousled head appeared in the crack of the door. "I woke and you weren't there. Darling, I'm sorry I disbelieved you. With all that's been happening how could I have been so stupid? Come to bed. Of course you weren't careless, I – What is it?" He stared at her ashen face, realising belatedly that something was wrong. "Rosemary?"

"Did you hear the tapping?"

"Tapping?" He frowned and shook his head. "I haven't heard a thing. I woke, felt for you and woke up as I remembered our quarrel. What's happened?"

Suddenly she didn't want to tell him. The tapping had stopped as soon as he began to come down the stairs. It was him. It must have been him. He was trying to terrify her. The reasons she didn't even try to work out. For some reason he wanted her to leave this house. Just as determinedly, she made up her mind to stay.

"Larry, I think you should leave."

"Because of the quarrel? I said I'm sorry and I meant it. I'll never doubt you again."

"I want you to leave. Now, as soon as you can collect your things."

He moved towards her, and she was very afraid. She backed towards the kitchen. She saw the concern on his face change to shock as she almost screamed, "Keep away from me. Don't come near me, ever again! I don't know what you're game is, but you aren't playing it here any longer, d'you hear me? Go!"

"I can't leave you like this."

"Go, or I'll call the police and tell them everything that's happened."

"But what *has* happened? What's this about tapping? You heard something tonight and think I'm involved, is that it?"

"That's only a part of it. Get out, and leave me alone."

"Tell me what happened. If you're in danger I can't leave you. I love you, you must believe that?"

"I don't believe a word you say."

Larry recognised from the wild look in her eyes, the terrified expression that made a stranger of her, that she wouldn't listen to him.

"I'll go. Of course I'll go if that's what you really want. But darling, I won't be far away. Please remember while you sit trying to unravel this mystery, that I am on your side, whatever happens. I love you. I'll come like the wind any time you need me. You don't even have to explain. I'll never doubt you again. If you say you heard tapping, I believe you. Stranger things than that have happened. And I've shared them with you. Do you want to tell me about the tapping?"

The realisation he was humouring her, that he was pretending to believe her to persuade her to talk to him, was the very end.

"Get out. I'll put the rest of your things outside the front door for you to collect. I want you out of here."

"Like this?" He attempted a smile as he gestured towards the towel he was wearing, fastened around his waist.

"Just get dressed, and leave," she said more calmly.

The house seemed unnaturally silent after he had gone. She turned on all the lights and walked from room to room, convincing herself that the atmosphere of menace that had

Search For a Shadow

been present in the very air she breathed was gone. Larry's departure had ended the haunting of her home. It was hers again. Once she had put out all his things, the final vestige of a minatory presence would dissolve with the last of the darkness.

As she had once before, she pulled the covers from the bed and bundled them into a black plastic sack. She might not throw them away, as she had after the intruder had lain on her bed, but she would wash and wash them to get out the last lingering hint of his very existence. She struggled and managed to turn the heavy mattress over. Larry was gone and would never return.

To her surprise, when she pulled back the curtain, it was daylight. She stared at the clock in disbelief. It was past nine o'clock. She was late for work!

She washed, then looked in the wardrobe for something to wear and stared at the two sides of the hanging space. On the right were the clothes she had bought since she had known Larry; bright, fashionable, out-going styles. On the left, were the remnants of her old self: the browns and beiges, the sensible shoes and practical suits. Was she a split personality, being someone for Larry and someone completely different for the rest of the world?

Almost reluctantly, considering it another episode in the ending of her relationship with Larry, she chose from the left. A mid-brown skirt with a cream shirt-blouse over which she put on a dark, long-line cardigan with large pockets. Looking at herself, she saw a dowdy, shapeless young woman, who would continue to look the same until her hair changed to grey and she became old and shrivelled. With a defiance that almost brought a smile, she brushed her hair and piled it into a bunch. Around it she plaited a coloured scarf in greens with touches of yellows and reds. "'Dead, but you won't lie down'," she told her reflection, with a wry grin.

She felt almost light-hearted as she left for work. She glanced back at the house and thought that now she had at last faced up to the obvious, admitted to herself that she had been deluding herself, that Larry was indeed the instigator of all the troubles, the house was no longer frightening. She picked up the key that Larry had ostentatiously handed to her as he left, and tucked it into her handbag. This evening, she would put it back in the shed, where she had always kept it. The danger was faced, dealt with, and could now be put behind her.

Megan was delighted to hear her news.

"Thank goodness you've come to your senses at last!" She hugged Rosemary. "What say we go out at lunch-time and celebrate?"

"Better still, come home with me this evening and we'll eat too much and drink too much and forget Larry ever existed."

"Still nervous, aren't you, for all your new bravado? Not that I blame you. It'll take time for you to realise that it's all over, that the house is yours again."

"I'm not nervous," Rosemary smiled happily. "I felt a return of sanity the moment the door closed behind him. Honestly! All right! To show you I'm no longer nervous, let's leave it for tonight, and you come tomorrow night. There, are you convinced?"

"Convinced! But, is this why you've changed your image? To show how easily he's being forgotten?" Megan touched the long skirt and turned her head quizzically.

"I don't know." Rosemary frowned. "I only know I don't want to do or be anything that's remotely reminiscent of Larry Madison-Jones – or whoever he really is. I've had a lucky escape. I don't know where it would have ended if I hadn't come to my senses."

Despite her brave words, she was apprehensive as she undressed for bed that night. Larry's belongings had disappeared from the front step so she presumed he had called to collect them before she came home from work. Several times she thought she heard the Citroën and her heart began to race, but each time it was only her imagination. She slept without incident until the alarm warned her that it was time to rise.

On the following evening, Megan – and Sally, who had coaxed an invitation from her – came home to the cottage. By majority vote they went to the local public house to eat. There were several people from the village there, including Muriel and Henry, and they spent the evening chattering and laughing with them. Rosemary relaxed and glowed with the return of her sense of "belonging" that had vanished after her holiday earlier in the year.

"It's as if I've been away since early June," Rosemary explained when Sally commented on her high spirits. "I didn't realise how much I've missed them. Gethyn and I used to come over here often before June, we'd sit in the garden or the bar and have a drink. We never stayed long though, he was always so fearful of his mother needing something and not be able to ask him."

"How is he coping on his own?" Sally asked. "Has he heard anything more about his house?"

"I'm ashamed to tell you I don't know. Of all the friends I've neglected, Gethyn is the one about which I'm most ashamed."

Later, they sat idly watching the late-night film and Sally picked up the newspaper in which Rosemary had been attempting to complete the crossword. She noticed the series of crosses and circles and asked about them.

"What's this, morse code?" she asked.

"Morse code? I didn't think of that!" Rosemary explained that was how she had written down the tapping she had heard on the night when she hadn't gone to bed. Although doubtful, she reached for a dictionary and found the translation of short and long taps. Sally read the numbers and gradually they began to translate.

"Four dots, that's 'H'. One dot, that's 'E'. Two dashes, that's 'M'. Two dots and one dash, that's 'U'."

"It's nonsense," Rosemary protested. "What can HEMU mean?" But Megan continued, and under their startled gaze, the letters revealed the short sentence, HE MUST GO.

Rosemary threw the paper from them and watched as it curled up and disintegrated in the flames of the fire.

"Who's doing it?" she cried.

"Boy Scouts, practising for their badges," Sally joked. "Forget it."

It was a long time before any of them slept. In their separate beds they lay listening, half expecting something to happen, becoming wider awake rather than more sleepy as imagination took them in its grip. But the night passed without incident.

The following Saturday, Rosemary called in at number three. Gethyn was there, sitting beside Mrs Priestley.

"What's this, another party?" she asked.

"There's a bit of bother we thought you might like to know about, love," Muriel said, handing her a drink. "Sit down by there, next to Gethyn while Henry gets out the papers and then we'll tell you all about it."

Search For a Shadow

Henry shuffled his large frame into a captain's chair near the window and began.

"By accident I found out. I was talking to Trevor Trew who works in planning and he told me what was happening, gabbling on about it as if it were general knowledge! I was crafty mind, didn't let on I was ignorant in case he stopped 'gabbling on' and I'd have missed something."

"About what?" Rosemary asked, her mouth suddenly dry. She felt anxious. All her memories of the recent troubles flooded back to haunt her. Was this going to be a return of them? Or an explanation? She wondered which would be worse.

"Come on, Henry, stop keeping the girl guessing," Muriel said giving him a shove. "Tell 'em quick now, or I will!"

"A group of local businessmen is hoping to buy all five cottages and turn them into an hotel. There now, what d'you think of that?"

The news when it came caused the three guests to frown. But in Rosemary's case, the frown quickly faded as she began to wonder if the hotel scheme had been the reason for the attempt to drive her from her house. This question was promptly followed by the realisation that if it were true, it was the consortium planning the hotel behind what had been happening – and not Larry.

"Tell me more," she said and she tried to hide the relief that had lightened her heart.

"It seems that when they heard of your plan to sell, then learnt that Gethyn's house was only rented and with a tenancy no longer valid, they came up with the idea of buying the rest of us out and making the row into a small, exclusive hotel.

"There's a fair bit of land at the back, and the stream to add a bit of scenery at the front. It would be a good centre for country rambles, bird watching and botanists. But it's only a good proposition if they can get the whole bang lot of them cheap. I suspect," Henry went on in his deep slow voice, "they each planned to make a purchase as a private individual so we wouldn't catch on and demand a higher price."

"How far would they go to make sure we sold to them, Henry?" Rosemary asked and she saw from the sympathetic look from both Muriel and Henry that her thoughts about Larry's innocence were shared.

"I don't know who is involved, so I can't answer your question, but I'll be very surprised if there isn't some connection between the hopeful purchasers and the things that have been happening to you," Henry said with a thump on the table to emphasise his conviction.

"We think you ought to go back to the police, love," Muriel said.

"No." Rosemary shook her head. "It's enough to know the reason. It's not knowing why, that's kept me awake at nights. That and the fact I blamed Larry. No, I won't go back to the police."

"I think you should," Muriel insisted.

"I agree," said Mrs Priestley. "Best we get them businessmen off our backs. I don't want them to start pestering me."

"I'm sorry. I didn't think of that!" Rosemary said with a startled gasp. "Of course. If they want mine, they'll want yours too. Yes, I suppose I must."

"I won't move. Ever," Mrs Priestley went on. "I need to stay in case – well I suppose it's a foolish dream after thirty years, but I won't move no matter how good the offer, in case my son comes home."

"What about you, Henry?" Gethyn asked. He was very pale. Rosemary guessed that for him the news made it

Search For a Shadow

extremely unlikely that the tenancy would be transferred. It was the death of his hope to stay in the cottage that had been his only home.

"I don't want to let you all down," Henry said, "but we have been thinking about selling and moving to Bala. And this might mean a better offer than we'd otherwise have."

"We won't go yet though," Muriel said. "We'll delay as long as we can. Perhaps if they know that Mrs Priestley is definite about staying, and the Powells won't want to sell and have nowhere to come home to when they leave Australia, they might give up the idea and look elsewhere. And you, Rosemary. Will you be staying now you know the reason for the incidents?"

"I honestly don't know."

Her mind was less on what was being said than on places she could try to get in touch with Larry. The problem of someone buying up the cottages was far below the top of her list of priorities now she knew that Larry wasn't involved. There were still many things unexplained, but knowing she had been wrong about his causing the things that had frightened her was lifting her spirits like a runaway balloon.

"What do we do?" Gethyn asked. "I've sent a request for my tenancy to be confirmed but there's little chance they'll agree. You see, my house is owned by the same people who own the local pub. It's the same sort of business, leisure industry they call it, and they won't let go to please someone as unimportant as me, will they?"

Muriel suggested letters to the paper, and a bit of local stirring, believing that publicity of any kind would harm the prospects of the consortium succeeding.

"They'll only have to wait for me to die, they'd get my place then for sure," Mrs Priestley said with a wan smile. She stroked the cat and shook her head as the others began to protest. "No, I'm getting on in years and it would only take a push at the wrong time if they really wanted me out of the way. I'll be the stubborn one you see, renting and not having any money to make out of moving."

"A push at the wrong time! Don't start worrying about things like that, love," Muriel said. "They aren't murderers for heaven's sake! If they did plan a few shocks for Rosemary, it was only to get things started. They wouldn't have gone to any greater lengths that a few tricks."

"Perhaps." The old lady's eyes wandered briefly to Gethyn, and she said quietly, "But you won't get me wandering up on the mountain on my own for sure."

"Whatever did she mean by that?" Gethyn asked as he and Rosemary left. "She doesn't think Mam was attacked so someone could buy the house?"

"No of course she doesn't!" Rosemary spoke with a conviction she didn't feel. "She's afraid of dying before her son returns, that's all. Fear of a bad fall is always in the minds of the elderly. It's the biggest danger to their mobility and mobility is what they value most."

"Perhaps you're right." Gethyn didn't look convinced.

"I was intending to come and see you tomorrow morning," Rosemary said to change the subject. "I wondered if you'd like to come for lunch? Since I went on holiday we haven't had a good long talk."

"Is the American likely to be there?" he asked with an attempt at lightness.

"Larry has gone. It – didn't work out," she said.

"Gone for good? Not just gallivanting off somewhere?"

"Gone for good."

"Thank you, I'd love to come. About half-twelve?"

"I'll look forward to it."

But in fact she almost forgot it. She spent all evening

and most of the following morning trying to get in touch with Larry.

Gethyn arrived on the dot of 12.30. She was pleased to note that his clothes had improved. He worn a pair of jeans and a smart shirt and no tie. His shoes were comfortable trainers. He looked at her with open admiration in his dark eyes and he seemed more confident, more sure of himself. And, she surprised herself by thinking, far more attractive than she had realised.

"Gethyn, you look super," she smiled as she invited him in.

"So do you. But you always look beautiful, Rosemary."

She handed him a drink and he sat on the settee where he could watch her through the kitchen door as she put the finishing touches to their lunch. On the floor beside the settee was the telephone book and a paper on which she had been scribbling lists of phone numbers then crossing them off.

"Been trying to find someone?" he asked casually.

"Yes, as a matter of fact, I have."

"The American?" She nodded.

"Yes. Larry. His name's Larry."

"Then don't! Rosemary, it's really best that you don't."

"I have to, I owe him an apology."

"Then don't say I didn't warn you."

He stood up and was watching her with a slight frown on his face, his handsome face, she realised with a start of surprise. Gethyn was really rather handsome and in this new, more positive mood, perhaps more than just the boy next door.

Chapter Fifteen

Rosemary spent most of her spare time during the following weeks trying to locate Larry. She tried the numbers he had given her at various times, over and over again in case he had made contact. She asked everyone she could think of if they had seen the red and white Citroën.

she also spent some time with Gethyn in spite of her fears that he would misunderstand and read more into her visits that she intended. The night when she had heard that frightening tap-tapping, she had seriously considered the idea of the mysterious visitor being the ghost of Gethyn's mother. That crazy explanation for the visitation vanished as the dawn pushed the darkness aside, but there remained the guilty feeling that she had ignored Gethyn in his grieving. She had let him down.

When she had time to sit and have a conversation with him, she encouraged him to talk about the sudden loss of his mother but he seemed reluctant to do so.

"Every time I think about it, I feel a wash of shame flood over me," he said one day when they were walking up on the mountain to look for likely places to gather her Christmas holly. "I know that 'if only' are the two most useless words in the English language, but I can't help repeating them. If only I hadn't argued with her that day. If only I hadn't allowed the disagreement to continue. And worst of all, if only I hadn't gone to town and stayed out for such a long

Search For a Shadow

time. I'd never left her for so long before. Not since I was a child. She was over seventy. I should have been more caring."

"What was the quarrel about, Gethyn?" she asked. She had asked before but he had always been evasive. It was no different now.

"Nothing. That's the terrible part. It was over nothing at all."

"But there must have been something? You never lost your temper and certainly not with your mam. Can't you remember what it was that she said to upset you? I'm sure it would help to ease your mind if you could."

He frowned and shook his head. His eyes looked into hers and the frown softened and became a smile.

"Let's forget it, shall we?"

"I want you to forget it, Gethyn, but I don't think you will, not until you've talked it out of your system."

"I can't."

"But you can remember what the quarrel was about, can't you?" she coaxed. But he wouldn't be drawn.

"Nothing," he repeated. "Nothing at all." She could see by the strained expression on his dark face that he did remember and the memory was eating him up.

Gethyn's house was still in a mess. When she went to see him, he showed her into the tiny room at the front of the house. This room was reasonably comfortable and obviously well-used. She sat near the iron fireplace in which a fire burned. Gethyn sat near the window and she could see from the squashed cushions in the old wooden armchair that he spent a lot of his time there.

One day, while he was fetching her the fresh mint she had asked for and which grew in profusion in his garden, she sat down in the well-used chair and looked out. Allowing for Gethyn's extra height, she could see the chair gave a clear view of the wooden footbridge and the car-parking space in front of the cottages to the right of him. To the left the path went to the foot of the steps leading up to the road and the road bridge. The parapet of the bridge was low enough to see the top half of people walking across. There wouldn't be much going on at the five cottages that he didn't know about.

She remembered with an ache how Larry had called Gethyn "the queer fellow" and remarked on how often he was at the window, looking out. How strange that he hadn't seen at least something of her mysterious visitors. But most of the occurrences had been at night, and even Gethyn had to leave the window and sleep, she told herself with a chuckle.

The Hughes's seemed to bring everyone in the cottages closer together now they were home again. Rosemary hadn't realised how much they had been missed. They were often waiting for her when she arrived home from work; they would be silhouetted against the light spilling out of their door, a cup of tea freshly made on their kitchen table. Rosemary rarely said no. Their genuine welcome was balm to her in her loneliness.

She had refused overtures from her friends to revive their once regular meetings. Apart from the occasional visit to the aerobics club with Sally she met socially with no one. She visited her parents once or twice to eat up the long, lonely weekends. But each day was heavy with waiting and hoping. Weeks had passed without a word from Larry. It was as if he hadn't existed, apart from in her heart.

"Perhaps he's gone back to America," Muriel suggested one evening, and Rosemary could only shrug.

How could she know? She would probably never know. The world, instead of becoming smaller, seemed now to have to increased in size and emptiness.

* * *

Search For a Shadow

One evening when she answered the invitation shouted across the bridge – this time by Henry – she found Gethyn there. He stood up and smiled a welcome that warmed her. Large, comfortably familiar and dressed in warm sweater and corduroy trousers, his feet were without shoes, the cuffs of his trousers steaming in the heat of the fire.

"I've been pulling firewood out of the stream," he explained. "Pushed down by the winds of last week and beginning to block the passage of the water. Handy for winter fires, so I was doing myself a favour as well as clearing the stream."

"Frozen stiff he was, I had to rescue him and make him a cup of tea," Muriel laughed. "Soaked he was too. Fifteen inch wellingtons and sixteen inches of water would you believe!"

"Thinking of firewood, Gethyn," Henry said, as his wife poured tea for Rosemary, "what about this fireworks party you mentioned. Done any more about it, have you?"

"I don't think I'll bother after all," Gethyn said. "Huw and Richard and the others are going to one of their friends, Mrs Priestley is frightened for her cat and, I don't really feel ready for a party. I thought I'd give the fireworks to someone in the village. Someone with children. Who d'you think would like them?"

"Are you sure, love?" Muriel asked. "We'll all join in if you want to have a bonfire. We'd scrape up a few more from the village for sure."

"No, it was a mistake, I'd rather give them to some children."

They discussed who would be the recipients and Gethyn said he would take them the following day.

"There's only a few, hardly worth making a fuss about," Gethyn said deprecatingly.

After he'd gone, Henry said, "Typical of him to make light of his gift. Huw said he bought boxes of them."

"Such a shame he's so reserved," Muriel sighed. "There's so much kindness and love in the man but he hasn't anyone to share it with." She nodded towards the teapot. "More tea, love?"

"Where have you been? You look frozen!" Gethyn asked one morning when Rosemary had returned after a walk up on the mountain.

"I couldn't sleep, so I went for a walk."

"Not still worrying about the American, are you?"

"I wish he'd write or phone. It's crazy for us to part in anger without time for explanations. It was all my fault," she said, as she unlocked her door and invited him inside.

"Nonsense," he said. "If he really loved you, nothing would have separated you one from the other."

"I accused him of flooding the house, of trying to frighten me away from my home, abusing my hospitality and using me, pretending to love me simply to use me." She fought back precipitant tears that seemed, these days, to be always there.

"What's happened to make you believe you were wrong?" Gethyn asked with a hint of sarcasm. He went into the kitchen and put on a kettle for tea. "Shall I make us some toast?" he asked, when there was no immediate reply. "You look as if you could do with something to warm you up."

"Gethyn, I know you never liked Larry, but he wasn't responsible for what went on here. I know that now and I regret my stupidity in allowing myself to think he was. I'd give anything to talk to him, beg him to forgive me. I think he'd understand how fear had twisted my common sense into what was almost hysteria."

Search For a Shadow

"I asked what had changed your mind."

"It's obvious, isn't it? Someone has been trying to get us out of here so a business consortium can buy the houses and change them into the hotel they want. The cottages are in such a beautiful position. It's a perfect place for holiday accommodation." She sighed deeply and took the tea Gethyn offered. "And I thought Larry was doing it. What motive could he have had? I was so stupid!"

"I know you won't like my saying this, but can you really believe that professional men would stoop to such depths simply to persuade you to sell?"

"You hear about such things."

"Perhaps, in London or New York. But here? In our small village?"

"I've heard of people being frightened out of their homes," she insisted.

"I've heard of two-headed ducks but I've never seen one!" He was rewarded with a smile and he turned back to the toaster which was about to toss its brown offering up into his hand.

They crunched on the toast and sipped the tea companionably while Gethyn quietly tried to convince her that Larry was an enigma.

"He's what Mam would have called a dark horse."

"Gethyn!" She laughed. "Now you're being melodramatic! What did Larry gain? Nothing!"

"But there must have been some reason behind his coming here and behaving as he did towards you? Perhaps you sending him away when you did saved you from further disasters."

"Nonsense." She swallowed the last of the toast. "If you can't talk sense, then feed me. Can I have some more toast?"

* * *

In the weeks after Larry's departure, Rosemary and Gethyn spent more and more time together. They took to walking at weekends, occasionally taking a small rucksack of food and drink and spending a day in the mountains. It was usually in their own area where the car was not necessary, but once, Gethyn asked to go to Aberangell.

Although her emotions railed against visiting a place where she had Larry had been so happy, she defied her instincts and they went.

Then there was the heart-stopping moment when they saw a Citroen Dolly, and it was all revived. She ached with longing for him and was tormented by the belief that she had misjudged him, and her dismay at the final ending of a wonderful affair.

"It's not him. It can't be," she whispered. Gethyn smiled at her but didn't comment.

"There must be more than one red Citroën," she whispered.

He touched her arm, and gently pulled her away from the side of the road where she had been standing looking at the car that had driven past them.

She realised with a mild surprise that it was the first time since they were children that Gethyn had touched her. In all their meetings he had never once even held her hand. Suddenly she wanted him to.

She put a hand through his arm and said brightly, "Come on, we'll find a pub and have a drink." His hand closed over hers and as they approached the village through which their walk would take them, his hand was warm and comfortingly familiar.

All through the half-hour they sat in the cosy bar, his eyes continually darted to catch her gaze. Perhaps to convince himself she was really there and with him. She smiled and began to realise that he was very dear to her. A warm feeling that was nothing to do with the blazing fire in the corner, overwhelmed her like a baptism of love.

"Rosemary," he said thickly. "I've so enjoyed getting to know you again. You were drifting away from me. Are you back now?"

Warning bells clanged ominously in her ears. She knew that if she didn't speak now he would be convinced that she was begining to fall in love with him. She looked at his eyes, regarding her, a question clear in their depths.

"Gethyn," she said lightly. "I've never been away. You and I are friends, aren't we? We'll always be friends."

"You're more than that to me," he said. "Something better than friends."

"We have an affinity based on years of companionship, Gethyn. What better relationship is there than good loyal friends?" To soften her words, she put her hand over his as it lay on the table beside her. "I value your being there for me whenever I need someone, more than anything."

She saw the nervous glance he flickered between her face and the check table cloth spread in front of them and wondered if she had been strong enough in her denial of love. His face was relaxed and half smiling. She hoped he had accepted what she had told him in the way she had intended.

There was no change in his mood after their stop and their conversation. She was still happy to have his company as a bridge between her loss of Larry and a return to her previous life. For him, she imagined she filled a gap left by his care of his mother. She was someone to look after, even though at some distance.

That he had been encouraged by her words did not occur to her until she found a huge basket arrangement of flowers waiting at her door on returning from work on the following day. When she saw them, in the light of the torch that was necessary now to guide her from the car park across the footbridge and to her door, she almost shouted with delight.

"Larry!" she whispered aloud. She trembled as she pushed her key into the lock and held her breath as she switched on the light and opened the tiny envelope that held the message. Then her heart plunged like a dying bird. The card was from Gethyn, thanking her for a wonderful day.

She closed the door, conscious of the fact that he was probably sitting in his chair by the window watching for her, expecting a response, but she was unable to even thank him. Anger was highest in her emotions, not pleasure or even polite appreciation. She was angry with him for boosting her hopes. It was Larry whom she wanted. It was Larry whom she loved.

There were letters on the floor and she picked them up, her lips tight, not even glancing at them, scrunching them in her hands as if they too were an irritation.

It was when she had washed up the few dishes and settled to watch television that she remembered her post. Amid an assortment of junk-mail was an air mail letter. With trembling hands she turned it over to read the addressee. It was the girl in New York, Barbara, who was also a friend of Larry.

It was brief, Barbara's large bold handwriting covering the flimsy sheet with only a few lines. She would be in London in a few days' time. Would Rosemary meet her? it asked. There was a phone number and although it was late, she dialled the number, which was an hotel, and was told that Miss Barbara Tate was booked in for three days' time. She left a message to say she would meet her at the hotel, on Saturday at two o'clock.

She went in then to thank Gethyn for his flowers and when she had told him how much she had loved them, hoping he wouldn't come in and see them thrown casually across the kitchen table, she asked, "Gethyn, will you keep a special eye on the house at the weekend? I'm not so worried, now the mischief seems to have stopped, but I'd be happier if I knew you were watching it for me."

"Of course. Going to visit your parents, are you?"

"No, in fact I'm off to London."

"Larry!" he expostulated. She shook her head.

"No, just a friend, another American, as it happens, but a woman this time. Her name is Barbara Tate and I met her on my holiday back in June."

He seemed slightly mollified by her explanation and again she felt the resurgence of guilt for not being more honest with him about her feelings. She was leading him on, unintentionally, but never the less unkindly. But how could she state baldly that she could never love him? That she was still in love with Larry?

"Thanks, Gethyn." She didn't step further inside than the small hallway although he stepped back and eagerly invited her to do so. She was determined that at least she could start being less friendly, stop popping in so frequently, stop treating him like more than a kind neighbour, using him to fill the emptiness.

"Won't you come in?" he asked with a frown of disappointment.

"It's late, I have to write a letter and—"

"All right," he laughed, "I know when I'm getting the brush-off. See you tomorrow, sleep well, my love."

The words "my love" startled her. They took her by surprise and without realising it, she touched her hand to her lips and blew a kiss. It was something she did often, and to the slightest of acquaintances, but the thought that for Gethyn it might be misconstrued, clutched her heart with dismay. Then she snorted with exasperation at herself.

Really! She was getting paranoid! Gethyn probably felt the same for her as she felt for him and nothing more!

She left the car in Aberystwyth and caught the Euston train with a less than excited feeling of anticipation for the few days ahead. To her it wasn't an unexpected holiday but another pilgrimage to places seen and enjoyed with Larry. Everywhere she and Barbara might go she would be shadowed by memories of her previous visit, with the image of Larry, laughing beside her.

The hotel was not the grand one to which Larry had taken her, but a small guest house in Chiswick. She alighted at Turnham Green underground station and looked around her. She wasn't expecting to be met, but she waited until everyone had left the platform, then made her way outside. Opposite was a park and she stood for a moment watching as children exercised a playful puppy. She was in no hurry to meet Barbara and have to listen to questions about Larry.

How foolish she had been to come. How foolish she'd feel admitting that having lived together for months she didn't even know where he was! The map in her hand marking the position of the hotel, fluttered in the cold wind, a reminder of the moment they had first met. She pulled up the collar of her fluffy-lined jacket and headed for the main road.

A glance at her watch told her she had plenty of time, and she dawdled, relishing the evocative aroma of Greek bread and other assorted ethnic foods that were floating on the crisp cold air from the wonderful assortment of shops.

The hotel was in a quiet road and she went into its enveloping warmth gratefully. There was a sign pointing to a lounge and when she opened the door and looked in, she looked first at the two women sitting beside a table, drinks in front of them. Neither of them looked like Barbara and she began to retreat, wondering if in fact she would recognise her friend again.

"Rose Mary," a voice called and she looked into the corner as Larry stood up and smiled at her.

"Larry!" The room spun and she stared at him. She stood like a statue, her face frozen with shock, as he walked over to her and took her arm. "Larry," she said again, like an idiot.

"Darling, forgive me," he said.

Then she was in his arms, arms so familiar it was like putting on a perfectly fitting garment to warm her from an icy coldness of which she had hardly been aware.

"I heard from Barbara and she allowed me to cheat on you and meet you this way. Darling, I was so afraid you wouldn't come if you knew I'd be here."

"I've been searching for you," she whispered. "I've pestered all the hotels I could think of and all the places where you'd once stayed. I couldn't find you. I thought you'd gone home."

He held her tighter and kissed her hair.

"This, my love, is home."

"Then why—?"

"Have you booked a room?" he asked.

"No, I wasn't sure if Barbara would be staying here more than the one night."

"Wait there, don't move." He kissed her gently, as if she were something fragile and likely to break, then went to change his room for a double. "My wife has joined me," she heard him explain.

They made love with an intensity that left them breathless.

Explanations were spasmodic and hardly relevant. Each knew the other regretted the separation, and neither cared much for wasting time listening to apologies or illumination.

"Where is Barbara?" Rosemary managed to ask later that evening when they had managed to separate far enough apart to eat supper.

"At the theatre this evening, then tomorrow she heads north for some conference or other. You aren't sorry not to meet up with her, are you?"

"I can bear it," she smiled.

It was as she was repacking her suitcase for leaving that she asked, "Larry, what now?"

"I'm sorry?" he asked.

"I'm going back to Wales, where are you going?"

"This isn't the brush-off is it for heaven's sake? I'm going with you of course!"

"I was afraid we'd – that you—"

"Rosemary," he began, running his hands through his hair in that familiar gesture, "Barbara is a sort of cousin. There's no one else in my life, if that's what's on your mind." It wasn't, but it would do for now. The least said was, at this moment, by far the better. Words could be damaging.

"Is there anyone in your life?" Larry asked. "I mean, what about the queer fellow, you haven't been consorting with him behind my back I hope?" He surprised a slight blush on her cheeks and added, "I'll kill him if you have."

"I've seen rather more of him since you left, but he knows it's you I love. I've never made a secret of the fact." She surreptitiously crossed her fingers and hoped that it was true.

Chapter Sixteen

When they reached Rosemary's cottage, Larry, as always, went first to the kitchen to fill the percolator. Rosemary rang Megan.

"It's me, Rosemary. Oh, Megan, he's back!"

"I know, and it's wonderful! I knew from Gethyn and Huw, they saw him in town."

Rosemary hardly registered the words. She went on, "Larry and I met at the place I expected to meet Barbara and, oh, it's fantastic! Everything has been sorted out and, well, he's back. I'll tell you about it tomorrow."

Megan told her that Sally had visited Mrs Priestley and spoken to the students, and added a few items of news but apart from that, she only managed to make the few necessary responses to the news, given little chance to do more than gasp and repeat how pleased she was. She knew she would have "chapter and verse" on the following day, and laughed excitedly at Rosemary's obvious delight.

"I'll see you tomorrow morning," she said. "And Rosemary, I'm so pleased that everything has been settled between you."

Rosemary replaced the phone feeling guilty of deception. Larry was back and she was happy about that, but she had lied by pretending everything was sorted. She pushed aside the slight misapprehension and smiled as Larry came downstairs ready to leave.

"Come on honey," he said impatiently, "I'm starved."

"Pity it's so late," Larry said as they were walking back from the restaurant. "I'd like to invite Henry and Muriel in for a drink. Huw and the others too. D'you think they'd come?"

They walked past Gethyn's door and as they reached their own, their feet crunched over something. Larry struggled to take out the torch, then shone it at their feet. The ground was littered with broken glass. He swung the beam of light across the path, then towards the house. They both gasped with shock as the thin beam revealed that the front windows had been broken in.

Before they could do anything else but gasp, shapes moved out of the shadows. Henry and Muriel had obviously been waiting for them to return and Muriel ran to hug Rosemary. A tall figure revealed itself as a police constable. From number five, Huw and Richard came, walking along the path, each carrying a torch so the scene was like some bizarre *son et luminaire*, with lights, sounds, but with the actors invisible. A shadow edged from the doorway of number one, and Gethyn said, with a nod at Larry, "I see you're back then!"

They had all been sheltering against the frosty evening in doorways, waiting to comfort them, but to Rosemary there was something ominous in the way they had remained hidden until they had found for themselves the damage done by some mysterious attacker. The police must have instructed them to wait out of sight, hoping they would give something away in the manner in which they reacted to the damage.

Larry was once more the prime suspect.

They went inside, with the neighbours hovering near, and the policeman asked Rosemary to check in case anything was missing.

"We don't think anyone entered, mind, we think it was some youngsters on a bit of a prank," the constable said, but Rosemary saw the slight glance he gave Larry and knew that some mischievous children were not what he really suspected.

"Been together have you?" he asked.

"All evening," Rosemary said in a whisper as she stared at the glass-covered carpet, the rocks lying on the floor where they had landed after being lobbed through the glass, and the curtains, torn and ruined.

"All the time?" the constable asked. "You didn't separate?"

"All the time!" Larry snapped. "Now, can we get started on clearing up this mess?"

"You didn't lose sight of each other for an instant?" the uniformed oficer persisted.

"I went for a pee! Rosemary didn't go with me!" Larry almost shouted. "Now, can't you see how distressed Rosemary is? Just go catch this sonofabitch will you?"

"We'll do everything we can, sir."

Muriel and Rosemary made tea in the stupid way people do, mainly for something to occupy themselves. Henry, Larry and Richard made a temporary boarding for the windows, both the front room and the bedroom windows were smashed, and they gathered up the broken glass fragments and put them into a bucket supplied by Gethyn.

"Other police have been and they've investigated and said they'll be back to help board the windows temporarily if we need them, but I said we'd manage," Henry explained to Larry, while Rosemary was comforted by Muriel.

"Investigated? You really think they'll find who's doing this?"

"I don't know. It might be as they said, some boys fooling

about and going too far. Boys do," he smiled, "I know, I was one myself, once, a long time ago."

"Shoot straight, Henry, what d'you really think happened here? What's going on? Why is someone picking on Rosemary?"

"Rosemary, or you," Henry said quietly. "Is there something you ought to tell us, boy?"

"How's that?" Larry frowned, staring at the face of Henry, which was now uncharacteristically serious.

"Isn't there something that you're keeping back from us, something that might explain all these incidents?"

"I just wish I knew." Larry spread his hands in exasperation, then ran them through his hair. Henry frowned and stared at him, trying to will him to add something more, but Larry said, "Well, I guess that's all we can do for tonight. Gee that certainly sobered me up. I think a cup of coffee is in order."

They slept uneasily, both waking at intervals, wondering with differing thoughts, who it was causing them so much trouble. It was as the alarm began its jarring demand that Rosemary remembered Megan's remark that she knew Larry was back. He'd been seen by Huw and Gethyn. And she remembered also, the few minutes when Larry had vanished, purporting to have visited the men's room. He'd been gone a long time. Long enough to smash a few windows?

She began to shake. There were so many uncertainties, had she been stupid to allow him back into her house, her bed? If only she dared to face him with it all, but the fear of losing him was stronger than her conviction he was guilty of anything serious. No, somehow, Larry was the catalyst, not the instigator.

The morning's post brought a letter with the postmark

Search For a Shadow

Birmingham. Rosemary recognised the writing. It was from Barbara. It was long and full of chatter but one page set the see-saw of her emotions and fears plummetting once again.

"Sorry we couldn't meet," it said, "But Larry explained about you not being able to spare the time from your conference after all. What an unfortunate coincidence that it fell on the very weekend I was in London. Better luck next time, O.K.?"

More chatter, then in a postscript it went on to say:

"I hope Larry owned up to the joke about the parcel and the letter he had me send you from New York. He never did explain it!"

It was raining steadily and with the intention of continuing all day. The wind was touching the trees and making them dance. Rosemary left for work, running across the footbridge over the gurgling water that was already swelling with the downpour. Larry promised to arrange for the glaziers to fit new glass.

"I'll buy paint and in a few days you'll never notice the damage," he promised, kissing her through the car window as he saw her off. The rain had soaked him on the short run to the car and his face felt cold.

"What about transport?" she asked. "Don't you want a lift?"

"It's all right, Henry is going to take me to where I left the Citroën," he said. She was afraid to ask where it was, she didn't want any more lies, there were enough to deal with already.

Megan was quiet over lunch as Rosemary told her all that had happened.

"Why didn't he want you to meet Barbara?" she asked. "It's obvious he made certain you'd miss each other."

For an answer, Rosemary showed her the letter she had received and which she hadn't shown Larry.

"Then you still think Larry is behind all this?"

"He can't be! – Can he?"

"Sorry to say it, love, but there's only one way to find out. You'll have to ask him."

"But he'll be so hurt that I can even for a moment believe he's responsible!" Sally who had been invited to listen, blew an unladylike snort of irritation.

"I can't understand people like you, Rosemary! You sound like one of those gullible victims, heroines in a corny, badly written romantic novel! If your relationship is that insecure, then isn't it best you finish it anyway? How long will it last if you are constantly under the threat of some secret being revealed? Come on, Rosemary! You aren't that stupid for heaven's sake!"

"It isn't that easy. Something deep inside me believes him. I'm not deluding myself, I really think he's innocent. I know there have been untruths. But I have to trust him and believe that once whatever it is has been resolved, he'll explain."

"Face him with your suspicions! He was here when he told you he was in America!" Sally had difficulty controlling her irritation. "He deliberately prevented you from meeting his cousin! Huw and Richard saw him around here when he was supposed to be elsewhere! What more d'you want?"

"I want to believe him," Rosemary said quietly.

The night was black with no moon and the wind was rising, shaking the trees and touching the water into ridges in the

Search For a Shadow

light of her torch. She imagined people standing in the shadows, threatening figures, about to lean out and stop her in her path, prevent her from reaching the cottage. But, she didn't want to reach it. Hollow-eyed and malevolent, storm-lashed and alien, it wasn't her home any more. What would be waiting for her there? Since Larry had come back, the fears and wild imaginings had also returned to haunt her.

She ran across the bridge as if pursued by demons and knocked on Henry and Muriel's door. There was no reply. Hastened now by her own invented terrors, she ran to number one. Gethyn was in, she knew he was in. There was music playing inside. She banged on the door, called his name but the only response was for the music to increase in volume. He didn't want to speak to her.

A branch groaned, creaked and fell. It skittered across the grass to the swirling waters to be swept away. She wanted to run, and not even pause to get into the car, her feet were all she could rely on, but she gripped her hands tightly around the torch, and gritted her teeth with determination. She wouldn't be driven from her home. She would go, but only when she chose, not when someone else wanted her to leave.

Shaking with the anticipation of some further horror waiting for her behind her door, she thrust the key into the lock and pushed the door wide while keeping her feet on the outer step. Remembering how a hand had once closed over hers when she had reached for the light-switch, she hit the wall time and again with the torch until it finally touched the switch and flooded the hall with a bright light.

Closing the door behind her she leaned against it and listened. The wind had lessened with the barrier of the door closing, the music from Gethyn's house had stopped. While the wind moaned a low accompaniment to the pattering rain outside, within the house there was a silence that seemed like a held breath. Slowly, she went into the living room.

It looked ordinary. The fire was set ready to light, the window had been replaced, and the curtains were neatly sewn so the tear damage hardly showed.

The room was very cold, any residual warmth had been lost through the broken windows, but she didn't attempt to light the fire. The background heating was hardly enough to take the chill off the air, but she sat, still in her outdoor clothes and waited for Larry to appear.

She couldn't go on like this. She had been acting like a simple, lovesick schoolgirl refusing to face facts. From the moment they had met, in London at that hotel, Larry had been evasive and dishonest. Now, sitting in her inimical front room she faced the facts. She had been so afraid of facing life without him she had ignored things she would never have tolerated in normal circumstances. Love is blind indeed! She had deliberately closed her eyes against reality!

She didn't hear the car. The sound of the wind was rising and beginning to lash against the walls. When she heard the key in the door she didn't even look up. Larry found her sitting with her shopping at her feet, looking utterly weary.

"Baby, what is it? You look pooped. What d'you think?" He waved at the repaired curtains and the pane of glass through which the shadows of trees were waving in the wind could be seen. He picked up her shopping, and taking her arm, led her into the living room.

"Larry. I want you to tell me why you're here. I want to know everything."

He stared at her for a moment, then said, "All right, I guess I owe you that, but I'd hoped—" He broke off and said lightly, "But first, a coffee I think."

Search For a Shadow

He pushed the matches into Rosemary's hand and gestured towards the fire as he went past her to the kitchen. She still didn't move. He was whistling as he busied himself with the percolator and cups. When he brought in a tray containing two coffees and some biscuits, she was exactly as he had left her, staring into space, the matches balanced on her hand as if she were unaware of them being placed there. He put the tray down beside her and lit the fire, piling on logs and pieces of coal as it grew in strength. It roared almost immediately as the wind whipped the air from the chimney and he concentrated on it until it blazed satisfactorily.

"Now," he said. "Where do I start?"

"What are you doing here?" Her voice was flat, as if she were half asleep. "Why did you make my acquaintance in London?"

"I am looking for a member of my family," he began. "We lost sight of him years ago and I think someone is trying to stop me finding him."

"Why the mystery?"

"Because the disappearance was such that if someone knew I was searching, I'd get the fast shuffle and they'd cover their traces so fast the paint wouldn't be dry! I thought that if I stayed here, incognito, near where it happened, I stood a better than evens chance of learning something." He took her hand and made her look at him. His eyes were steady and full of sincerity as he said loudly and firmly, "But, my darling Rosemary, the reason I'm here, now, with you, is because I grew to love you. At first sight I thought you were rather cute, sorta British and stilted and reserved, but cute. But I soon discovered a wonderful person whom I can never let go. Believe it," he pleaded.

"Then all this isn't anything to do with the plans to built an hotel?" she asked, ignoring his declaration. At that moment it seemed frivolous and artificial and she was embarrassed rather than flattered by his words.

"An attempt to drive you all out and change the cottages into an hotel? I doubt it. I think the events here are aimed at me, an attempt to get me blamed and sent away with a flea in my ear."

"Why did Richard's father hit you?"

"That's easy to answer and the joke's on me! I thought, for a while that he was someone who had some information, someone who could lead me to what happened. I was wrong, he got overly angry and swiped me good and hard so I wouldn't forget it!" Her hopes plunged further into the depths. That wasn't the truth either.

"When you said you were in America, when you sent the presents and the letter, you were here, weren't you?"

"Of course I was in America."

Another lie. Without a word she showed him Barbara's letter.

"Shit!" he said softly. "I don't believe this girl!" He handed it back to her and nodded. "I was still here, I didn't fly anywhere but my reason, my *only* reason, was to keep whoever was trying to get at me, away from you! I left, in the belief that they would leave you alone if I disappeared from the scene."

"How did they know you were back?" she asked, her voice still low and depressed.

"I guess I was kinda careless. I saw Huw watching the car and thought I'd given him the slip, I ducked and dived around the cafes and shops in Aberystwyth like a clockwork 007!" he joked, "but he saw me driving off. I kept my head low but he saw me all right."

"You think it might be Huw?" For the first time she appeared animated, the hope that he could end this by revealing who was responsible gave her hope.

Search For a Shadow

"I doubt it," he admitted. "It just that this is such a terrible place for 'running off at the mouth', everyone would have been told within a few hours, and I mean everyone!"

"You still haven't told me why you're here."

"And I don't intend to."

"Please."

"No way! It's no good, darling, I still have the uneasy feeling that this house has ears. As we sit here and talk, I can feel the words being whipped away to other ears but ours. Now isn't that stupid? You've gotten me believing in ghosts after all!" He smiled and pulled her to her feet. "C'mon, let's see what's to eat. I'm starved."

They unpacked the shopping but nothing she had bought seemed to tempt them.

"What say we leave it 'til later and I go for some fish and chips. Dammit, you're making me more British by the minute! My folks'll never believe all this! Imagining this is a haunted house, and now, going out to buy fish and chips!"

A few moments later, Henry knocked and asked whether he and Muriel could be included in the fish and chips order. When he went out, the door was slammed back against the wall as a sudden gust hit the row of cottages.

"Hell, I hope the windows hold! And don't forget to lock up!" he shouted as he hurried towards the car.

From the front window she watched as the torch wavered, occasionally showing his faint silhouette as he walked towards the footbridge. Then suddenly the beam of light seemed to rise in the air and falter, to suddenly snap off as he reached the middle of the bridge. For a moment she hesitated, thinking he had dropped it, and even when it didn't come back on, she thought it had fallen somewhere he couldn't reach.

She picked up her own torch that was in its usual place

near the front door and, grabbing a hooded coat, ran out to give it to him. Walking down from the road was dangerous. The rain was pelting down and a gust of wind made it necessary to hold on to the wall of number five as she made her way to the bridge. She waved the torch about, surprised at how high the water had risen after the day of rain. There was no sign of Larry. On the side of the bridge to the right, the trees were overgrown and formed a barrier that touched the side of the bridge like a wall. Hawthorn and elder, sycamore and hazel, their branches bare of leaves but still impenetrable at the level of her shoulders, were lit by the thin beam.

Then she pointed the torch downward where the branches were less thickly grown, down into the rushing water. There was a bundle. She frowned and stared, then almost abandoned the attempt to decide what it could be. People threw rubbish into the stream all the time, even though requested not to. Then she moved the light across it again and screamed. It was Larry.

He was face down in the water and any moment he would be released by the spurs of branches that held him, to be dragged down to where the stream joined the Dovey, a fast and dangerous, flooded river on its impatient way to the sea.

Chapter Seventeen

Rosemary didn't stop to think how she could achieve it, she just jumped down into the swirling water and hauled him to the bank. The banks were mercifully lower than further down, where the stream joined the large river. She found strength she couldn't have imagined possessing as she tugged at him and took the weight of him, exceptional with the addition of the water-sodden clothes, as he began to flow with the storm-water that almost reached the top of the banks.

He recovered sufficiently to crawl out, dazed and, once he was clear of the cleansing water, blood-spattered, from a cut on his temple. He sat up on the slippery bank in the pelting rain just clinging to her and catching his breath. His first words were, "Don't tell anyone about this, Rosemary. Not a soul."

"But Larry, why not? What happened?"

"Not a soul. Promise me. Someone pushed me with a swipe on the head for emphasis. I want whoever it was to look surprised to see me."

"Don't let's talk about what happened at the moment," she said, not believing him but recognising the need to humour him. He had simply fallen. The wind, that was still behaving like a hooligan on the loose, was probably the cause. The wind must have tossed a branch over the bridge. He just imagined there was someone wielding it.

"Go and get the stupid fish and chips, will you?" he said. "And get something for Henry, Muriel, and the queer fellow, it doesn't matter what. Bring it to me and by that time I'll be changed and ready to deliver it. Someone will be extra surprised and I want to see that surprise."

"Let me at least help you to the house?" She didn't try to argue with him, although she couldn't believe that the Hughes's and Gethyn could be in league against him. She put her arms around him. "Come on, it won't take a moment to get you inside, I'd be happier if I knew you were safe."

"No. I'll creep around the road and down the steps and try not to be seen. Hell, this is getting better than a James Bond movie," he joked, but there were no laughter creases on either of their faces.

She watched as he began to move away from her.

Taking a deep breath, she stopped dithering and decided to do as he asked. She turned away from the spot where he had been lost to her view and at which she had been staring, and fought her way through the storm to his car which he had parked near the road.

There was a sense of unreality as she stood in the queue in the steamy shop and waited for her order. Fish and chips, when Larry had just almost drowned? What was she thinking of, standing here as if nothing had happened? If he had been correct and someone had been waiting for him in the darkness, they were still there and would try again! Why had she left him? She must be going mad!

She stepped away from the counter as if to run. She was stupid, her brain wasn't functioning properly. She stood poised to run, unable to decide whether to believe Larry or not. If she did believe him then she shouldn't have left him.

"What would you like, *cariad*?" the smiling assistant

asked and she obediently abandoned her intention to flee and gave the order she had been chanting in her head like a child learning the times-tables.

With the paper-wrapped bundles on her arm she ran back to the car. The rain and wind were relentless and she felt the car roll as she negotiated a junction.

The cut on Larry's temple was a swollen, angry lump, but he seemed to have survived without serious harm. He had showered and dressed in a comfortable tracksuit and his newly washed hair was darker than usual and flattened to his head. She threw herself into his arms, wet as she was and he laughed.

"Goddammit, woman, I've spent the last half-hour drying myself and now you—" Her lips silenced his mock complaint.

"I want you to come with me and watch as I walk in. Check? We're looking for a surprised look, a disappointed look, or perhaps an angry look. I'll just get an anorak."

When Muriel opened the door and saw Rosemary's bedraggled state there was no opportunity to walk in and surprise the others. She shrieked with laughter and called the others to come and look.

"Orphan of the storm!" she shouted and the others came to look through the door and share the joke, their faces only shadows with the light from the living room behind them, their expressions hidden. If anyone hadn't expected him to return, they would have had time to recover from the surprise and disappointment by the time they were able to see their faces.

Larry showed himself, his hood pulled across to hide the bruise and Muriel laughed even louder.

"Thank goodness it isn't halloween! You two would have put the fear of God into me! What happened to you both? You didn't have to go and catch the fish, did you?"

They refused an invitation to go in, wet as they were, and the door closed on their laughter.

"That was a washout!" Larry snorted, back in the cottage, taking off the wet clothes and helping Rosemary out of hers.

"But there was only Gethyn and Henry and Muriel there. You can't think one of those—?"

"Who else knew I was going out and what time I was going?"

"I'm curious about Henry and Muriel knowing about the fish and chips we'd just decided to have," she said. "I know coincidences happen all the time but this, it's hard to accept as pure chance."

"My thoughts too, honey." He was thoughtful for a while. They undressed completely and put on night-clothes and settled before the fire. It was almost out, only a small area of redness was visible far back in its grey ash.

"The fire's gone next door," Rosemary laughed. "That's what my Gran used to say."

"Next door where the Hughes's live? I wonder if other things go next door too? Rosemary, I looked around that house when I broke in there that time, but meeting Huw discouraged me from a proper search."

"Huw," she mused, "he keeps popping up unexpectedly, doesn't he? And it was he who reported seeing your car in Aber, when you were supposed to have been in America."

"And he's studying electronics!"

"Could he be involved?" she wondered. "We don't know him, do we? Only as a temporary neighbour."

"Or what about the queer fellow?" he whispered. "Although I'd have difficulty in believing in him as a present day private eye!"

They both laughed, muffling their laughter guiltily. "What about the Hughes's?" he went on. "D'you think they could be involved in all this?" he asked.

Search For a Shadow

"All what, Larry?" she asked. "You haven't told me, remember?"

He moved close, holding her in his arms and spoke in a low whisper.

"After tonight I don't intend to. This maniac – whoever he is – has changed from hurling rocks at me and means business. He wants me out. Sorry, but I can't tell you why I'm here, not until I've sorted out what I want to know, what I came all this way to find out. Darling, tonight, someone tried to kill me. It's no use trying to wrap it up in softer words. He wants me dead. Whatever I'm seeking must be goddamned important to someone. And that someone seems able to read my thoughts, know exactly what I'm going to do next. Someone is behind it all and I sure as hell know it isn't you or me! So, what *do* we do next?"

"The police again?"

"I'd rather play this cool, pretend nothing happened tonight. You never know, it might unnerve who ever pushed me, make him careless and give us a clue. Seeing me about and uncomplaining, he might think he pushed the wrong man." His voice was barely audible, the breath of the words touching her ear and it added to the creepy sensation of being overheard.

"Do you remember anything about who pushed you?"

"Only the impression of someone large, but who wouldn't look large on a night like this, bundled up against the weather?"

Rosemary shivered and looked around her at the familiar room. It was no longer friendly. What was happening?

"Please, Larry, you must tell me! I can face anything if you'll let me into your life and allow me to face it with you. Please. I want to know. Whatever it is I want to know."

He looked at her then, as if he had made up his mind, he took a notebook from his pocket and wrote:

"I know this sounds melodramatic, but I think someone can hear everything we say. Tomorrow, we'll leave together, early, before it's really light, and I'll come back, hopefully without anyone seeing me and wait here, watch and listen. Perhaps, if the gods are with us, I'll discover something."

She stared at him, began to reply but was stopped by his finger on her mouth.

"Come on, let's go to bed."

"We haven't eaten," she said, looking at the packet of fish and chips still wrapped in the white paper, "but I'm no longer hungry, are you?"

"Only for you," he said, taking her arm and leading her to the stairs.

In an obvious attempt to cheer her up, Larry whistled and sang an accompaniment to a "Beach Boys" record as he prepared toast and coffee the next morning. He made a flask of coffee and packed some sandwiches and biscuits for his vigil in the loft, which was where he had decided to hide.

At six, when the light was still poor and the wind still howled around the houses, he left the house with Rosemary, talking loudly in case someone was watching for them. Taking the two cars, they kissed goodbye on the footbridge and Rosemary drove off. Larry walked to where his car was parked, up near the road then drove off after her.

He drove the Citroën down a narrow lane, turning in

through a farm gate and rolling it down behind the hedge. The leafless hawthorn didn't give much cover, but it was unlikely that anyone would be passing such an unlikely spot, on a lane which led only to a farmhouse.

The darkness was weakening as he ran across the fields, his sneakers squelching in deep mud, the wind flapping his anorak hood like a torn sail. He tied it around his chin and hurried on. He wanted to get in place before anyone was up and prowling around.

Passing well south of the wooden footbridge he made his way in a large circle to the back of the row of cottages. There were lights in all but number two and through the uneven hedging at the end of the gardens, he could see people moving about in both number five and number three. He kept to the shadows and made his way to the back door of number two and slipped inside. They had left the door open so he needn't make a sound.

He collected his bag of food and added a couple of cans of beer before hauling himself up into the roof-space and pulling the door-flap up after him. It was cold. He had not imagined it could be so bitterly cold. The wind, although not so fierce as the day before, was still gusting occasionally and the draught between some of the ill-fitting slates was as cutting as a knife.

Thankful for the blankets Rosemary had insisted on, he zipped himself firmly into his anorak and settled into a wig-wam made of the thick, Welsh woollen blankets. For a long time he didn't move, allowing the warmth to build up around him. Then, he carefully lowered the door-flap using a string loop which he fastened around a convenient nail. By moving only slightly, he could see anyone coming up the stairs and hear quite clearly if anyone entered the house. But the draught was bitterly cold and cut into him so that he doubted if he could stay there.

He tried to think of a place that would do as well. The closet under the stairs was a possibility, hardly much warmer but at least out of the cruel wind that whipped through the door-flap and caught him as it made its escape between the slates. But he was reluctant to move. A sudden noise when someone listening believed the house to be empty would be a disaster; both in warning any intended intruder off and letting him know that they were aware and trying to catch him out.

In the library Rosemary was unable to concentrate on her work.

"Your friend's just come in," Sally called, and at once she ran into the main room, expecting to see Larry. But it was Gethyn who stood there. She forced herself to hide her disappointment.

"I hope you didn't mind my asking for you," he said. "I wanted to see if you were all right after the soaking you had last night."

"Soaking?" She frowned. "Good heavens, Gethyn, I only went out in the rain."

"Covered in mud you were. How did it happen. Did you fall?"

She felt her shoulders droop and the fear and anxiety for Larry overwhelmed her.

"Oh, Gethyn, someone pushed Larry into the river. Don't tell anyone, will you? Someone was standing on the footbridge, hidden in the darkness, and hit him with a stick or something and sent him into the river."

"What? Are you sure he didn't make up a story to impress you?"

"No mistake, he almost drowned."

"How did you get him out?" he asked. "The stream was deep and very fast yesterday with all the rain."

"I don't know how. I went out to find him when the light from his torch disappeared and he was – Oh, Gethyn, it was terrifying. If I hadn't been able to haul him to the bank he'd have – I would have lived with the memory of watching him drown all my life."

"Where is he now?"

"At home."

"That's what he's telling you. There was no sign of his car when I left. You really can't trust him, believe me."

"He's moved the car and he's hiding," she defended at once. "Up in the loft he is, hoping whoever is doing all this will come in and show himself. I'm so afraid for him."

"Would you like me to go in and keep him company? If he really is there," he couldn't resist adding.

"Larry is telling the truth," she said hotly.

"He hasn't always told you the truth and I bet he hasn't told you the whole story even now." He saw from her expression he had hit a sore point and added softly, "I'm sorry, but I can't help mistrusting him. He's a stranger and I worry for you, I care for you," he added softly, "far more than you know."

It was the strongest hint yet of how much he cared and he looked at her anxiously, waiting for the reaction to his words. There was none. She continued to stare into space and there was such despair in her lovely eyes that he felt a churn of guilt at the way he was warning her against the man who obviously meant a great deal to her. But, he reassured himself, all that would change once she had realised where her happiness lay.

"Have you had lunch?" he asked.

"All I wanted."

"Pity."

"Gethyn, I have to go, there's work I must do today." She smiled regretfully, not wanting to part from him. He offered security and strength in a world fraught with unseen dangers and seemingly false friends.

He stood to leave and she felt his love and protection enfolding her. He was tall, strong and so familiar and comforting. Impulsively she stretched up and kissed him lightly on the cheek.

"Thank you for listening to me," she said.

"I'm always here for you, Rosemary, remember that," he said as he turned and walked out.

Rosemary went back to the staff room and found Sally standing there, white-faced, her red hair seeming brighter by comparison.

"Sally? What is it?" she asked. "You look as if you've had a shock."

"I have, but not this moment. Rosemary, I have to tell you something. I've befriended you for a purpose."

"Join the club!" Rosemary retorted. "It seems it's the only way I make friends, by someone wanting something!"

"I think Mrs Priestley is my grandmother."

"What?"

"My father left my mother when I was small, I know nothing about him, but I've searched and – well, I'm almost certain he was Mrs Priestley's son, Leonard. Everything fits. Dates, areas and ages – Rosemary, I'm sorry I've used you and sorrier still that I couldn't tell you. Will you come with me and talk to her. I can't go alone and you know her and – please?"

"He went to Australia or Canada," Rosemary said stupidly.

"Perhaps he did, but not before he married my mother and fathered me."

"But your mother would know where he is, surely? She'd have told you about your grandmother?"

Search For a Shadow

"She died when I was born. That's why Dad left I believe, he couldn't cope with a small baby, could he?"

Rosemary shook her head. She stared about her at familiar things and wondered if she were really sleeping and involved in a dream. All these years she had lived among people she didn't know.

"Of course I'll go with you to talk to her. But I don't think she'll be anything but pleased." She hugged the girl to reassure her.

Inside number two, Larry sat huddled in blankets and anorak in the chilly loft-space. The coffee flask was almost empty and he couldn't risk turning on the electric kettle, knowing how sharp and clear the sound of a switch was in a silent house. He had climbed down once to use the lavatory but had remembered just in time not to pull the flush.

Hours had passed without a sound to suggest anyone was near. A box tucked away under some books intrigued him and he pulled it out and unpacked its neatly arranged contents.

It was clothes, baby clothes, but whose, or even whether they belonged to a girl or a boy, he couldn't guess. He put these aside with the diary he had also come across, to show Rosemary. He thought of his own mother's stories about storing the clothes for a next child and guessed they had been packed away for a baby, who had perhaps never arrived.

The wind rose again and, collecting the items he had left out to show Rosemary, he climbed down onto the landing. His idea had failed and he wondered doubtfully if he could face a repeat of his vigil on the following day. He didn't go upstairs again but sat in the armchair in the darkening room. He wanted to light the fire but with the curtains open to the darkness outside, it would be a giveaway. He couldn't even use the electric bar, and he sat and watched the numbers of his watch marking the slow passing of time.

As five o'clock chimed in the house next door, he stood lethargically, facing the window. He didn't attempt to look at anything at first, staring blindly at the blackness, allowing his thoughts to wander idly, his eyes sightlessly roaming across the blank windows. What a waste of a goddamned day!

Gradually he saw objects grow out of the darkness and he began to recognise a few trees, and the banks of the stream; the water the colour of lead in the gloomy autumn evening. He realised he had failed.

Chapter Eighteen

He shared the events of the day with Rosemary, making light of its tedium and the cold that had steadily eaten into his bones. She in turn confessed to having blurted out to Gethyn in the library Larry's soaking at the hands of the unknown assailant the night before. "I'm sorry," she said miserably, "I know I promised I wouldn't tell a soul." Larry stood up, walked around the room for a few moments then turned and glared at her.

"You did what?" he shouted.

"I'm sorry, Larry, but I was dreadfully upset and I needed to tell someone and—"

"I've had it up to here with your lack of trust!" he yelled at her. "I've wanted to help you but I can't. Not any longer. I'm leaving, here and now."

"Larry, you can't go!"

"You'd better believe it!" He ran upstairs and came down only moments later with a bag packed untidily, the zip caught in the sleeve of a sweater that hung out, dragging the floor. Under his arm he had a sleeping bag.

"Larry! Don't go, please, not at this time of night. Please!"

"Lock all the doors and make sure the bolts are fixed tight. If you're frightened, call for Gethyn! You obviously trust him more than you trust me!"

Suddenly he was gone. Rosemary stared at the door,

wide-eyed, her hands on her cheeks, bewildered at the speed of the transformation. Too numb to cry at first, she stared at the cold fireplace, foolishly wondering if she should light it or manage with the electric bar. Dulled as she was from thinking clearly, she knew she wouldn't attempt to go to bed. This room was where she would stay until dawn. The rest of the house was no longer her domain, but a place in which she feared to trespass.

She stretched her neck to look inside the coal scuttle like a stranger peering through a window into someone else's home, and saw the coal was low. There was not enough to last the night. That seemed to be the last straw, and a wail of despair filled the room like an echo of the dying wind.

Outside in Rosemary's car, huddled against the chilly night and the biting wind, Larry sat and watched the house. He wished he'd made a flask of coffee, and remembered with sudden pangs that he hadn't eaten either.

He was pleased with the way he had been able to cause a quarrel. The realisation that Gethyn knew about him being pushed into the stream was a gift and, if his rapidly growing theory was correct, then the quarrel would have been overheard and he was certain it would have sounded genuine.

As the first minutes passed he had moments of regret that he hadn't warned Rosemary of his intention, but she was an innocent and not convinced of her danger – or, he thought sadly, of his own lack of guilt, and she might have again trusted someone against his plans. The wrong someone.

He smiled in the darkness as he imagined their reunion once the situation had been made clear to her.

Rosemary allowed herself the luxury of crying unrestrainedly and when there was a knock at the door she at first didn't hear it, then decided it was Larry and refused to open

Search For a Shadow

it. She hadn't thrust the bolts home and was hardly surprised when the door opened. Larry had his key. She forced the crying to an even louder pitch. She wasn't even going to talk to him after what he had done. Not now or ever!

She glanced into the mirror through swollen eyes and saw, not Larry, but Gethyn entering.

"Sorry to come in uninvited, Rosemary," he said in his quiet, caring way. "But I heard you crying and, well, I had to come and see if there was anything I could do."

The gently spoken words, undemanding of explanations, a well-known face and arms held just slightly towards her were enough to make her sob louder and run to him.

"Oh, Gethyn, it's—"

"Hush love." He pressed her face into his shoulder, bent his head to hers and made soothing, murmuring sounds and encouraged her to take comfort from him like a child with its mother.

He smelled of soap, and warm wool and there was the faintest touch of wood-smoke about him and it was all she wanted; familiar scents, familiar touch and the soft, caring familiar voice.

There was another knock at the door and she stared up at Gethyn, who was looking at her, his eyes large, dark and lovingly aware.

"If that's Larry back I won't see him," she said thickly, her voice strange after all her sobs and tears.

Gethyn left her and she heard him open the door, knowing that in spite of her words she wanted it to be Larry. But it was Huw who walked in and came to stand beside her, an arm at once touching her shoulders.

"Rosemary? Are you all right?" he asked. "I went for a last breath of fresh air and thought I'd knock in case you were frightened."

"I'm fine. Gethyn came when he heard me crying but everything is all right now."

When the fire was burning brightly and she had made them all a cup of coffee, Rosemary tried politely but firmly to persuade them to leave. Huw took a pen and wrote his phone number in large numbers on a piece of paper which he propped up against the telephone.

"Come on Gethyn, the lady wants us to go," he said. "Call me if there's the slightest worry, Rosemary, I can be here in seconds." He took both her hands in his and stared down at her from his extra height, making her look at him, making sure she listened. "I want you to promise that if anything disturbs you, even if it's a passing owl, you'll tell me; I want to know about it. Promise?"

"I promise," she smiled.

"I don't have to make you promise, do I?" Gethyn said, touching her cheek lightly with his lips. "Anyway, I don't intend to leave for a while. I want to know you are relaxed and calm before I go.

"Rosemary, I want to talk. I know you were upset earlier but now you're calm. We have so much to say to each other."

At once Rosemary regretted allowing Huw to leave before Gethyn. She had fallen once more into the trap of giving Gethyn the impression there was more than friendship, by the way she had clung to him and allowed herself to be comforted.

"Gethyn, there's nothing for us to talk about. We're neighbours and good friends, when I was in trouble you comforted me as I would you. That's all. Now, if you would leave me, I'm so exhausted."

To her alarm he came towards her, his eyes full of an unfamiliar wildness. He put his arms around her but now there was no comfort in them, they gave her a feeling of vulnerability and alarm.

"Rosemary, I love you. We belong together. Tell me you know it, that we'll marry and stay here where we both belong."

She struggled to be free of his searching lips and for a moment his strength refused to release her. She struggled and called for him to let go and suddenly, his arms fell to his sides and his great shoulders drooped.

"You are my dearest friend, Gethyn," she said, her voice trembling, "but it's Larry I love. I'm sorry, so very sorry."

He didn't reply, he lumbered from the room and across the hall like a wounded bear and she followed after a few moments and locked the door behind him.

Outside, Huw waited until Gethyn had gone into his own house and Rosemary had thrust home the bolt on her door, then he walked slowly back to number five.

Larry was attracted by the swinging of a torch as Gethyn walked from his own house to Rosemary's. He saw, in the uneven beam, Gethyn standing there, having obviously knocked on the door. Then after a while during which the door remained obstinately closed, he saw the light focus on the keyhole and Gethyn appeared to open the door with a key and walk in.

Larry opened the car door and stood outside. The sonofabitch didn't waste much time, did he? he muttered. He was carefully walking to the beginning of the bridge when he was halted by the sight of another shadow easing itself from the trees and saw the tall, skinny figure that could only be Huw, heading for Rosemary's door. He followed, and watched as Gethyn let him in, then settled against the front wall to listen at the window, trying to hear what was being said.

He ran to hide when Huw, then Gethyn, came out and he was about to return to the car when he made up his mind. He had to take a chance and trust Huw. Turning back from the bridge he ran and knocked on number five, reaching there just as the light on the landing went off. It came on immediately and Huw opened the door.

"Time for a skull-session, I think," Larry said as he walked past a surprised Huw into the house.

"First," he said after making sure there was no one else in the living room, "first, I have to tell you that for a while I thought you were involved in all this. Now, well, I have to trust you. Dammit, I'll go mad if this isn't sorted soon! I have to talk to someone!"

"Start at the beginning?" Huw suggested. "Like what you're doing here?"

"That will have to wait. Sorry, but although I once thought differently, I now think it's irrelevant. What's happening isn't anything to do with why I'm here." Huw turned away and opening a cupboard, he handed Larry a can of beer.

"You wouldn't have a sandwich would you? I'm starved!" He followed Huw into the kitchen and talked while Huw prepared peanut-butter sandwiches.

"I saw Gethyn go in and although I was too far away to be sure, he seemed to let himself in with a key," Larry began. "How can he have a key? I had the locks changed twice."

"I asked the same question of Rosemary. She looked surprised and said she always gives a spare key to Gethyn. It hadn't ever occurred to her not to. The key had been left with his mother by her grandmother and it was only natural for that to continue."

Search For a Shadow

"Ooo*ooo-o-oh shit!*" Larry snorted.

A knock at the door startled Rosemary. She rose and looked at the clock, then out of the window. To her surprise it was morning. She went to the door and began to unbolt it but remembered in time the need to be cautious and called to ask who was there.

"Gethyn," a voice said. "Please, Rosemary, I don't want to pester you but can I come in, just for five minutes?" She opened the door.

"I just wanted to say I'm sorry, I don't want you to think that I'll allow my love for you to ruin our friendship. That's all."

"I wouldn't allow that to happen either, Gethyn," she said. "Look, I've just woken, will you have some coffee?"

When she went back into the living room from the kitchen, with two steaming cups, he was examining the baby clothes. His expression, when he looked up at her made her stomach churn with shock. It was accusative.

"They aren't for me!" she said with an edge of anger to her voice. "Larry found them in – when he was looking for something for me the other day and brought them for me to look at. I suppose they ought to go to one of the charity shops."

"They smell a little of damp," he said. "Whose are they?"

"Well, I presumed they were mine, kept by my sentimental old Gran."

"Blue? Isn't blue the colour for boys?"

"Perhaps. But if they aren't mine whose can they be?" She laughed. "Perhaps my mother liked to defy the conventions! I'll ask her next time I talk to her."

While they sipped their coffee, she picked up the diary and leafed through its yellowing pages. The date was 1962.

"Wasn't that the year you were born, Gethyn?" she asked, showing it to him. When he nodded, she looked for his birth date, wondering if there was some mention of it. Living next door, her gran would certainly have considered that exciting news and worthy of a mention in a diary.

There were several references to his mother, Marged. In early June, it noted that she was at a hospital in a distant town. Marged had hinted at a long awaited pregnancy. "But," the pages remarked, "this has happened so many times before." He moved away from her, his face revealing shock, but Rosemary didn't notice his ashen colour or how silent he had become, as she muttered the dates on the pages for June. What she then read aloud made him cry out in pain.

> "Today, Marged brought home a baby. She admitted that it wasn't hers but one she had stolen from a pram in the streets of Aberystwyth. I have pleaded with her to return him, but to no avail. I know I should report it but as the hours pass my resolve weakens. I am so ashamed that I have condoned, by my lack of action, the loss to some unknown mother of her child."

"She promised me she hadn't told a soul!" Gethyn groaned. Rosemary didn't hear the words.

"What does it mean?" she whispered. "Surely you can't be – No. There must be a mistake! There was another child and she returned him. This doesn't concern you at all. It was a momentary madness, that's all. My grandmother would never have allowed this to happen."

"Not even when my mother tried to hang herself?" Gethyn said softly.

"It's true?"

"My – 'mother' – told me just before she died. The

accident and her death were a punishment. I couldn't grieve for her. When I think how she deprived me of a life among my own family, perhaps brothers and sisters, and cousins and uncles – I hate her."

The vehemence in his voice was reflected in his eyes, staring eyes, staring at the clothes.

"They were the clothes I was wearing when she stole me."

"Perhaps it isn't too late." Rosemary was bewildered, she was on a merry-go-round completely out of control, everything was crazy, the world insane. For a moment she wondered if she were going mad. Surely none of this was happening? She forced her fluttering thoughts to earth and said, "It isn't too late to find your family. There would have been reports in the papers of the time, you'll be able to find them without any difficulty."

"I can't. I'm nearly twenty-eight. A child could adapt, but not a grown man, with a mind made small by a restricted upbringing by a stupid and probably unbalanced old woman. They'll be rich, confident people and I wouldn't fit in just because our blood is the same! She ruined my life and when she told me, with that silly grin on her face, she expected me to be pleased! Can you believe that? She thought I'd thank her, tell her how glad I was she had stolen me from my family!"

He sneered and Rosemary looked into the face of a stranger.

"She honestly believed that when she explained how much she loved me that day, when the sun shone on my dark curls and I – a baby of only a few weeks – looked at her with what she called 'recognition', she honestly believed I'd thank her."

Rosemary didn't know what to say. She sat there hardly daring to breathe as his face showed the torment within him.

Then he suddenly rose and ran from the house, out into the mist of the late-autumn dawn.

Across the stream, Larry sat dozing. He and Huw had spent several hours discussing with complete truthfulness their thoughts on the mysteries surrounding Rosemary and the second cottage in the row and coming to the same conclusion, had agreed to combine forces to protect her. Larry had abandoned his watch during the night when he thought Rosemary was safe and set the alarm on his watch for six-thirty. He didn't see Gethyn enter number two and didn't stir when Gethyn ran out and headed for the church.

Rosemary guessed where Gethyn was heading. Taking an anorak she ran after him and was in time to see him hacking at his mother's grave with a post torn from the fence surrounding the small graveyard. He was muttering, "Stolen child, stolen child", his face a swollen red mask of fury. She was afraid, then, to approach him but she stood close by and waited for the fury to subside.

Chapter Nineteen

Larry woke guiltily to see Rosemary's door wide open and, running across the footbridge, realised to his alarm that she wasn't there. He ran to find Huw and together they searched the area. First they went to Gethyn's house and that too seemed to be deserted. Huw decided to look in the hills in case they had gone for an early walk.

"The car is there, so they can't be far," Huw said. "You stay close by and whistle if she appears so I know to come back."

Larry went into Gethyn's house.

The door was locked but he forced a window without any difficulty.

He went from the small, overfilled front room in which he found himself, across the hall and into the main living room. The place was such a clutter that he despaired of finding anything to help him in his search for information. But when he opened the large cupboard that stood out from a corner in an untidy way, he gasped with shock.

It was filled with electronic equipment. He recognised several tape recorders, some machines that looked like radio receivers. A large-volt battery stood against the wall behind the couch, connected to something that disappeared through the wall below the level of the skirting board. Cursing his ignorance in such matters, he blundered around the room wondering what to make a note of and how to deal with what he had found.

Seeing everything, yet understanding nothing, he knew that if he wasn't careful he might lose the advantage he had been given. Somehow he must record what he'd found in case something happened, like being caught and treated like a thief.

He tried to calm his mind and take a cool look at what he had found. He looked at the boxes of tapes, picked one at random and stuck it in his pocket. He felt bemused by what he had found. In his wildest imaginings he hadn't thought of anything as complex as this. He stood looking at the cupboard with its boxes and wires spilling out, but not seeing what it all meant.

He shook his head to clear his mind, pressed the heels of his hands into his eyeballs, ran his hands through his hair and began again.

At once a slight tear in the wallpaper caught his eye. An examination showed it to be a tear on three sides of a square. Lifting the flap that had been created, he saw it was hiding a hole that had been drilled through the shared wall, right to the wallpaper in Rosemary's room.

A slight touch with a pen and he was through with a view of her room, too small to be used for spying, but good enough, he guessed, to hold a microphone attached to a recorder. All the time he had been living there, Gethyn had been watching and listening.

Rosemary could see from the drooped shoulders and the exhaustion in the lines on his face that Gethyn had come out of the rage that had engulfed him. She waited until he turned and looked at her then walked towards him slowly, but trying not to show her fear of his returning to the anger of a few moments ago. To her relief

Search For a Shadow

he smiled and when he spoke, his voice was low and gentle.

"That's been building up ever since my mother told me about how I became Gethyn Lewis," he said, taking her hand and slipping it through his arm. "I'm sorry you witnessed it but so very glad you didn't go away. Just knowing you were there helped me cope with it."

"I have to go, Gethyn," she said, trying to keep her voice light. "If you're sure you're all right, I have to get ready and leave for work. Walk back with me will you?"

He held her, stopped her from walking on and said, "I know you don't like me saying it, Rosemary, but I love you and feel our destinies are linked. If you would tell me you feel the same, the way I came to be here doesn't matter. To think that I was taken from a street in Aberystwyth all those years ago and brought to live in the house next to your grandmother . . . doesn't it seem like fate? You can't deny that it was meant to be."

He was holding her hand and squeezing her arm against him so tightly she began to feel the pain of it. His grip was like a clamp, threatening to stop the blood from coursing around her body. His eyes were wider than usual, giving his usually gentle face a fanatic stare. She began to be afraid. Instead of the negative answer she intended to give, she said, "I do know what you mean, Gethyn. Fate takes a hand and we hardly realise it most of the time. Only in very exceptional circumstances do we see clearly how our future is mapped out. Tortuous threads lead us to the here and now, and we accept what the day offers without considering how we reached our position, our—"

"Destiny," he said softly.

"But Gethyn, I really must go now. We can't have me being given the sack, can we?" She pulled away from him and he released her arm after a few moments with a puzzled look, as if he hardly knew it was there. Or perhaps had not expected her to want to be free, she thought with a shiver of apprehension. His tenseness was unnerving her and she was glad when he looked at her with his face returned to normal and said, "Go on, my darling. I want to wander around here for a while and think about what we do next. You know, don't you, I'd never have let you go, not to the American. Somehow I'd have prevented you leaving. You belong here, with me, and this is where we'll stay."

"I'm not going anywhere," she said, praying he would believe her lies.

Gethyn watched her go but instead of wandering as he had stated as his intention, he took a short cut down through the dangerously steep, wooded hillside, where boulders and ravines blocked the path of the inexperienced. He jumped over the fencing where it was low and was back at his door long before Rosemary, who had walked the usual way, had even come in sight of the cottages or sound of the stream.

She sensed the emptiness of the cottage long before she reached it. Without Larry there it was no longer a home. But she had to face the fact that Larry had lost patience with her and was gone. She was alone and the word, "alone", seemed a more emotive word than "deranged", she decided. She could escape from a deranged neighbour but not from being alone. "Alone" represented a lifetime without Larry.

Larry was looking, with gradual understanding, at the collection of equipment gathered in the living room of Gethyn's house.

He had searched the walls by smoothing the wallpaper with his hands; had been horrified to find a second hole drilled through the wall. Gethyn had been listening to their conversations and intimacies both in the living room and the bedroom.

Returning to the ground floor, reeling with the shock of the discovery, he began to untangle the intricacies of the wires and recording devices with greater determination. He daren't try listening to one of the tapes although the idea was tempting; if anything were disturbed, Gethyn would be sure to guess. He felt in his pocket but decided to keep the tape he had taken from one of the boxes. He had to take away something to show the police. He daren't stop and listen to what it contained, it was hardly likely to be a fairy story!

The first sound at the front door made him freeze and he stood half hoping that whoever it was would go away, the mailman perhaps? But the key, finding the lock and turning with a swift movement, unlocked his muscles and brain as well as the door and he fled into the only cover he could find, the closet under the stairs. As he pulled the door to, Gethyn entered the living room.

Rosemary knew as soon as she went inside and threw the bolt that she couldn't go to work that day. She wouldn't ever come into the house again if she left it now. She looked at the time and decided she would catch Megan before she left for work. She hadn't intended to offer more than the mild excuse of a headache, but the friendly voice on the other end of the line soon had the story pouring from her.

At number one, there was a click, and reels began to turn.

She described the sensation of fear when she realised the depths of Gethyn's instability, and ended by telling her friend that however long it took, she would find Larry. Megan listened to her and promised to both make her excuses that day, and help her search for Larry.

"Although I don't know where we start, do you?" she said.

"I think he went a long way away," Rosemary said. "His car isn't here and from the way he stormed out yesterday, I don't think he'd have stopped until he'd put a couple of hundred miles between us. I've been such a fool."

"Don't be ridiculous! How could he expect trust when he was so lacking in it? He still hasn't told you why he's here, remember. Are you really sure enough of him, even now? He's kept you in the dark about so much of his life."

"There's a good reason and he'll tell me when he can. I haven't been the most confidential person, have I? He's asked me to keep a secret and I've told Gethyn. And the key. We made such a fuss, getting the locks changed and I, in my stupidity, gave a spare, as I'd always done, to Gethyn. And now it seems that Gethyn's, well, deranged."

"Should you be talking like this now, if Gethyn can overhear?"

"It's all right, I left Gethyn up on the hill; I'd hear him if he came back. The house is empty so he can't be listening to me. But I will be careful once he's home. Megan, it's very frightening."

"Want me to come, love?"

"No. Thanks, but I have to face this or be a coward for the rest of my life."

"Don't open the door, whatever you do."

"Not a chance!"

Larry was watching from the partly open door of the cupboard, wondering how long he could stay in such a cramped position without straightening his legs. Gethyn was standing with his back half towards him, his dark face in profile. He was watching the turning spool on a large tape

Search For a Shadow

recorder. Larry heard the click as it stopped and saw Gethyn press the button to begin to play it.

His own voice came clearly, and he was able to relive the quarrel he had contrived with Rosemary. It sounded good and from the way Gethyn was now smiling, he was satisfied too. Larry hoped he had convinced the man that he and Rosemary were finished. Her safety, her very life, might depend on it.

Gethyn played the quarrel over and over again and Larry waited, dreading discovery. The stiffness of his limbs began to trouble him and he hoped he could manage not to move while Gethyn was so close. The need to stretch made him lose his concentration and he was jerked from thoughts of his discomfort by a low growl of anger from Gethyn.

The recorder had stopped repeating the quarrel and Gethyn had allowed the tape to run. He had reached the conversation between Rosemary and Megan. Larry went cold as he saw the change in Gethyn's expression. Rosemary was pouring out the story of the encounter at the graveyard, and her thoughts that Gethyn was "deranged". She spoke emotionally of her love for Larry, and this enflamed Gethyn and made him growl, low in his throat. His hands twitched and he kept mouthing the words, "the American, the American", and Larry feared for his own life.

How could he escape? Larry ran all the possibilities through his anxious mind. He daren't show himself, not now he knew how much Gethyn hated him. In his confused mind, the man was obviously blaming him for taking Rosemary from him; he wouldn't be persuaded that even without Larry's arrival, Rosemary would never have loved him.

Talking to Gethyn would not be the solution, especially if he showed himself as an intruder, who had uncovered his secrets. He settled for a long wait, dreading the possibility of moving and making a sound, or of the dusty surroundings creating the need to sneeze.

His heart almost failed him when Gethyn began to step over the piles of clutter towards him. He held his breath, expecting the door to be flung open and be dragged from his hiding place but the man went past the cupboard and climbed the stairs, his footsteps creaking the boards above him.

It was now or never. Larry shot out of the cupboard and, half imagining seeing Gethyn staring down from the stairs, he reached the kitchen and looked frantically at the door. If it was bolted then he wouldn't get out without being heard, but miraculously, and typically, it wasn't even locked. He turned the brass knob and escaped out of the house into the clean, crisp air.

Above him, he heard the chain being pulled in the bathroom and on weak legs he reached the back door of Rosemary's house and fumbled for his key. If it was bolted he could make his excuses, better that than be seen running like a bat out of hell down the side of Gethyn's garden.

Gethyn's voice called to him and nervousness made him drop the key. Bending over to find it gave him a few seconds to recover. He pretended to have just locked the door.

"Women!" he said. "They want to own you, every inch. They give you the runaround then expect you to apologise. I've had it up to here with this one. Hell, they expect too much of a guy, don't you think, Gethyn?"

"I think wicked women should be punished," Gethyn said quietly.

"Hell, don't I just agree! Well, I'll be off, and glad to shake the dust of this place off my shoes." He edged away from Gethyn, intending to make for the bottom of the garden and the lane beyond the fence, but Gethyn stopped him.

Search For a Shadow

"What d'you think is the right punishment for wicked women, then?"

"Leave 'em flat, man. If there's no future in it, get away and as far as you can."

"I mean really wicked."

The last thing Larry was capable of was a philosophical discussion, and unnerved as he was, he said the first thing that came into his head.

"Some need their brains blowing, some need a kick up the ass. Some want locking up. But an ordinary quarrel, well, I guess it's best to move right away and that's what I intend doing, right now." He hurried down the path and out of the gate on legs that seemed to be made of unset jelly, and once outside, he leaned on the wall to recover.

Gethyn went back inside and began to sort through the untidy collection of unlikely items he would need to punish the American with for pushing his way into his life and for hurting Rosemary. Pulling the cloth off a low table, he pulled from beneath it, where it had been hidden by the folds of the cloth, the box of fireworks he had bought and never used.

He gathered together a light bulb, some electric fittings, a file, some tubing and a length of electric cable. The punishment should be aimed at Rosemary, women were the evil ones, but now it had to be the American. Larry was the only suitable target. That was much more satisfactory. Rosemary wasn't really wicked, she only weak and soon, she'd belong to him. His eyes glowed with an excitement and his face showed a contented smile as he began his preparations.

Larry walked across the fields to collect his car that had remained undisturbed since he had hidden before his sojourn in Rosemary's loft-space. Driving carefully out of the muddy field, he made his way into town. He hoped Rosemary was at work, he needed to convince her of Gethyn's insanity and he needed to do it fast, before she went home. Unaware that he had been close to her as he had left Gethyn's house, he drove away from her and went to the library.

"She's at home," Megan told him and he groaned with frustration.

"I can't go there and I can't phone her," he said. "If Gethyn sees or hears me, there's no knowing what he's capable of doing."

"Police," Sally said firmly and she reached for the phone.

"No!" His hand went out to stop her. "I want to get Rosemary away from there before he's warned. Can you get a note to her?" he asked and when Megan agreed to go during an early lunch-break, he added, "And warn her not to discuss anything while she's in that house. That sonofabitch listens to everything that goes on there, and I mean everything!"

Sally found him some writing paper and he wrote down his reasons for coming there, telling them both the story first in case the note was, for some reason, not read. He admitted that he had overheard her telling Barbara at a New York party where she lived and had acted on it by following her to London and faking an introduction by pretending to be a stranger there.

"I promised my mother that one day, I'd go to Aberystwyth and search for my missing brother; the coincidence of Rosemary belonging in the area was too good to miss," he said, as he hurriedly wrote down his explanations.

"How was your brother lost?" Sally asked. "Did he go missing at sea or something like that?"

"No, he was stolen from his pram when he was only weeks

old and I – What's the matter? What have I said? D'you know something that would help trace him?" He stared at Megan's startled face. "For heaven's sake, woman, spill it out, and fast!"

"Just before Gethyn's mother died, she admitted to him that he was a stolen child, taken from a pram in Aberystwyth in 1962."

"What? Then Gethyn's my – oh my God!"

Megan hurriedly explained about the entry in the diary.

Rosemary had looked out of the back window when the voices of Gethyn and Larry reached her ears. What was Larry doing at the back door? What was he discussing so amiably with Gethyn? Why didn't he come in? If he was there to make up the silly quarrel why didn't he come in? She watched in disbelief as he walked down the garden and disappeared through the gate.

Some minutes later, standing at the front window looking, hoping, for Larry's return, she saw Gethyn hurry up the steps to the main road. He was obviously going to catch the bus to town. He didn't usually go to town apart from market day, but he had his shopping bag in his hand so there was obviously something he needed in a hurry. He looked strained, and in his haste was tripping over the stones on the rough path to the steps.

Over the top of the road bridge parapet, she saw the bus driving past and, realising that the house next door was empty she decided to look inside. She thought of the crashing of furniture and the fury at the graveside and wondered if there was a connection. It was a perfect opportunity to find out. The bus from town wouldn't bring him back for several hours.

The key to number one was hanging where it had always hung, forgotten for years, inside the cupboard under the sink. She lifted it from its hook and went outside. Guiltily she turned it in the lock and stepped inside Gethyn's house, feeling like a thief, although all she wanted to steal was his secrets.

The big cupboard was closed but when she opened the door she saw what Larry had seen. The first sight of the black boxes with the digital dials and the cassettes that were visible through clear plastic covers were enough to convince her that Gethyn had been listening to all that went on.

She felt sick: all the conversations and the love and the silliness and the passion, it had all been overheard by Gethyn. She sank down onto a chair, her legs weak with the shock of it. Her heart racing, she stood shakily, holding her head against the giddiness she suffered, and looked again at the recording equipment. She guessed that was what it was. Gethyn had been listening and recording them so he could play their conversations over and over again.

Everything was still among the reels and dials. It all looked benign and innocent, no tape was turning. So far as she could see nothing was working. He had presumed she and Larry had parted for good and there was no further need to listen. He was out of the house, and if he had gone to town on the bus, he'd be gone for hours. It was safe now, to use the phone and call Megan.

There was no phone in Gethyn's house, she would have to use her own. She had to talk to someone, she didn't know what to do next. Oh, if only Larry were here, he would handle everything and make sure she didn't do anything stupid. She always seemed to make the wrong decisions. Supporting herself against the walls, she went out.

She relocked the door, went back to her own house and dialled the library number. Sally answered and said at once, "Larry's here." Then Rosemary heard his voice and she knew that somehow everything would all be all right.

"I've been into Gethyn's house and I saw all sorts of electrical equipment," she said, then listened as he almost shouted.

"Rosemary, get the hell out of there, and fast! Go to Megan's. I'll meet you there."

"I'm quite safe, Gethyn caught the bus to town, he won't be back for ages yet."

"Thank the Lord!"

"I wanted to tell you that I believe you, and—"

"Darling, that's wonderful news, but get out and we'll talk when you're safe. Just get out of there, please baby, I don't want to frighten you but I think you might be in danger from Gethyn. I know you've known him all your life, but believe me, he's more than a bit crazy."

"I'll drive to Megan's and meet you there in about an hour."

The car slowed to a stop and the passenger thanked the driver for the lift in a vague way and waved goodbye. He stood where the car had left him and looked down on the row of five cottages, sleepy and quiet in the weak sun. The door of the second one opened and he leaned on the parapet to watch as Rosemary closed her door, pushing against it to make sure it was secure. His smile was gentle and affectionate.

"Sorry I have to kill him," he said aloud. "But I did warn you that I couldn't allow him to take you away from me. You should have listened. Your punishment is to lose him. Wicked women should always be punished. The American will understand, he agrees with me. Wicked women who take babies from prams. Wicked women to leave the ones who love them for another.

"My mother had to be punished, she stood on the edge of that ravine admiring some rabbits at play and I sent her down to join them. One push. My hands were guided, so I know it was the right thing to do. Wicked women, they all have to be punished. The American agreed."

Gethyn watched as Rosemary, carrying a small case, went to her car. She drove off and Gethyn guessed she had gone, not to Larry but to stay with Megan. He waited until the sound of the car had faded and went into number two to begin his preparations. He knew exactly what he needed to do and his fingers worked fast as he rewired the pair of switches above the kitchen units. The coffee percolator was now on the other switch of the pair. To the switch previously used by the percolator, he connected the contraption he had prepared, and which he hid inside a saucepan. The first thing Larry always did when he came in, was to go into the kitchen and make a cup of coffee.

Using Rosemary's phone, he rang the library and asked for Sally.

"Is Rosemary there?" he asked.

"No, but – wait a moment." Sally muffled the voice-piece and told Larry, who was sitting near her, who it was. Larry elected to speak to him.

"I've no idea where Rosemary is, can I help?"

"I've fallen, I've done my leg I think, it's very painful. I seem to be unable to get up, can you come and help? I'm in Rosemary's house, a parcel came and I brought it in for her and slipped on the mud on my shoes."

Larry didn't know what to do. He frowned, undecided whether to be harsh with the man or try to reason with him. The risk to Rosemary had to be the greatest priority. He hesitated only a moment, then said, "Tough luck fella! Call yourself an ambulance!" and dropped the phone into its rest.

He looked thoughtfully at Megan.

"I won't be happy until Rosemary is safely locked in your

house. If the queer fellow phones again, tell him she's on her way to London or something, will you? I'll go to your house now and wait for her, if that's okay with you?" Megan handed him the key and he drove to her home at the edge of the town.

He had been gone less than ten minutes when Rosemary arrived at the library.

"I thought I might have found Larry still here," she exclaimed in disappointment.

"He left a minute ago!" Sally explained. "There was this call from Gethyn saying he'd fallen and was hurt, then Larry told him more or less to get lost, and went to my place to wait for you."

"Forget about it and go to where Larry is waiting for you," Megan almost shouted.

"Gethyn was hurt?" Rosemary asked. "What happened?"

"Said he'd fallen but Larry told him to get himself an ambulance. In your house he was, mind. So he could have phoned for help."

"But why speak to Larry?" Rosemary frowned.

"Wanted you, he did, but Larry took the phone and was told he'd fallen, was in a lot of pain and couldn't get up."

"Megan, I have to go and see if he's all right."

"Don't be a fool! The man can call for help, you can't go back there! – Rosemary!" she called as her friend turned and made for the entrance. "At least go and find Larry first!" But Rosemary was running and already holding the keys to her car.

People looked up from their books in surprise; the silence of the library had been broken but no one complained. This was a very interesting conversation to liven their day.

Frantically, Megan ignored the people waiting to have their books stamped and dialled her own number, but there was no reply. Larry couldn't have reached there yet. She allowed it to ring, willing him to be quick and not to have stopped for anything on the way.

Larry slammed the receiver down when he heard what Megan had to say. He ran out of the house to find that someone had parked across the drive and the Citroën was blocked completely. He shouted his rage then ran to the road staring left and right, hoping to see someone whom he could persuade to take him to the cottages.

Further up the road he saw a man about to get into a Rover and he ran to him and asked, begged, for a lift. The man was about to refuse and Larry wasted no more time. He pushed the man aside after grabbing the keys and drove off before he had even closed the car door, leaving the man shouting for someone to call the police.

The Rover swerved around the corner, the driver's door swinging open, Larry leaning out with his hand reaching to close it, his foot pressing the accelerator and the tyres squealing.

Gethyn was sitting beside his cupboard. He had heard the car arrive and heard Larry enter number two. Smilingly, he waited.

The second car arriving puzzled him and he stood up then and went to the front window. He saw the door of the Rover open and Larry striding across the footbridge and he stared at the shared wall as if trying to see through it and find the explanation.

If Larry was just arriving, then who was inside?

"Rosemary!" he gasped.

He ran out of the front door and reached it just after Larry had gone inside. Gethyn ran after him and, the door being open, saw him put an arm around Rosemary and lead her towards the kitchen. He heard Larry say, "First a cup of coffee, then you'll explain why you won't ever listen to me." As he stepped towards the percolator, there was a shout from Gethyn, making them aware for the first time of his presence.

"No! Don't touch it!" Gethyn warned.

Rosemary saw him then, running toward her as if to murder them both with his bare hands and she tried to close the kitchen door against him. As the door closed, Gethyn burst through. Larry ran for Rosemary and threw her to the ground as the flash and roar of the explosion disintegrated the room around them.

Rosemary came to her senses with the belief she was deaf and blind, as fire burned, giving a deafening roar and filling the destroyed room with smoke. The weight resting on her was Larry, she knew that. She thought from the heaviness and stillness of him that he was dead. Confused, she couldn't begin to imagine what had happened, she only thought that they were going to die together. Then she remembered Gethyn, an enormous, flying figure coming towards her, his face distorted and wild, and exploding into this, fire and pain and grief and despair.

Then Larry's weight was lifted from her, and gentle hands came and moved her out of the hell that had been her kitchen, and she was carried outside into the cool, sweet air, with the sound of the stream and dazzling bright light from the sky.

"Larry?" she called, and a strange voice said, "He'll be all right. He has a nasty cut on his shoulder from some jagged debris, metal it was, but he'll be fine."

"Gethyn?" she asked, slowly opening her eyes and seeing a policeman bending over her, wiping her face with a cloth dampened in the stream.

"Now don't you worry about a thing, he'll be all right, for sure."

"The maniac!" another voice said.

"Go easy with the poor guy," Larry whispered, raising his head and looking across at the figure of Gethyn.

Gethyn's clothes were torn into shreds, blood seeped from numerous cuts, a blood-soaked bandage covered a gash on his head and his face was one black bruise. He wasn't moving.

"Don't treat him roughly, guys," Larry whispered hoarsely. "He doesn't know it yet, but he's my brother, stolen from my mother when he was only a baby."

When Muriel visited them in hospital, almost invisible behind a huge bouquet of flowers, she said, "Rosemary, Larry, I blame myself for this. I had a strong feeling that Gethyn was more than just upset by his mother's death. The story of her accident just didn't ring true. I knew he was unbalanced by something and suspected all along that he had pushed her to her death. I knew he was like an unexploded bomb and I didn't warn you. Couldn't face the truth I suppose. A dangerous sort of loyalty. I'm sorry."

"How *could* you believe that Gethyn, whom you'd known all your life, was dangerous?" Rosemary comforted her. "He's one of us and immune from such things as murder. That's what I thought, that's what we all thought. Who would have believed that a neighbour, someone we'd known all our lives, was bugging our homes and learning how to make bombs?"

"I won't keep things to myself any more." Muriel leaned closer to Rosemary and whispered, "New Year's resolution – a bit early but never mind. There's something else I've been holding back. I know where Mrs Priestley's son is and I'm going to tell her, now, today. He's just around the corner from my daughter, in Bala, he never went abroad at all. His first wife died soon after their daughter was born and he never found happiness with the second. Divorced he is, with one son and a daughter who was adopted. Very unhappy he's been and he blames his mother for interfering all those years ago, between him and Megan. I'm going to ring him and tell him the time has come when he should forgive his mother for her interference and come home."

"I'm glad. She's so lonely. And for Sally! She's got a brother, or half-brother. Oh, Moo, there'll be a wonderful reunion!"

"Sally? What's Sally go to do with it?"

Rosemary explained Sally's relationship to Mrs Priestley and they excitedly planned how the news of Leonard would be told, Muriel imagining a huge party to which all members of the new family would be invited.

"Lovely it'll be."

The tapes Larry had taken from Gethyn's collection were quite revealing. One was a recording of their conversation during which Rosemary told Larry she had decided to sell her house. The conversation was followed by the sounds they had heard, much later that same evening – presumably when he had listened to the recording – of him using his axe on his furniture in rage. The day following, they had witnessed him burning the remaining evidence of his fury and anger.

"What now?" Rosemary said when they were home again, bandaged and bruised but safe.

"Well, baby, I don't think I could face much more of the peace and tranquillity of the Welsh countryside! What say we go to New York and get married there? It's a darned sight safer!" While Rosemary stared at him he went on, "I tried to ask you once before, but you seemed to sense what I was about to say and you put me off."

"I remember the moment," Rosemary said slowly. "I thought you were trying to tell me goodbye. Darling, Larry, that's a word I never want to hear from you."

"Then it's yes?"

"After we've sorted out some help for – the queer fellow?"

"You'd better believe it."